MW00831892

MURDER
IN
PARADISE

PARADISE SERIES,
BOOK 4

DEBORAH BROWN

This book is a work of fiction. Names, characters, places and incidents are either the product of the author's imagination or used fictitiously. Any resemblance to actual persons, living or dead, or to actual events or locales is entirely coincidental.

All rights reserved, including the right to reproduce this book or portions thereof, in any form. No part of this text may be reproduced, transmitted, downloaded, decompiled, reverse engineered, or stored in or introduced into any information storage and retrieval system, in any form or by any means, whether electronic or mechanical without the express written permission of the author. The scanning, uploading and distribution of this book via the Internet or via any other means without the permission of the publisher is illegal and punishable by law. Please purchase only authorized electronic editions and do not participate in or encourage electronic piracy of copyrighted, materials.

MURDER IN PARADISE
Copyright @ 2014 by Deborah Brown

Excerpt from Greed in Paradise @2014 by Deborah Brown

Published by: Paradise Books June 2014

Cover: Natasha Brown

ISBN-13: 9780990316602
ISBN-10: 0990316602

PARADISE SERIES NOVELS

MURDER IN PARADISE

Chapter 1

Dark gray thunderclouds filled the sky, threatening to pour big fat raindrops at any second. With the mugginess stripped from the air, the temperature began to drop and streaks of lightning flashed to the west. I opened the back door of my Tahoe and put Mother's birthday gift on the back seat. Creole, an unofficial cousin, had called in a favor and gotten me an invitation into Patron's Cigar Factory, an appointment-only cigar bar where I scored a small handmade teak humidor filled with hand-rolled Cubans, the kind that Mother enjoyed.

Sliding into the driver's side door of my Tahoe, I had one leg under the steering wheel when someone jerked me from my SUV.

"Hey, bitch, I'll be taking this ride."

I elbowed my assailant hard, making contact. He yelped, twisted me around by my hair, and tossed me airborne until I landed in the middle of the busy street. "Get up and I'll shoot your ass," he said as he pointed his gun at my face. He jumped behind the wheel, spinning the tires as he squealed off down the street.

A beat-up sedan honked furiously, screeching to a halt just inches before rolling over me. The driver put his car into gear to go around me and yelled from the passenger window, "What the hell's the matter with you, lying in the street?"

Carjacked––and in broad daylight no less.

Sylvia, Patron's wife, rushed out of the cigar bar. "Madison, are you okay? My daughter is calling 911." Her big brown eyes checked me over.

"I'm fine. I need to place another order." I'd waited six months for the humidor I picked to come in, and now I refused to be empty-handed.

"You're a good daughter," Sylvia said. "The best birthday gift for your mother is that you're not hurt."

A Miami police car flew up the street, lights flashing. If this had to happen, it would've been nice to have been closer to home where I knew the sheriffs on a first name basis, for a variety of reasons, both good and bad. The officer climbed out of his patrol car.

"You the one who got jacked?" he asked, as he pointed at me.

"Come back inside when you're done here," Sylvia said.

The officer's name tag read, "Durango." I gave him the straight facts, veering away from the tabloid-style I enjoyed when relating details to friends. I knew when not to overplay the drama.

"Here's my card. I wrote the report number on the back for your insurance company." Durango looked bored. "If--when--we find your vehicle, you'll get a call from the tow yard. Cancel your cell phone and credit cards if they were left inside."

Standing in Little Havana, reality set in that I was an hour away from home and I knew no one. I had no ride, no money, no phone. Mother's birthday party started in less than two hours and I needed a stand-in to handle the last minute details. I also needed someone to break it to Mother that I'd be lucky to get there before her party ended.

I went back inside Patron's and asked Sylvia if I could use their phone. The aroma of tobacco from the open boxes displayed filled the air. The family-run business specialized in cigars rolled on site.

Bitsy answered on the first ring. "Famosa Motors."

"This is Madison Westin. Tell your boss it's urgent." It could be loosely said that I work for Brick Famosa, trying to get hours for my PI license. He calls me when there isn't another person in town who will accept the job. At least tracking down a missing urn of ashes didn't land me in jail.

"Red, you in trouble?" He gave me that nickname because I have red curly hair, and lots of it.

"I got carjacked. I need one of your rentals; my insurance will cover the cost." He owned the largest high-end car lot in South Miami.

"Did you shoot him?"

I knew Brick would be disappointed with my answer. If he had his way, the bad guy would wind up dead every time. "He grabbed me from behind. My gun was the only thing he didn't steal." I reassured myself by touching the holster at the small of my back.

"I'm on my way out. You can choose any rental on the lot — Bits will give you the key." Bitsy was a former employee at Brick's gentlemen's club whom he'd promoted from stripper to receptionist. The customers at Famosa Motors loved her bubbly personality and ginormous assets.

"Don't hang up," I said. Brick had a tendency to be abrupt when ending calls. "I need a ride from Patron's to Famosa's along with one of your phones." He ordered phones by the case, along with phone cards.

"Your ride's on the way. When you're done, take the SIM card out and throw the card and phone away." He clicked off, not giving me an opportunity for another word. Pure Brick!

Brick had been named Cuban entrepreneur of the year. In addition to the car lot, he owns The Gentlemen's Club out in Alligator Alley, a string of pawnshops, a bail bonds place by the courthouse, and he's a private investigator.

Fabiana Merceau, my best friend and roommate, would be annoyed that my next call wasn't to her, but I knew she was spending the day with her underwear model boyfriend, Didier. To put it bluntly, she lacked hostess skills.

I dialed my brother Brad, instead. "I need a favor," I said when he answered. "Are you with Julie?" Julie, my brother's girlfriend, was the perfect choice to attend to last minute details for the party. "First off, I'm okay."

"What the hell does that mean?"

"I got carjacked. A rental car is on the way. I need you and Julie to see to the last minute details of Mother's party. Cook knows what I have planned and everything is ready, except for last minute stuff like ice. You need to open up Jake's, turn on the lights, and put out the 'Closed for Private Party' sign." I didn't give Brad a chance to interrupt.

"You better be okay."

"You're the best brother ever. One more thing, I need you to tell Mother I'm going to be late and why. I'm borrowing a cell phone so pick up your calls and I can let you know when I'm on my way."

"You're bratty," he snorted. "Any

problems, you call me."

Sylvia held a Patron's shopping bag out to me when I was done with my phone call. "Your Mother will love this. It's a small personal humidor that holds a half-dozen of her favorite cigars."

"I'll send you a check." I almost started to cry.

"It's the least we can do since this horrible thing happened in front of our store." Sylvia patted my shoulder.

"I'll tell Mother it's from the both of us and she'll love it even more."

* * *

A black Land Cruiser pulled up to the curb. The window rolled down and I could see Gunz sitting behind the wheel. "Get in, crazy," he called out to me. "Brick sent me. He owes me, and so do you." After I slid into the passenger seat he handed me a phone and an envelope with cash in it.

Gunz, short for Theodore Gunzelman, is big-boy material, dressed in all black that's an enigma I hadn't begun to understand. If one needed a new identity, he'd be your first call. He stopped painting his bald head with fake hair paint, which was a big improvement.

"What the heck happened to you?" I asked, since there was tape across his nose from one side of his face to the other.

"I had to have a little cut-and-paste on

my nostril." Gunz shook his head. "Mango and I got into a disagreement, and her tooth got lodged in my nose."

"Owwey," I scrunched my nose. "Who's Mango?"

"Stripper chick from The Gentlemen's Club; she's a little excitable," he sighed. "They were able to extract her tooth, but the dentist said it wasn't reusable."

Gunz turned into Famosa Motors. "So, which car are you taking?" he asked.

"Brick said I could have my pick. Thanks for the ride." I climbed out and looked around. I saw the SUV I wanted and went in to get the keys from Bitsy. I slipped behind the wheel of the black convertible Hummer knowing full well my insurance wouldn't cover it, but thought that maybe I could work a deal on the difference with Brick.

Chapter 2

Getting carjacked forced me to stop at home to shower and change. I couldn't show up to a party with dried blood on my arms and legs, not to mention the little pieces of gravel that embedded themselves into my skin from the pitch and roll. After going through my closet I chose a black lacey push-up bra and spaghetti strap dress. My first dress choice lay on the floor, a large unrepairable hole along one side. Since one of the heels had snapped off my shoe, I opted for a pair of black wedge designer flip-flops.

I inventoried the cars in the parking lot of Jake's and determined I was the last to arrive. Jake's, my favorite sports tiki bar, was under new management. Jake, one step ahead of heavy hitter collectors, had transferred his entire interest to me for safekeeping. Word had it they wanted their money, or him dead. I hadn't made any major changes to the exterior, but I hired a contractor to make long-needed repairs and to add more outdoor lighting. All the palm trees were wrapped in lights with colorful annuals planted at the base of each.

As soon as I put the Hummer in park, the door handle jerked open and I screamed. "How did you know it was me?" I grabbed

Zach's head and curled my hands in his thick black hair. Bringing his mouth to mine, I met him with a hard, hungry kiss.

Zach Lazarro is my boyfriend, practically from the first moment I laid eyes on him. We had a fun relationship, although lately I had to remind him more often that I wasn't a stay-at-home, bake cookies kind of girlfriend. I bought them from the bakery and passed them off as homemade.

"You have a driving style all your own that the previous pimp owner of this auto would never emulate." Zach lifted me up, our bodies fitting together, softness against hardness. "Why in the hell didn't you call me?" He pushed me away, his deep blue eyes checking me over.

I licked my lips, staring at his, hoping to forestall the lecture that waited on the tip of his tongue. "Talking and driving is out of the scope of my skills and although there's a phone inside, I need the owner's manual to learn all the tricks."

"What strings did Brick attach to this little baby?" Zach looked over the Hummer in appreciation for its mechanical capabilities. I choose it for its hotness. "Why couldn't you go to a regular rental car place and get a nice two-door sedan?"

"Brick takes insurance."

Zach laughed. "I put a man on locating

your SUV. We'll get it back, then beat the hell out of the guy and drag him to jail."

Zach, a former Navy Seal, owned AZL Securities, which boasted an impressive clientele and provided a wide variety of investigative and security services, including extreme ass-kicking.

"How's Mother?" I asked.

Recently, she sat at my kitchen island with her drink of choice, a Jack on the rocks, while lighting up a cigar she knew I forbid inside the house. I decided not to mention it because her topaz-colored eyes had turned a deep brown when mad, like my own. She issued a new order that under no circumstances was she to be the last person to "know" anything. Or she'd kick my adult butt.

"I saw her wagging her finger in Brad's face and knew you were in trouble again. I only exhaled when Brad assured me you hadn't been shot," Zach said.

"On the angry scale, one to five…"

"You skated again. Whatever Brad told her, she relaxed. Then he made her laugh and put his arm around her." Zach nibbled on my bottom lip, covering my mouth with his. "I can't believe you're throwing your mother's birthday party here at Jake's. She doesn't have the same attraction to dive bars that you do."

"Jake's is the perfect place. We have the best Mexican food in The Cove and all the Jack

Daniels Mother can drink. Haven't you noticed the improvement?"

"What are you going to do when Jake slithers back to town and wants his bar back?" Zach bit my earlobe.

"That's going to be a problem. We'll have to work out a co-ownership or something. I have big plans for this place."

"I knew it," Zach groaned, "You couldn't be happy to just pop the top on a beer and slide it down the bar."

"Party-face time, honey. We can argue later, *after* sex."

We walked through the door; Mother spotted me and ran over. I held out my shopping bag two step-lengths in front of me.

"Gift," I said.

"Oh, stop. I'm happy you're here and in one piece." Mother looked me over. "You better go make up with Fab. She's not happy she wasn't your first phone call. That boyfriend of hers wished me a happy birthday in French; so sexy sounding."

"I think Didier could say, 'Take out the trash,' and make it sound sexy."

Mother had changed her look; she still had the blonde bob, but gone was her usual conservative knee-length dress, replaced with a wildly colorful three-quarter length tropical sheath with deep slits. I eyed her open-toed striped linen wedges, thinking they'd look good in my closet.

A finger tapped me on my right shoulder. Only one person had that annoying habit. I looked left. "No chance to shoot your jacker?" Fab slinked up behind me.

"By the time I picked my butt up off the ground he had disappeared. Wait until you see my rental."

"Brick?" Fab smiled knowingly, scooping up her waist-length brown hair and putting it behind her shoulders. She traded her cars in every three months or so in exchange for unspecified jobs that she never talked about. I knew some of her methods pushed the limits—others were outright illegal—but sometimes you have to stack the deck when dealing with a dirtball.

Liam ran up and threw his arms around me. I groaned, several places on my body tender to the touch. "When Brad told us the story, I was happy to hear you were okay."

"We have a date for the aquarium this weekend. I'm not missing that."

Liam was fourteen going on thirty, an atypical teenager. Mother and I already claimed him as our grandson-nephew even though his mother, Julie, and Brad were only in the dating stage. Neither of us entertained the idea that Liam wouldn't always be a part of our family.

Familiar arms wrapped around the front

of me, turning me around. "This place looks like someone actually cleaned it." Creole scanned the restaurant and each guest; it would make his night to haul in a drug dealer. Only a handful of people knew he was an undercover cop. "Food's good; I came in the back and sampled my way through the kitchen." His lips looked ready to zoom in on mine. I turned my face away at the last second and he kissed my cheek.

"If you start a fight with your best friend at Mother's birthday party she won't be happy."

"Zach just gave me the finger. It's nice being friends again, but he knows if he screws up and you dump him, I'll be banging on your door."

Creole, aka Luc Baptiste, is an unofficial cousin in our family; only family knew his real name. My Aunt Elizabeth had adopted him with her heart, giving him protection from an abusive home life. As a young boy, he grew up several houses down from her. They formed a bond that was as close as mother and son. Mother had warmly welcomed him into the family. He was actually a good fit, which annoyed Zach. Creole dripped sex, had caramel-colored skin, and he'd cut his black ponytail that hung down to the middle of his back, in favor of shoulder-length hair.

Creole ran his hand slowly down my

back to my waist. "Where's your gun?"

"Thigh holster."

"Why is Mother kissing that criminal?" Brad pointed to Mother's boyfriend, Spoon.

"He's a reformed criminal," I said, patting Brad's shoulder, "How could you not know? She's been sneaking around with him for forever. She's terrible at it." My brother is a straight-up nice guy with sun-bleached hair from long hours spent out in the Gulf waters as a commercial fisherman. No one ever says a bad word about him.

Spoon and Mother shared the love of a good cigar. They started out as smoking buddies. Brad couldn't help but notice Mother looked happier since her hook-up with a younger, edgier man.

"There's a nice doctor and CPA in town, they're both single," Brad fumed. "She's not going to date him anymore."

"I dare you to go over there and get the 'I'm a grown woman' speech," I taunted. If only Brad would stop being so hard-headed and get to know Spoon. Well, he still wouldn't approve, but he'd stop with the wishful thinking that Mother would hook up with a nice older gentleman.

Brad pushed his chin forward and started in their direction.

"Toss back a beer with Spoon and you might be surprised," I called after him.

Zach and Creole answered their phones at the same time. Work probably beckoned the both of them. Creole turned a short-term assignment with the Miami Police Department into a permanent one. He mingled with drug dealers and other lowlifes, climbing the ladder of dirty dealings to the man at the top. They were both now staring at me. I groaned inwardly. Now what?

Zach walked over to me. "The fire is out."

"My house?" I ran for the front door. "What about Jazz?"

Zach caught me in his arms. "Cat's fine, it's not your house. Cottage ten caught fire and burned down. The good news is the front steps are still intact, and thankfully, there's no damage to the rest of the property."

I sighed with relief, "Good thing it was empty." Brad moved to my side and heard the conversation.

"Go check on the property," Brad said as he hugged me. "Get back as soon as you can. Julie and I will make sure everything goes fine here."

* * *

I took the shortcut to The Cottages. There was no reason to drive along the beach, since there was nothing to see at night except for total darkness. I saw Fab and Didier sneak out of the party earlier for some more of their

15

jungle sex as she liked to call it. Late one night, I'd gone down to the kitchen for a snack and heard them giggling, Didier making animal noises. My cheeks turned bright red and I raced back upstairs.

As it turned out, Brad and Julie were the only ones to stay behind and clean up after Mother's party. Brad called to tell me he'd bring the birthday cake to my house. My mouth watered at the thought of eating a piece of the strawberry perfection: white cake, hollowed out, filled with sliced strawberries, and iced with whipped cream.

Liam rode with me and set my radio stations, got the time right on the clock, and was currently setting my home address on the GPS.

"Wow look at that!" Liam said in awe. "Glad it wasn't our cottage. Mom and I like living here."

I parked the Hummer on the street in front of the office. Cottage ten was now a burned-out hollow shell. "How does an empty cottage burn down?"

Liam shrugged and jumped out before I shut off the engine.

Tomorrow it would be a tourist attraction. It sat closest to the street, separated by the barbeque area. Thank goodness an individual parking space separated each cottage or the fire could have leapfrogged down the driveway.

"Hey, Kev, what the heck happened?" I asked Kevin Cory, a local sheriff who'd been assigned to this area as long as I owned the place.

Kevin and Liam high-fived and did some sort of knuckle-bump ritual. Kevin and Julie were brother and sister. Kevin wasn't happy that Julie decided to date Brad, until they met and he learned crazy only ran on the female side of the Westin family.

Kevin pointed to the still-smoldering rubble. A fire truck sat curbside. "Who was living in there? It surprised me we didn't find a dead body or two; wouldn't be the first time."

"Somebody died in there?" Liam asked with fascination.

I spoke up quickly, never wanting the dead body subject to come up again. Hey, I didn't murder the man, but that didn't make for an interesting story. "It had been out of rotation for plumbing repairs, an insidious leak that turned into a remodel when the floor had to be ripped up."

Kevin loved to lecture, my guess, about what a poor adult role model I made. He looked at Liam and changed his mind. "Well, someone lived in there. The fire chief stopped by on his way home from dinner, his investigator suspects it was a meth lab."

That should rule me out as a suspect, I

thought; I've never done drugs and had a no tolerance policy. "Did you talk to the rest of the tenants and guests?"

The Cottages is a ten-unit property that I inherited from my Aunt Elizabeth, Mother's only sibling, and to say the regular tenants were eccentric was putting it nicely. The tourist guests, mostly from the UK and Scotland, were repeat customers, along with their referrals who came and went and gave the property a sense of normalcy. Despite the turnstile of trouble the property attracted, the out-of-towners never seemed fazed by the occasional shooting, brawl, or dead body.

Kevin's blue eyes sparkled with anger. "Not a single damn one of your so-called tenants would answer the door," he seethed, brushing his blondish-brown hair from his eyes; he wore it longer than most sheriffs did. "I know they're home. A couple of them had the audacity to turn off their lights after I knocked. And now look, they're staring out their windows bold as brass."

I couldn't help myself. I laughed. "What about Joseph?" Joseph, a Vietnam vet, had lived at The Cottages the longest and one of my aunt's first tenants.

"That piece of shit yelled, 'Go away,' and turned off his light. I'm calling his probation officer in the morning."

"I'll save you a dime, Joseph's off

probation." That was the only good thing about his last girlfriend, his first grade teacher. She kept him out of trouble long enough to finally close the drunk driving case. Closing that case also wiped out a grand theft auto charge, a car stolen from a friend of course, drunk in public, and peeing in the alley files.

Kevin motioned to Zach, who walked up. "I'll let you know when we're done with the cleanup," Kevin said. "I'll take Liam with me."

Zach spoke up. "Actually, Julie is at Madison's with Madeline's birthday cake. Liam's expected there." Zach and Kevin were good friends, so Kevin wouldn't say "hell no" like he would if it were my suggestion.

I squeezed Zach's butt cheek in a silent thank you, knowing the last thing Liam wanted was to be left out of the fun. "Kevin, you're more than welcome to come for cake."

Chapter 3

The advantage to having my bedroom on the second floor overlooking the back yard, I didn't have to hang window coverings. The early morning sun streamed through the windows, signaling another warm day. Once I turned over, Jazz stuck his face in mine and meowed at the top of his lungs. Cat-speak for, "Get up and feed me."

If our roles were reversed and I had celebrated being over one hundred years old, would I rule the house, or still be his servant?

Zach had left early. We seldom shared leisurely mornings in bed. He did make a point of telling me for his birthday he'd like me to get rid of Fab as a roommate. I gave him my usual vague response that didn't commit me to an answer either way. If he had his way, my open door policy would change to "don't come by uninvited."

I scooped up the large black ball of fluff and headed downstairs. Halfway down, I noticed a nice-looking man with disheveled brown hair sitting at my kitchen island. "Who are you?"

"Bonjour, mon cherie." He looked me over in clinical detail.

I felt naked standing in my Dolphins

football jersey that hung mid-thigh. He must be another friend of Fab's––none of mine spoke French; a few had a hard time with English.

He raised a gun up off his lap and pointed it at me. "Take a seat."

Two days in a row I'd stared down the barrel of a gun; I needed to give my Karma a shining. "What do you want?" I stood rooted in place.

"Sit." He pointed to a barstool pulled away from the island. "Or my first shot will kill the cat."

Jazz howled, pacing in front of his food bowl. He had food, but demanded I refresh it in the morning.

"Shut that damn thing up."

My voice pleaded, "I just need to give him some food and water and he'll go to sleep." There was a gun in the drawer, but shooting the intruder before he shot me seemed highly unlikely. I hurriedly took care of Jazz and then sat on the stool.

"Just tell me what you want," I said.

"That's easy. I want Fabiana Merceau." His gray eyes were hard as steel.

"Fab doesn't leave notes as to where she's going. Why don't you check back later?"

He unleashed a tirade in French and then said in English, "You uneducated American. Get her here. Now."

"So you can kill her?" My stomach

muscles clenched.

"Killing my dear Fabiana would not get me what I want. Now call her." He punctuated this by pointing his gun at Jazz.

"This I can promise you, you'll never get whatever it is you want by shooting me or the cat." I reminded myself to remain calm and picked up my phone. *Why had we never talked about a code word? How was I going to warn her?*

Fab picked up on the second ring. "Cherie," I blurted. "Can you come back to the house?"

"What's up?" Fab asked. "Why do you sound weirder than usual?"

"Don't speed in my car." I hung up, hoping that because the conversation made no sense that would be code enough.

"Who are you anyway?" I asked.

"Shut up or I will shoot you and Fabiana will have to get over it," he sneered.

* * *

Fab walked through the French doors from the pool area, her Ruger LC-9 handgun pointed at our mystery man. "When did you get out?" She asked, clearly not pleased to see him. "Put your gun down, this has nothing to do with Madison."

The energy intense and electric; as I looked between the two of them, sparks from their eyes flew back and forth. This must be the ex-husband, Gabriel, I thought. Looks wise, he had a lot in common with Didier. Fab clearly had a type: tall, dark-haired, and with that delicious accent. Didier was sweet and flirted shamelessly, his blue eyes sparkled; this one's eyes were cold and calculating. The hair on the back of my neck told me he would bring Fab down.

Gabriel put his gun in his front waistband. "You're going to give me back what is mine and if you don't I'll blow up your life and everyone in it."

The tone of his voice sent shivers up my spine. His words shocked me; I'd never had someone who loved me speak to me with such venom.

Fab holstered her gun. "I don't have anything that belongs to you. I sold my ring and two other pieces of jewelry and fled France."

Gabriel beat his fist on the counter. "The painting." He kicked his stool over, clearing the space between them, and grabbed her face, smashing his lips to hers.

Fab gave him a hard shove with both hands. "Don't you remember I never had possession of the painting?"

Gabriel dug his fingers into both sides of her cheeks and squeezed. "You forget how well I know every inch of your sexy body and larcenous mind. You're a liar. Convince me as though your life depends on it that you had nothing to do with the fake that was left in place of the real painting. Even if you can, I'll still need another priceless work of art."

"You're hurting me." Fab shrugged out of his grasp. "Wait while I pull a masterpiece out of my back pocket."

Gabriel had lost all interest in me; he was locked in an intense standoff with "his" Fabiana. I slid over to the kitchen drawer and removed my Glock. "Step back, Gabriel." I cocked my 9mm.

Gabriel turned. "You won't shoot me." He spoke to me like a mere irritation.

"Yes, she will." Fab walked to the front door and held it open. "Leave here and don't come back. If I even see you in the neighborhood, I may have to shoot you."

Gabriel pinned Fab to the front door with his body. "Meet me in one hour at that dreadful café the two of you frequent. We'll catch up on how I did prison time and you're living in this dreadful hole." Gabriel shot hate sparks in my direction. He ran his finger down Fab's cheek, kissed her, and then disappeared down the driveway.

I exhaled when the door slammed shut. "Wow, we have terrible taste in ex-husbands."

"Jax would never shoot you. Gabriel wears vengeance like an honor badge." Fab rushed over. "I'm sorry. Are you okay?"

"You have options. I know people who

could make him disappear." I mentally ran down the list of my friends and knew two who could expedite him to a mere memory in twenty-four hours.

Fab wagged her finger at me. "I'm going to take care of this and you're going to stay out of it."

A bad feeling settled over me. "You know where the painting is, don't you?"

Fab shook her head. "I hate it when you just seem to know stuff."

"Give it back to him with the understanding he leaves town tomorrow." My hand shook when I pulled a coffee mug off the shelf.

"I'd have to steal it again." Fab covered her face with her hands.

My phone rang. Mac's name popped up on the screen. "More bad news?" I asked.

Mac Lane managed The Cottages and, for the most part, stayed one step ahead of the crazies.

"Koozie got arrested," Mac blurted. "He set cottage ten on fire using his cooking-meth-for-dummies manual. When one of his cooking pots exploded, he freaked and ran out the door. He didn't bother to call the fire department or anyone else, for that matter. Kevin's partner, Johnson, stopped by on an official visit and to chat it up with you."

"Blow Johnson off until later. Can you

start with estimates for cleanup, et cetera? Once I get the okay from the insurance company, I'm going to have the rubble hauled away." One problem at a time today, I thought.

Officer Johnson and I had an avid dislike for one another. "He started it," I told his partner Kevin when asked to be nicer. Johnson liked to snap his fingers and didn't like that I wasn't a jumper.

"On it already," Mac smacked her gum. "Several folks have stopped by offering services. I have business cards in two piles: second look and no way."

I hung up the phone. "Start from the beginning," I told Fab. "Try not to minimize the pertinent details." My heart pounded hard. I hoped Gabriel wouldn't be the end of our friendship.

"Gabriel and I made headlines as sexy cat burglars. Lucky for me, a security camera caught only the back of me in skintight black pants and a long-sleeve top. We were selective, had high thieving standards. We stole from rich people. Let's face it, they have the coolest stuff. My job was to gain entry. Rich people leave their windows open a lot, so I'd cut the screen and crawl right in. Most times we were invited guests—my parent's friends and those of their social ilk."

I couldn't imagine stealing from my parents' friends. I'm sure I embarrassed

Mother plenty of times, but this took it to a whole new level.

"The Evards, tennis partners of my parents, bragged about their newest 'little getaway' to Monte Carlo. What a perfect time to loot their mansion! The entire alarm system appeared to be as old as the house; dismantling it was child's play. Unbeknownst to us, behind every painting was a back-up system that sounded an alarm if moved. While Gabriel ransacked the downstairs, I swept the master bedroom, pawing through Madame's jewels, helping myself. Gabriel had the painting off the wall, admiring it, when the guards burst in. He managed to hang on to the painting, jump out the window, and lead them on a chase. He had a slight lead; apparently the guards weren't window jumpers and chose to go out the French doors. They struggled to get them unlocked, and then the pursuit was on.

"The master bedroom doors stood open to the garden below. I heard the commotion, dumped a handful of trinkets into my pockets, and slipped out through the library at the opposite side of the house."

"What happened to the painting?" I asked.

"They had Gabriel in custody within an hour, no painting. He managed to make it back to town before getting caught. Instead of using the painting to broker a deal, he kept quiet and gambled, trying to convince the court the guards chased the wrong man. After all, he didn't have it in his possession." Fab checked her watch. "I can't be late."

"My Glock and I will go as backup," I said. "Give me five minutes to change."

"You go take care of The Cottages and we'll meet here later." Fab grabbed her keys.

"I don't like this," I grumbled. "You tell Monsieur Bastard if I don't see you tonight I'll unleash every law enforcement agency I can on him."

"Promise me, you won't breathe a word of this to anyone."

"I can't keep that promise," I sighed. "You need to think very carefully before you agree to something that will have you in prison stripes for a very long time."

Fab waved and raced to the door, I was hot on her heels.

I yelled, "Tonight, Fabiana!"

Chapter 4

It took every ounce of self-control not to drive by our favorite place for breakfast, The Bakery Café, on the pretext of needing a latte or some other lame excuse. Fab was in more danger than when she faced down the drug dealer pointing a gun in her face, and besides I knew Gabriel would spot the inconspicuous Hummer in a second.

I was so preoccupied with Fab's problems, I couldn't remember driving along the beach, which was my favorite route from my house to The Cottages. Before last night, it had been a ten-unit, three-sided square building that had direct beach access. My strengths were used in renovating the units and grounds. For day-to-day management, I hired a double Red Bull-drinking manager. Mac handled the tenants and their flakey friends with tough love.

Turning the corner, I almost ran into Miss January, who'd wandered into the street pacing, holding Kitty. Miss January was another tenant I inherited from my aunt; a fortyish woman who looked eighty, was consumed with cancer, and self-medicated with vodka and cigarettes. There were no signs of dementia except where her cat was concerned, never acknowledging that Kitty had been dead a long time and was stuffed.

I pulled into a parking space reserved for the office, jumped out, and cut across the grass to find Miss January before a car hit her.

Tears streamed down Miss January's face. "Kitty's dying." She slid her hand from Kitty's side and showed me a gaping hole where stuffing had come out.

Mac loved to mind other people's business. She hustled up behind me and groaned loudly at the sight. Her auburn bouffant stayed stiffly in place by a half a can of Aqua Net.

I put my arm around Miss January's boney shoulders. "Don't worry, I'll take Kitty to the vet, and she'll be good as new." It never occurred to me to blurt out, "Damn it, the cat's dead." Instead I said, "Mac can help me."

"Yeah, sorry, I have a gyno appointment," Mac grunted. She rolled her eyes and headed straight for the office.

"Ever since I got cancer the doctor hasn't been interested in looking up there," Miss January shared.

"Let's put Kitty in the back of my SUV." I drew the line at touching it; I had picked it up before but had worn gardening gloves. It was another warm day, and I hoped Kitty had been dead long enough not to smell. Brick would flip.

"Joseph called me an old drunk." She tossed her limp hair. "You don't think I look old, do you?"

"Don't pay attention to Joseph. You know he says stuff he doesn't mean." I helped her up the stairs and into her cottage.

"I need a nap," Miss January mumbled, and flopped onto her bed.

I covered her with a blanket and did my best to walk calmly out.

"I swear if this office door was locked I'd be tempted to kick it open." I wanted to throw myself onto the couch, but sat in a chair instead. "You're going to hell."

Mac sat tipped back in her chair, tennis shoe-clad feet on the desk, sporting one of her tie-dyed hippy skirts and matching ill-fitting T-shirt.

"Party in the afterlife." She handed me a piece of paper. "I assume by vet you mean taxidermist. I could find only one down in Pigeon Key."

Feeling frazzled I said, "Koozie burnt the cottage down, how the hell did he even get in?"

"He got hired on the plumbing crew as trash dude. He knew it was empty and a perfect place—in his drug-addled mind—to set up shop. He'd also been living there, sneaking in at night." Mac threw her gum in the trash, putting a new pink piece in her mouth.

"The insurance agent is my neighbor and got us moved to the top of the list. He'll be coming over today to take pics and once the red tape comes down, we can start debris removal." I reached across to the bar refrigerator and helped myself to a cold water. "I'll call Kevin and get the green light from him; I'm avoiding his partner, Johnson. What does he want anyway?"

Mac sucked the giant bubble she'd blown back into her mouth. "Koozie claimed he did everything according to your orders and that the two of you would be sharing the profits. Officer Johnson is salivating to talk to you." Mac enjoyed the story, but then no one mentioned her name in the same sentence as selling drugs.

"Does anyone believe the crap story besides Johnson?"

"I haven't heard there's a warrant out for your arrest. And no sheriff's staking out the place, so I'll take a leap and say no." Mac flashed a fake smile.

I dropped the loaner phone this morning and it changed the ring tone to annoying. "Hi, Brick."

"Bring back my Hummer!" he yelled. "I do you a favor and you take a hundred thousand dollar automobile."

I held my phone away from my ear. Mac slid forward to hear every word, though people walking down the block could listen in. "You said I had my pick of cars. It didn't cost a hundred thousand new. Besides, it's used with twenty thousand miles on the odometer."

"Are you crazy? It's a one of a kind! They're not manufactured anymore!" He still yelled, but not quite as loudly.

"Let me drive it for a week. I thought if my Tahoe isn't found, I'd haggle you down on the price." I covered the mouthpiece so he wouldn't hear Mac laughing. "How about the work for auto program?"

"I want the Hummer back tomorrow."

I heard a loud noise in the background. He either hit his hand on the desk or threw something.

"You were coming in anyway because I've got a job for you. Straight-up investigation. I need someone to go out, be nice, and schmooze info, which––before you ask––is why I didn't call Fab."

"How can I work for you with no car?" My charming voice needed work; I sounded whiney.

"I have a nice Chevy Vega washed and gassed for you. Tomorrow morning, Red." Brick hung up.

Mac pulled open a drawer and held out a five dollar bill. "This says you're back tomorrow in the Hummer."

"I'm so happy I hired you and even

happier that I've never regretted my decision." Mac cornered me one day at the pool applying for the job, five minutes after the idea of hiring a manager left my lips. There's a party-line for gossip in the neighborhood that's unmatched anywhere. The idea of sitting in the office all day held not a sliver of interest to me. I'd have to drink starting in the morning.

Mac jumped up and raced to the window. "Look, another carload of people stopped to have their pictures taken in front of the burned out mess."

I opened the door. "Dare you to go out there and start charging people."

"A buck a pic? I don't want to make change." Mac headed over to the picture poachers and I left.

Chapter 5

I cruised into Jake's and parked my Hummer in the space next to the SUV I'd finally talked Mother into getting. I refused to barricade myself inside my home. Damn Gabriel for making me afraid in my own house. Not knowing what Fab was getting herself into didn't help. I almost forgot that tonight I had volunteered to fill in for my regular bartender; her young son is the star tomato in his school play.

Mother sat at the bar trading jokes with the day bartender, Phil. She nodded to me and disappeared into the kitchen.

"You did a good job on the deck," Mother hugged me. "I just enjoyed a cigar out there."

"Jake had a stack of code violations, all of which he ignored. The deck being the biggest problem, it had rotten, termite eaten boards and studs barely held together with rusted screws, and shorter than the code demands. How no one went tumbling to the concrete below is a mystery. I replaced the entire deck and cleared every outstanding violation. Once I got rid of the roaches and power washed the entire place, the 'C' rating got raised to an 'A.'"

Jake managed to evade being shut down by opening the deck on nights and weekends when he figured no inspector would show up. What he didn't know was that his luck had run out, and he'd been days away from being padlocked. He gambled his life into a complete train wreck. Had he stayed in The Cove, he'd be dead by now. The people he borrowed from took a dim view of late payments.

Mother looked around. "You've done a good job classing up this dingy bar."

Phil came out of the back with two racks of clean glasses, set them down, and then grabbed her motorcycle helmet and jacket. "See you tomorrow, boss."

She'd sauntered into the bar during renovations, the Help Wanted sign in her hand. "I'm your new daytime bartender." Dressed in short-shorts, a tankini bathing suit top, and cowboy boots, she'd bring in the business. I hired her on the spot.

"I have followers," Phil informed me when we shook on the deal. Under Jake's control, the bar was a ghost town during the day, the occasional customer coming in for verbal abuse from the unfriendly owner. We now did a brisk lunch business; the cook complained he didn't have enough time to talk on his cell phone.

"It's been fun. Word's spread; we get busier every day. Business has boomed since I hired people with personality and big boobs." I looped my arm through Mother's. "Come sit at the other end of the bar and I'll buy you a drink." She'd soon learned it was the best seat in the place to people-watch, and had the added advantage of no one being able to sneak up on you.

Filling a glass with ice, I poured her a Jack Daniels, her signature drink. "How often did you gamble in the back room?"

"Really, Madison." Mother said, looking flustered.

I stopped myself from rolling my eyes. "Don't bother to deny it; Jake ratted you out a long time ago. I'm thinking about re-opening the room."

"It wouldn't surprise me if I opened the door back there and it was all ready for play," Mother said, pointing down the hall past the kitchen, "even though it is illegal."

"A few of the old players have stopped by since Jake's re-opened, letting me know they missed the 'friendly card games.' I'm thinking invitation only, no cash on the table, buy chips ahead of time, and cash out after. Private bar set-up; small buffet and a private hostess."

"Can we smoke?" Mother asked. "When's the first game?"

A large group of beach goers, all coupled up, tried squeezing in the door at the same time, heading straight to the deck and claiming half the tables.

"Would you like to help me pick the cigars for the standing humidor? Did you know I hired one of your boyfriend's parolee friends? He comes with an impressive set of carpenter skills; less chance of word getting around."

Jimmy Spoon, Mother's boyfriend, had long ago done prison time and he paid back by mentoring newly-released felons; he gave them a chance at a fresh start with a job and a place to live. To my knowledge, he had a one-hundred percent success rate.

Creole walked out of the kitchen. The few days of facial stubble that shadowed across his face gave him an even more dangerous look.

"Hello, ladies," He said before he kissed Mother and sat down next to her. "I'll take whatever you have on tap."

I extended my cheek to him. "We have a front door." My phone rang. "It's about time," I answered, setting an ice-cold beer glass in front of Creole.

"I didn't want you to worry. I'll be away for a few days." Fab sounded stressed.

That worried me because nothing fazes her. "That's not acceptable." My voice went up with each word. "I'm here at Jake's. You tell that piece of crap ex of yours that if I don't see your face in one hour, I'm calling Brick. Tell Gabriel, tick-tock." Brick had a brother, Casio, who was second or third in command of Miami detectives. I knew him well enough to know he wasn't a rule follower and he owed me.

Fab shushed me. "Calm down. Really, I'm fine."

"Listen to me, Fabiana Merceau. One hour or I'm calling everyone I know." She rarely listened to anyone, but I wasn't backing down.

"We'll be there." Fab sighed and hung up.

"What the hell was that all about?" Mother demanded. "What kind of trouble is Fab in?"

"The felony kind. If either of you can't keep what I tell you a secret, let me know now." Both shook their heads, indicating that they would keep their mouths shut. I told them about Gabriel's morning visit. I noticed Creole's eyes turn to steel when I told them about his threatening to shoot me.

"Don't tell Fab she just missed me." Creole stood up. "I think I'll arrange a little meet and greet." He kissed Mother and slipped out the back door.

"We'll stop Fab from committing felonies." Mother patted my hand.

Gig, another new hire, was rapidly

becoming a favorite. The striking blonde worked her curvy assets and currently in her last year of college. "Two Buds, glass of your finest Cabernet, and a Pimple on Your Butt."

"You do this to me just so I'm forced to ask how to make the damned drink." I passed her the beers and screw top wine. "Here's a wine glass for your connoisseur," I chuckled.

She laughed and handed me a list of ingredients: vodka, coffee, triple sec. "See what happens when you class up the place?"

"What's happening out on the deck?" They were loud but laughing, having a good time.

She handed me another piece of notepaper. "They all ordered bottled beer. As soon as I deliver, I'll take the food order."

"You need help, yell."

Mother slid off her barstool as Fab came through the door, hugging her and whispering something in her ear. They both came and sat at the bar.

"What does he want from you?" I looked her over; she looked tired but had no marks anywhere. "Good to see you, by the way."

Fab smiled limply. "He wants us to burgle homes until he has the two million he was expecting from the sale of the painting."

"Do you or did you ever have the painting?" I hadn't forgotten she didn't answer the question the first time I asked.

"I had it briefly and used it to broker a deal for myself, getting the charges dropped and cover travel expenses to get out of France. My parents believed I was a pawn of Gabriel's and asked an influential friend of theirs in parliament for his help. He laughed at my 'pitiful' story, but in private he told me if I wanted his help, the price would be the painting. And not for altruistic reasons; he wanted it to hang in his house."

"Did your parents ever find out the truth?" Mother asked.

"I'd become an embarrassing disappointment to them and believe they were relieved when I fled France."

"Gabriel had the painting when he left the estate, but when apprehended, the painting had disappeared. What happened in between and how did you find it?" I asked.

"You know how snoopy I can be. Gabriel never knew that I went through his drawers, pants, cell phone; little did he know he had few secrets from me. He left the receipt for the storage locker on his desk. I slipped his keys out of his pants pocket and made impressions. Gabriel got captured a block from the place."

"Your snoopy ways are annoying to me." I pushed a lime and soda Fab's way.

"When I went to retrieve the painting,

the key didn't work so I ended up picking the lock. I'd already obtained an inexpensive copy. I figured he'd think the original had been a fake all along."

"That was clever," Mother said.

Fab looked defeated, which made me angry. "Tell Gabriel to take a hike. You don't owe him squat." I refilled Mother's drink. "You're spending the night," I told her.

"He's angry and bitter. He did prison time, I didn't. Getting the divorce papers in his jail cell stoked the seeds of retribution. He expected me to stand by him, visit, write, and be waiting with open arms when the steel doors opened. Instead, I fled and never looked back." Fab downed her soda. "I have to go. Gabriel's already suspicious. He's threatened your family, and mine in France. I'm not calling his bluff."

Mother took Fab's face between her hands. "Do *not* do anything illegal with this man. If you do, I'll have to hurt you," she said, using her no-nonsense mother voice. "You can hide out at my house and we'll make him disappear." She kissed her cheek.

Fab threw her arms around Mother. "I love you as though you were my own mother. I'll stall him as long as I can."

"Think of a plan B," I told her.

"I have to go. I'm surprised Gabriel hasn't burned up my phone. Love you both."

Fab slipped out the back door.

"What the hell is wrong with the front door?" I asked Mother. "Do I need to ask someone else to muddy their hands making that worthless bastard disappear?"

Mother's worry lines popped in her forehead. "Have you noticed Creole never came back?" She looked around.

"Maybe he's putting Gabriel on a slow freighter to a foreign country he'll never get out of." I crossed my fingers.

Fab rushed through the front door, out of breath. "Gabriel's gone."

"He stole your car?" Or more accurately, he'd stolen one of Brick's cars, and that would be a big mistake.

"The Beemer is still sitting there but Gabriel has disappeared. He couldn't get far on foot. I'll go out to the highway."

"No," Mother and I said in unison.

I looked at Mother. She had a smirk on her face. "Consider it a good sign from above. With really good luck, he'll never come back." We were both thinking the same thing: Creole.

Chapter 6

Black storm clouds gathered in the distance, an impending storm coming our way. Mother lay next to me on my king-sized bed, sending a message on her phone. "When did you push the chair under the doorknob?" I looked at the bedroom door. "Where's Fab?"

"I took Hairball downstairs to keep her company on the couch. Just sent another message to Creole; his phone is going straight to voice mail."

Jazz knew Mother called him names and every chance he got he rubbed his long black fur all over her white pants.

"Gabriel threatened to shoot Jazz first." The thought freaked me out. I knew he'd die one day, but not from a bullet.

"As of an hour ago, Fab hadn't heard from Gabriel––and no word from Creole." Mother brushed her hands together and continued, "I think one and one adds up to 'Creole took care of the problem.'"

"Hungry?" I wouldn't be convinced until I heard the words from Creole's lips. "I'm fixing frozen waffles."

"I should've gone to The Bakery Café earlier, but I was afraid you'd need me to shoot someone."

"Maybe next visit I'll arrange a shootout." I pulled the chair from under the knob, pushing it back to its normal place.

From the top of the stairs, I saw Fab sitting in the kitchen. "I'm cooking," I called to her.

"Putting waffles in a toaster is not cooking." Fab shook her head. "I'll have coffee."

Mother hugged Fab and sat next to her. "Make me a cup."

I shook my finger at them. "No talk about you-know-who until after breakfast."

"Where's Zach?" Fab asked. "I expected him to come strolling in last night."

"He and Slice are up in Tallahassee for a couple of days, new account." Slice was Zach's right-hand muscle man, just looking at him inspired fear. He stood well over six feet tall, with not an ounce of fat, and an angry scar ran from his forehead to his collarbone.

I set my new ceramic shell coffee mugs on the island. "Brick demanded my appearance in his office this morning to return the Hummer."

"While you're gone, I'm moving out." Fab turned her back and fiddled with the overpriced coffee maker only she knew how to work.

I never entertained the thought of a roommate, but Fab and I pulled off cohabitation without getting on each other's last nerves. "Fine. Do that and I'll track you down and drag you back by the hair."

"Gabriel's dangerous! The fact that he's disappeared without a word makes the situation worse."

"If you feel the need to move out, come to my house," Mother said. "Today, you're coming with us. I'm looking forward to meeting this Brick character, and then we'll go to lunch."

I enjoyed watching Fab's face. She itched to tell Mother that she'd do what she wanted, when she wanted, but good manners prevailed over her need to be in charge.

* * *

"Why couldn't I have driven?" Fab sulked, resting her head on the back of the passenger's seat.

We arrived at Famosa Motors. "I wanted to be an example to you, so you know that a person can drive within the speed limit."

"Do you want to know how many drivers honked at you or gave you the finger? You're damn lucky this isn't a road rage state." Fab sounded ready to explode.

"On the way back, you'll both ride in the back seat and I'll drive," Mother said.

I poked Fab, shaking my head. Mother had had enough of the "she touched me,"-- "no I didn't" bickering.

The doors to the showroom had been rolled open. "Hi, Bits." I waved. "Brick is expecting me."

"You think her back hurts with breasts that large?" Mother asked.

"You'll have to ask her; I don't have that problem." I looped my arm through Mother's and led her up the stairs to Brick's second floor office. The power seat came with a 180-degree view of the car lot and pricey South Miami commercial real estate.

"These are the worst chairs in the office, but there's nowhere else to sit," I told Mother, pointing to four chairs in front of his desk. "The floor sucks just as much." Brick once told me he chose the least comfortable seating he could find so that no one would stay long.

Brick hung up the phone with his traditional bang. "Give me the keys." He held out his hand. "Hello, ladies. Not to be rude, Fab, but I don't want you involved in this job." He slowly looked Mother up and down.

"This is my mother," I said, stressing the word 'mother', "Madeline Westin."

Mother extended her hand. "I've heard a lot about you."

Fab gave me a soft shove. *Uh-oh, what had she heard, and from where*? I thought. It irritated me the way Brick looked at Mother, like she was a tasty morsel. "What's the job?"

"Would you like something to drink?"

Brick asked Mother.

"No, but I'll take a cigar on the way out." Mother pointed to an open humidor on his desk.

Brick nodded. "A few months ago my niece, Katy, met the man of her dreams while skiing in Aspen. My sister is worried because Prince Charming is married, says he's getting a divorce. How many women have heard that line? Find out if the story is true." Brick handed me a sheet of paper. "Here's the name, address, everything I want checked out. I want this info yesterday."

I looked at the address, it was in a nice neighborhood. "What? I just knock on the door and ask questions?"

Brick snickered. "You're the wannabe PI, you figure it out. And don't let on they're being investigated." Brick held out his hand. "My keys."

I flashed my innocent smile. "Let me drive it for a week," I said. "My Tahoe can't stay gone forever."

"I know that look." Brick threw his pen on the desk. "I have a wife and a basketful of female relatives. I'll end up having to repo it to get it back."

Mother cleared her throat loudly, bringing all eyes on her. "Think of it as a nice way to say thank you after sending my daughter out on jobs where she got arrested and almost mauled by Dobermans." She stared icicles at him.

Dead silence.

Brick stared at Mother and she continued to stare back. "A week. If they haven't found your Tahoe by then, I'll trade you for a different ride, under 50K."

I wanted to jump out of my chair and do a toned down version of a happy dance. Ha-ha, he caved, go Mother! But there was still the issue of who ratted me out. It had to be Zach.

Chapter 7

Ramsey Sinclair lived in Gables by the Sea, one of the oldest, historical, and wealthier neighborhoods of Coral Gables. A private gated community, every estate boasts water views.

Fab cut through the busy streets of South Miami in her usual reckless abandon. I had to remind myself she hadn't been in an accident the whole time I knew her.

"How in the heck do we get in here?" I asked Fab, who stopped complaining now that she was behind the wheel.

"Watch this." Fab opened her briefcase and extracted a blank credit card. She inserted it into the box at the resident gate.

The double gates opened. "Where do I get one of those?" I asked.

"Make sure you get two," Mother said. "You never know when I could use one some time."

I called Mac on the drive over, gave her the address, and told her to get me the name of a previous neighbor on either side, and approximately when they moved. She called back as we turned into the gate. William and Lucille Cardinal owned the house across the street and sold it two years ago.

Every estate sat back from the street, with miles of front lawn and parking pads at the front door. Fab pulled up in front of the circular drive belonging to the Sinclairs. "Park in the street, I'll hike up the driveway."

Fab turned in her seat. "What are you going to say?"

"I've worked up a vague plan." I exhaled. "If I come back to the car with a person, Mother, you act like you've got dementia." I pointed to Fab. "You help her practice."

Houses in divorces usually got sold. If I were Lisa Sinclair, I wouldn't be happy. This house had it all; I guessed it to be ten thousand square feet, and the backyard was a tropical oasis that boasted a pool with a waterfall and tennis courts.

You know how to talk to people. I rang the doorbell and it reverberated throughout the house. A friendly looking middle-aged woman answered the door, small pruning scissors in her hand. This woman took care of herself; she was petite, tanned, and in great shape.

"Hi, Lucille Cardinal?" I smiled.

"No, dear, you have the wrong house. They used to live across the street," she said and pointed to a peach Spanish-style home. "They moved a couple of years back."

"Lucille was a friend of my mother's," I said, keeping my lying smile in place. "She's visiting from California and I thought I'd surprise them with a reunion lunch."

Lisa Sinclair's phone rang from somewhere in the house. "Just one moment." She ran down the hall.

I stood at the door, uncomfortable with what I'd already done. The living room reeked of wealth, decorated in comfortable-looking upholstered furniture. Lisa had been pruning a large arrangement of flowers that sat on the coffee table. Stems and blooms lay in a neat pile. I wondered if the roses and hydrangeas came from her yard. Dozens of rose bushes were planted along the entire front of the house.

Lisa returned carrying a phone book. "The Cardinals moved to St. Augustine to be near their children. I thought I had their new address, but I don't. We talked about getting together and never followed through."

A white Carrera Porsche pulled up to the front door and parked. The door opened and a middle-aged man got out, briefcase in hand.

He winked at Lisa. "Hello," he said to me, and kissed her cheek.

"This is my husband, Ramsey Sinclair. Where are my manners? I didn't introduce myself. I'm Lisa Sinclair."

"Madison Westin." I extended my hand to her outstretched one, despite the fact that I hated the whole hand-shaking ritual. "You've been incredibly nice. Thank you for the information and I'll tell Mother. I'll let you get back to your flowers." I backed up onto the walkway.

Ramsey set his briefcase down and put his arm around his wife's shoulder. "That's my wife, nice to everyone."

"Nice to meet you both, thank you again." I gave a friendly wave. I didn't know Katy but I'd be shocked if Sinclair left his wife for her or anyone else. If those were his current plans, Lisa Sinclair had no inkling.

"What an ass," I said, opening the car door.

"Damn," Mother said. "I was practicing being absent-minded without overplaying it and looking suspicious."

Fab rolled her eyes, happy I came back without any more drama in tow.

"It's my opinion Katy had sex in Aspen, not love. Lisa and Ramsey Sinclair look happy together and are a good fit, and it didn't appear to be an act. He didn't have the look of a man with one foot out the door; that, or he's a better actor than I give him credit for."

Mother said, "Men are stupid. Sinclair's mistake was choosing a woman to cheat with who can drive to his house. You should've scared Ramsey and told him to break Katy's heart gently, if there is such a thing, and keep his pants zipped."

"I didn't ask Brick, but if Katy is his brother Casio's daughter, Ramsey might want to watch his back," I said.

"What are you going to tell Brick?" Fab asked. "Let him break a few of Ramsey's bones and he'll skip the next Aspen trip."

"I'd almost rather run from dogs than be involved in this messy drama, especially if Ramsey ends up in the hospital."

"Where's my daughter?" Mother snorted. "You're the master of believable nonsense. Call Ramsey with a made up sob story in place for him to tell Katy, to break it off with her, one that's so sad she'll be forced to back away gracefully."

"You're the best, Mother."

Chapter 8

Mother's phone rang and she glanced at me before answering. "It's about time." She listened, said okay a few times, and ended with, "I'll tell them."

Fab lay on the couch, the most coveted place to sit in the living room because it was so damn comfortable. Mother and I sat in over-sized chairs facing her; I flipped my legs over the top and looked at the two of them from upside-down. The only thing on my mind, the raspberry cheesecake on an Oreo cookie crust waiting in the refrigerator. I knew the caller was Creole; the only question to be answered: what the heck happened to Gabriel?

Mother shook her head. "Madison, if you hit your head, I'm sending you to your room." She turned to Fab. "Gabriel's in jail. You have a three-day reprieve to figure out your next move, five if the paperwork gets lost."

"That's impressive," Fab said. "Any way to lose the key?"

"Creole was at Jake's when you called and let us know you were on the way over with your ex. He made this happen," I said. "You owe him."

Mother snapped her fingers. "You listen

to me, Fabiana Merceau. We love and care about you. You damned-well better not do anything stupid. I will be extremely disappointed if you end up in prison."

Feeling light-headed, I'd had enough of my childhood regression. I wanted to make a splashy finale by flipping over and standing up. Instead, I slid slowly to the floor, intensifying Mother's glare. "I agree with Mother."

My phone rang, breaking the awkward silence. I almost groaned out loud. Mac never called for anything fun, like, "Want to go get some ice cream?"

"The sheriffs are here snooping around, asking questions," Mac said. "They're tracking a black convertible Mustang that took out two cars and a pedestrian at the end of the block."

"I'll be right there." I thought about throwing the phone across the room, but I'd need it later. "Either of you want to tango with local law enforcement?" I asked Mother and Fab.

"You need to kick those tenants of yours to the curb," Mother said. "I'm going home while we have a reprieve from the Gabriel drama. Call me if you need extra muscle." She flexed her bicep and did a couple of air fists.

"I'm driving," Fab said.

Mother covered her ears. "Stop, you two."

"It's my car and you're doing all the driving. I call 'dibs' on the way home." I walked with Mother to her car. "Stay out of trouble," I whispered and hugged her.

Fab backed out of the driveway and pulled up alongside Mother at the stop sign and revved the engine.

"Stop it. Mother will take the challenge." The words had barely left my lips when Mother squealed her tires and took off.

We followed Mother to the Overseas and I breathed a sigh of relief when we turned in the opposite direction.

"I'm on call for a car repo job. Brick got smart and started outfitting his high-end rentals with GPS locators." Fab slowed as she went by The Cottages and continued down the side street. "Do you want me to pull into the driveway?"

"Looks like part of the street's blocked off." I turned in my seat and stared out the back window. "Let's park in beach parking; quicker getaway." Purchasing a parking tag enabled me to park in any beach lot without a pocketful of change.

"What would we be running from?" Fab looked interested.

"You and I both know stuff comes up at the last minute." We both laughed, a nice tension breaker from the specter of Gabriel.

"I'll wait in the office. I like Kevin, but

his partner gives me a rash." Fab barely had the door closed when she sprinted off.

I cut back to the street and walked up the driveway. I didn't want anyone to know about my alternate parking choices. Kevin and his partner, Johnson, stood where cottage ten used to be, the rubble cleaned away and the framing had begun. Couldn't they conduct their investigations in someone else's driveway? Two first time guests from the UK sat on their porches, taking in the excitement.

"Kevin, Officer Johnson." I nodded. "Does this accident involve anyone at The Cottages?"

"You wouldn't happen to know anyone who owns a newish black convertible Mustang?" Kevin asked. "Sideswiped two cars and hit a young woman. She seems to have disappeared, along with the driver of the car."

"No one here owns a Mustang." I wanted to add, *now leave*.

"We're not done here. I have a few questions about your involvement with Koozie." Johnson stared at me. "You seem to have ignored all my messages. And to think I was polite. I should've issued a warrant for your arrest."

Kevin's laugh set me off. "You know damned well, Kevin Cory, that I have no involvement with Koozie or with drugs. You couldn't inform your partner?"

Kevin turned red. "Don't blame me. Koozie implicated you in his crime. I excused myself from any questioning due to a conflict of interest." He stomped off in the direction of Liam who sat on his bicycle, leaning against the rail of his cottage.

I pulled out my cell phone. "This is Madison. May I speak to Cruz?" I asked his assistant, Susie.

Cruz Campion was one of the best lawyers in South Florida and he told me once, "Don't answer any questions until we talk." For once, I didn't have to play twenty "what do you want" questions before she put me through.

"Are you in jail?" Cruz asked.

"I'm here with Officer Johnson at The Cottages. A drug dealer by the name of Koozie used one of my cottages to cook up a pan of meth and implicated me. Johnson has a few questions and is threatening me with arrest."

"You know the drill, yes or no. Did you know this Koozie fellow?" Cruz asked.

I turned my back on Johnson. "Barely."

"So you might say hello, but anything else is out of the question?"

"Yes." I looked over my shoulder. Johnson had moved closer, listening to every word.

Cruz had perfected the long dramatic pause; probably learned it in law school. "I met

Johnson on my last case. He's a turd. Let me talk to him."

"Mr. Campion would like to speak with you." I held out my phone.

I wasn't a bit bashful about listening. They exchanged what seemed to be a few civil words. I knew Cruz was telling him I wasn't answering questions without my lawyer present.

Johnson and I rubbed each other the wrong way; I needed to work harder at being civilized so he wouldn't always think the worst of me. Heaven help me if I ever gave him a real reason to arrest me.

Johnson handed me my phone. "You didn't waste any time after we took down the red tape to start construction." He walked back to his car and turned. "You haven't seen the last of me."

Losing my temper would be stupid. I wondered what Cruz said to Johnson to get him to go away without putting me in cuffs. Cruz knew all the tricks, which made him the best. He had worked both sides during his previous incarnation as a District Attorney. Kevin gave a short wave, not stopping as he walked by.

Liam rode over on his bike, waiting until Johnson and Kevin both drove off in separate cars. "The Mustang is parked beside cottage seven."

"What are you talking about?"

"Johnson walked the property but didn't go all the way to the end," Liam confided. "From here you don't notice that four and seven have spaces on the far side. The driver pulled the Mustang all the way in, so you'd have to stand in the space to see it. Joseph came out and cut Johnson off before he got that far."

"Why didn't you tell Kevin?" If Kevin found out, he'd be back yelling about Liam and Julie moving again.

"He didn't ask. Besides, Mom and I have an agreement. I don't tell anyone squat until I run it by her first. She always knows the right thing to do."

"That's something we have in common," I said as I brushed his hair with my fingers. "I never tackled big troubles without my mother, and I still don't. Like your mom, she always knows the right thing. Did you see who parked it there?"

"Two seconds before Kev pulled in, I rode my bike by the space and saw the car. Word had already spread by then that cops were on the way. Joseph shook his head at me, which I took to mean I should keep my mouth shut."

"Don't do anything Joseph tells you unless you're sure he's one hundred percent on the up. In fact, don't follow anyone into

61

trouble. " That would be the end of Joseph; I'd show him the curb.

"Kevin treated me like a little kid. Instead of asking, he sent me back to my cottage and ordered me to not to leave the porch."

I get that Kevin's overprotective; he wants to protect his sister and nephew. But the smarter choice would be to ask the person who knows everything that goes on in the neighborhood and is much more reliable than Joseph. Liam doesn't sugar-coat the truth. Kevin probably didn't want to acknowledge how streetwise Liam had become.

"Where's Joseph now?"

Liam pointed to the yellow house. "He's across the street, where they smoke pot on the porch, and when they run out, they boil the stems and seeds and drink it. Have you met his new girlfriend?"

"Please, tell me she's nothing like the last one." To say that I was happy to see her go would be an understatement.

"Totally different. I'm not telling you anything until you get introduced." Liam laughed. "There's my mom." He waved. "Brad docked earlier today, cleaned his boat and we're going to dinner. I chose hotdogs on the pier."

"Have a great time. Tell Brad to call his sister once in a while." I waved to Julie and cut across the drive to the office. Now that Brad had met someone he liked, he no longer scheduled back-to-back fishing trips. Once he sold off his catch, he stayed docked for a few days.

I barely got the door closed and looked out the window just in time to see the black Mustang at the corner. The giveaway — the bashed in passenger side, which apparently didn't impair the ability for a quick getaway.

"Did you see that?" I pointed.

"Who was driving?" Mac jumped as the car rounded the corner.

"I change my mind. I didn't see anything," I said. "I don't need any black Mustang drama. I know nothing and I'm very happy it's not on the property anymore."

"I'm only resting my eyes, I'm not asleep." Fab lay stretched out on the couch. "I need a ride to the airport to pick up a car for Brick."

"Oh good, I can practice my hot-wiring skills." Mother and I had nagged Fab until she taught us in a group class. As usual, Mother was a much better student. What surprised me, Julie ranked up there with Mother, and I got a C.

"We don't have all night," Fab sighed.

Chapter 9

"Why didn't Fab shoot you?" I shoved another pillow under my head. Fab enjoyed pointing her gun at Zach when he snuck in like a burglar in the middle of the night.

Zach stood at the foot of the bed and stripped off his shirt, unbuckled his belt and let his jeans slide to the floor, as efficiently as he did other things. I never tired of looking at him naked, his darkly tanned skin and well-defined muscles. "Every time I ask you when she's moving out, you give me some vague answer that gives me hope it will happen tomorrow."

"Do you really want to fight before sex?"

"No, and not after either." He climbed onto the bed like a feral cat, leaning on one elbow, caressing my cheek and teasing my lips in a soft kiss that quickly turned hot. Zach pulled me on top of him, and I rested my head on his shoulder.

He brushed my hair out of my face. His breath played across my cheek as his lips found the side of my neck, teeth and tongue grazing my skin, pulling me to him, kissing me hard on the mouth. His hands slid down my body, pulling my T-shirt over my head. I groaned, my pulse quickening with the rush of familiar sensations flooding my body, chasing all thoughts from my mind, fully aware without needing to be told how much Zach wanted me. It's a mutual level of desire we feel for each other.

* * *

"You still here?" Fab asked Zach when we walked into the kitchen.

Zach ignored her as he poured himself a cup of coffee.

I motioned to Fab to take her coffee and go eavesdrop where Zach couldn't see her. "I should've been upfront the first time, and all the other times you asked about Fab moving out, but I don't like to argue. I don't want to throw her out." I took a quick breath to calm my racing pulse. "Besides, how can I trust you when I find out you snuck behind my back and told Mother I was working for Brick?"

"I worry about you." Zach gave me a lame smile. "I can't believe your mother told on me."

Mother would never rat him out, since she sees an opportunity for info in the future. It only took me a second to realize it couldn't have been anyone else. "How would you like it if I ran to your mother and told her stories to scare her and manipulate you? Oh, that's right, I've never met your family. Ashamed of me?"

"You're making something out of nothing," Zach's blue eyes turned stony.

"Why haven't I met a single Lazarro?"

"If I take you to a family dinner, my mother will think we're serious. I don't take a woman I date home to meet my parents. Or introduce you as my girlfriend, Madison. 'We sleep together, she uses me for sex, never listens to a single word I say, and doesn't want to commit to anything more.'"

"I'm sorry…"

"The hell you are. If you really were, you'd start by listening. You're so busy minding other people's business you're going to end up dead. I'm leaving before we say things we can't take back." He threw his coffee in the sink and banged out the front door.

Fab rushed in from the living room. "I'll move out tomorrow."

Tears slid down my cheeks. "I guess I won't be meeting his parents anytime soon. Sounds like he's embarrassed by me."

"Zach Lazarro is a man who's always in control. He tells people what to do and they jump. Let's face it; he doesn't have a fifty percent success rate with using that tactic on you."

"Don't move out. What if one of our ex-husbands come back?" I turned the kitchen faucet on, splashing my face with water.

"Can you imagine if they both showed up at the same time?" Fab shook her head, making a face. "Your phone's ringing," she said, pointing.

"You answer and pretend you're me."

"What the hell do you want?" Fab answered. "It's for you." She handed me the phone.

I didn't want to, but I took the phone and looked at the screen. "Sorry, the moral here is that you shouldn't let Fab near your phone."

Creole laughed. "Good news, your Tahoe was found and towed to the police impound. I'll text you the address for your insurance company."

"No more excuses. I'll have to give back the Hummer," I said. I missed the Tahoe but the Hummer's a fantasy ride and when I got to drive it, I liked it a lot. "Brick will be happy."

"More good news — well, maybe, sorta."

"Fab will shoot you if you make me cry again." I sniffed for effect.

Fab stood next to me, listening. No one else I knew had that kind of nerve.

"You're going to need a new car. The Tahoe was found stripped to the frame, looks naked."

"Thanks for the update, seems like Fab and I both owe you." I liked the smell of a new car and that there wouldn't be a bunch of empty water bottles rolling around. First I'd have to submit to severe haggling over sticker price with a salesman.

"You'd call me if you were in trouble, wouldn't you?" Creole asked. "I almost forgot I actually have real good news. Koozie recanted his story."

Fab gave me the thumbs up.

"Aren't you turning into a Fairy Godfather?" Thank goodness the meth lab drama had come to an end without my having to incur big lawyer bills. "How did you accomplish that?"

"Not me, Harder. He grilled Koozie, who after declaring you a Queen Pin, didn't know the color of your hair, and in fact, he got you mixed up with Miss January. Koozie lives at home with his mother and apparently she's not easy to live with. He wanted to move to Mexico, grow pot, and live on the beach. Harder offered him drug rehab—a get out of town card—in exchange for some worthwhile names."

"Koozie's stupid. He'll never be able to move back into his old bedroom. Screwing drug dealers tends to shorten your life expectancy."

"He gave us names, dates, and other useful information on a couple of dealers we've had on our radar, which I'll be using to my advantage soon," Creole said.

"Be careful. Don't forget if you need a place to hide out, Casa Madison is always open."

"I know Fab's listening, so 'bye to both of you." Creole hung up.

Chapter 10

"What are you doing?" Fab asked.

"Now that my phone's been replaced, Brick told me to get rid of his loaner." I grabbed a pair of scissors from a stainless steel utensil holder on the stove. I removed the back of the phone and took out the SIM card, cut it into pieces, and threw everything in the trash.

Fab slid the Hummer keys off the counter and was half way out the door. "Let's go check out the Tahoe. I can tell you if your insurance will pay off or fix."

"Then take me by Brick's so I can negotiate keeping my ride." I jumped in the passenger side.

Fab revved the engine. "Buckle up." She squealed out of the driveway. "About Brick, did you report back yet on the messy love triangle?"

"First I dealt with Ramsey Sinclair. I called early this morning and reintroduced myself and told him showing up at his house had been a ruse.

"I asked him, 'Have you seen your lawyer about divorcing Mrs. Sinclair?' 'Mind your own damn business,' he said to me in a snotty upper crust tone. So I said, 'Look, don't hang up. If you want to continue to breathe you'd better listen very carefully.' Then I gave him a colorful description of Katy's father and uncle. After a long drawn out silence, he told me he'd call Katy today. I told him exactly what to say. Then told him, 'If you don't want your wife to find out, or for you to end up in the hospital, don't be lame and deviate from the script.'"

I looked at Fab. "He actually said thank you and sounded like he meant it. I got off easy with Brick, his phone went to voice mail. Lies are always easier on the phone."

Some days a seat belt wasn't enough; I had to hang on tight to the sissy-bar. Digging through my purse, I pulled out my ringing phone and put it on speaker. I didn't want Fab to wreck trying to listen.

"I thought you'd want to know," Mac said, sounding muffled. "She's not dead."

"Miss January? Is it the cancer again?" Miss January had been diagnosed with cancer several years ago and told to go home and die. Instead, she told them to go to hell, went to doctor's appointments sporadically, and self-medicated with vodka and cigarettes.

"It's not her cancer and she's fine. Miss J hit her head and has already been released from the hospital and is on her way back to The Cottages," Mac said. "I can give you the deets when I see you."

Fab rolled her eyes. "Found drunk in

the bushes again?"

Fab cut diagonal across two lanes. I looked in the side view mirror and was relieved to see the nearest car didn't have to slam on their brakes. Fab hooked a turn down a gravel road, dust flying. Swamp lined one side of the road and the other side full of commercial lots, with an auto repair business and junk yard. At the far end, the tow yard took up half the street and had eighteen-foot fencing, barbed wire, and surveillance cameras.

"Have to go, be by later," I told Mac and threw my phone on the console.

"Did Mac sound weird or what?" Fab pulled into the driveway, missing the rather large pothole. In Florida, you might not realize it was a sinkhole until it swallowed up your car. I didn't want to be immortalized in the driveway of a tow yard.

I got out and looked at the No Trespassing, Dogs, and Shoot to Kill signs. "I've learned not to overthink Mac Lane." Thanks to Fab, I came with all the right paperwork and shoved it under the bars at the window.

The big burly woman inside the window looked around. "Where's your tow truck? You're not driving this thing out of here; lack of tires is the least of your problems. And I'll need the nineteen hundred and fifty, cash only."

"My insurance company will make those arrangements," I told her. "I'm here to pay my respects, and to see if it's time to start shopping for its replacement."

She took the cigarette that wobbled between her lips and put it behind her ear. "Note here, your insurance company called, will be here this week." She dragged the microphone across the desk. "Lude, get up here," she yelled. "Wait here, you'll be escorted. You have three minutes."

The fence opened and a broom handle with hair stood there, tobacco spit flying over his shoulder. He leered. "Why is it the women always want to be the ones to say a teary good-bye, it's not a dead relate? Men are at the car lot already." He motioned with his greasy stained hand to follow.

"Girly stays here with me!" the woman in the office yelled, pointing to Fab.

There were several hundred cars parked inside the fence in various states of disrepair, from cars that looked like they needed a long overdue carwash to burned-out shells. The hike to my Tahoe took longer than the three minute allotted time. I thought Creole exaggerated in his description; turns out, in addition to being stripped, it had been set on fire. Definitely time for a new ride. I snapped a couple of pictures with my phone and turned in time to see Lude take his finger out of his nose and wipe it on his shirt.

"Thank you, Mr. Lude." I forced myself not to run back to the gate.

"Wait up, you have to be escorted. Company rules. The boss don't want you stopping and jacking a part off another car." Lude caught up and walked beside me. "You got a boyfriend?"

"Yes and we're very happy." Well, some of the time we're happy. Even if I didn't have one, the answer would be the same.

He pulled out his wallet, took off the rubber band. "Your girlfriend got somebody?"

"We both have boyfriends." Lude didn't know how lucky he was that Fab stood on the other side of the fence. She'd pistol-whip his butt.

He handed me two business cards. "One for you and one for your friend. Call if either of you get single." He unlocked the gate, wiped his hand on his pants, and extended it.

Freaked out, I damn-near jumped. "I just got over the flu, wouldn't want to shake your hand and make you sick," I said, racing through the gate. "Thanks for your help." I nodded and waved his business cards.

"Time to go car shopping." I handed Lude's business card to Fab after we got inside the Hummer.

"What's this for?" Fab read the card.

"Lude wanted you to have his contact information."

"Who?" Fab looked around the tow lot while backing up.

"You know, that nice man who escorted me to my Tahoe." I bit my lip so I wouldn't laugh. "He thinks you're hot and wants you to call him, go out on a date."

Her eyes shot icicles. "You're lying."

"Once he found out I had a boyfriend, he asked about you. Wanted me to tell you to give him a call if you dump the boyfriend." I couldn't hold it anymore and burst out laughing. Pranking Fab never got old.

Fab rolled the window down and threw the card out. "Were you dropped on your head as a child?"

"Take me to The Cottages."

* * *

"What is Mac doing?" Fab asked, pulling into the only available parking space at The Cottages. "Who knew a woman her age could Hula-Hoop?"

"She's better at it than I am." I shook my hips in my seat. "The best I can do is three twirls before it drops to the ground."

Mac walked over to the car, pulling her skirt out of the top of her yoga pants. "I'm sorry for my part in this."

What now?

"Am I going to need a latte?" I asked.

"Miss J's home and resting. I'm the one who encouraged her to join The Cove Walkers, a group of older people who get together and walk around town once a week."

"That sounds like a great idea." I had seen the group many times around town.

Mac unwrapped a piece of gum and rolled it between her fingers. "Miss J hooked up with two other women. They formed their own group and got on the trolley to Custer's. During a game of drink or dare, Miss J agreed to a keg stand."

Custer's is a rat-hole bar and favorite hangout for the local drunks who enjoy cheap drinks and tourists who want their picture taken in front of the adobe-like hovel and the pink Cadillac. They were mandated by the Alcohol Board to serve only canned beer and screw-top wine.

"You're telling me two people suspended Miss J by her ankles over a keg, and she guzzled cheap beer?" I asked.

Fab clapped, the Hula-Hoop dropping to the ground. She'd been showing off her hooping skills.

"The best part was that under those ugly housedresses of hers, she had on a red G-string, no granny drawers for her," Mac snorted.

I stuck my fingers in my ears. "Stop. That's a horrible image to have burned in my mind."

"How did she end up in the hospital?" Fab asked.

"After her successful keg stand didn't kill her, she attempted a hand stand and fell on her head, knocking herself out." Mac enjoyed being the first in the know.

"I don't believe you." I shook my head.

Mac stuck her hands on her hips, thrusting out her girls. "Thank you for thinking I could make all that crap up on the spur of the moment. I don't need to make stuff up to entertain you. Have you met Joseph's girlfriend?"

"Is she as hideous as the last one?" Fab asked.

"I'm not going to spoil the surprise. She's quiet, has a pleasant smile, and she's not mouthy like that last one." Mac's mouth twitched, clearly holding back laughter.

I looked at Joseph's cottage. "Is the happy couple at home?"

"Svetlana doesn't get out much," Mac hooted.

I dreaded the short walk to Joseph's door. The last girlfriend wanted me dead, so I hoped the new one would be an improvement. I used my cop knock on his door, knowing it scared him.

"I'm watching a movie with Svetlana, now go away." He shut the door.

I banged again and yelled. "Let me in, or I'll evict you."

He opened the door. "You want a beer?"

I brushed past him. "You need to shine your manners." The new girlfriend apparently didn't have the same house cleaning skills as the last one. Newspapers were everywhere, he had a full trashcan, and discarded pants and shirts littered the floor. Sitting in the chair next to the couch, an attractive blonde in a green leather mini skirt showing off her long, sexy legs, wide open bringing attention to her matching G-string.

"Svetlana?" I stared at her, my mouth dropping open. A beautiful woman, with large blue glossy eyes, large breasts that peeped out from a lacy chemise also in green, skinny waist, round ass, and realistic hands and feet. I traced my finger softly along her cheek—one hundred percent rubber.

"Remember old dead Twizzle? He left me Svet in his will and all of her outfits." He sucked hard on an electronic cigarette. "None of my other dead friends ever left me anything."

I couldn't believe how real Svet looked. "I'm happy for you, Joseph." I didn't know what other lame thing to say, I just wanted some fresh air.

"Best girlfriend ever," He moved her to

the couch, caressing her arm.

"Nice to meet her." I reached for the doorknob, jerked the door open, and waved to Joseph. I covered my mouth and laughed all the way back to my SUV.

Chapter 11

Fab turned south on the Overseas toward the house. "I thought you were taking me to Brick's," I said.

"I've got a job that needs my attention-- and before you ask, it's for Brick and I can't talk about it. He emphasized not telling you."

I stared out the window. I didn't want to let Fab out of my sight.

"Promise me that no matter what happens, you won't call the cops. I know you're worried about me but I'm good at slipping out of tight situations."

"As long as I hear from you every couple of hours. You'd make me do the same thing if it was me eluding a crazy ex-husband."

Jax Devereaux's biggest crime is that he's a drunk, which is preferable to Gabriel, who steals and threatens to kill people. I hadn't seen my ex since he'd been released from jail for boating under the influence. A quick kiss on the cheek and Jax got in a car with his cousin and they went back home to South Carolina. I'd heard through the grapevine that he was sober and getting married.

"No need to start worrying. Besides, Gabriel's in jail." Fab pulled into my driveway and flipped me the keys. "I'll be back in a few hours. Don't worry so much." She jumped in her Mercedes and squealed out of the driveway.

The sound of an engine revving came from my purse; an alert from my phone that Fab and I had a business call. We had really cool business cards, the only problem—we couldn't come up with a name. Zach had seen the cards and rolled his eyes, commenting they weren't professional; his partner, Slice, gave me the thumbs up behind his back.

I listened to the message; Tolbert Rich wanted a call back. I decided I'd return the message in person, and climbed over into the driver's seat, a perfect day for a drive to Pigeon Key. The Overseas Highway was a one-of-a-kind two-lane highway that ran over water to the southernmost tip of the United States, Key West, surrounded by the Atlantic Ocean and Gulf of Mexico. I sang along with Jimmy Buffet, enjoying every mile. I'd met Tolbert when his son, Cosmo—who had been best friends with my brother—was murdered.

The paved road ceased and became gravel as we turned off the main highway. I bumped along until turning into The Wild Bird Farm. The arch overhead comfortably sat fifty or more brightly colored parrots, all of them bright green, their under parts variations of very light green to yellow. In its usual parking space sat the church bus, named Church of the

Traveling Jesus. Every Sunday Tolbert, a pastor, picked up his congregation along the main highway, preached an uplifting sermon, and followed it with lunch. Jimmy Spoon had been instrumental in getting the new bus and had it repainted in its patriotic red, white, and blue theme when the old one was vandalized beyond repair.

The Bird Farm was a snapshot into the Old South in its day of rambling old houses on large lots. The property boasted dozens of willow trees, their graceful limbs hanging to the ground, all filled with an assortment of birds. The private pond attracted ducks and egrets, walking along the shore. A pedal boat sat tied up to the short dock. There was a peaceful calm, no traffic racing by or noisy neighbors; the only sounds were that of nature and kids screaming and laughing when they were out of school.

Tolbert and Grover, a Golden Retriever, stood on the porch, probably wondering who was invading their peace and quiet in a gangster-mobile. As I came around the front of the Hummer, Grover barked and came running, skidding to a stop. I leaned down and hugged him, rubbing his neck. Grover and I bonded when he lived with me for several months after I rescued him from the side of the road and nursed him back to health. The worst day had been when I found out he had an owner who loved him and hadn't stopped looking for him.

Tolbert waved. "You didn't have to drive all the way out here. Come, we'll sit on the porch. I always have tea in the fridge."

"A little slice of heaven is just what my day needs and you offer that and more," I said, and kissed his cheek.

I walked up the stairs of the sprawling white plantation-style home to the signature wide veranda with comfortable cane seating. I snatched up a couple of faded colorful pillows, sun-bleached over time, and relaxed in a wicker chair. Grover sat by my side, his head in my lap. I put my arms around his neck.

"You look great, big guy. Jazz and I miss you."

Tolbert kicked open the wooden screen door and carried out a large tray of tea, ice, and those brown sugar cubes I liked. I noticed the plate of yummy looking shortbread cookies right away.

"Where's Miss Fabiana?" Tolbert asked. He was definitely smitten with 'Girl Wonder'. She'd charmed him with her stories of an all-Catholic, girls-only school education and trying to hold her own with the nuns.

"Fab's off taking advantage of bad guys. I should feel sorry for them, but I don't." I hoped when I got home she'd be sitting at the island, tempting Jazz with people food.

Tolbert chuckled. "Speaking of bad guys, that's why I called. You remember my neighbor, Gus Ivers? He's got a business property in town and needs the tenant evicted. He's older than dirt, like myself, but he can afford to pay full-price." He handed me a glass of iced tea with orange slices.

"You're lucky my mother isn't here to hear you say that," I said and wagged my finger, "since I know you're close in age. You look great; having your grandchildren living with you will keep you young." Tolbert, who was tall and lanky, had a big heart and still had a full head of hair. He won full custody of his grandchildren after his son's murder. The mother, a drunk, found herself "a daddy," and left town on the back of a motorcycle.

"Thank you for referring me to Cruz Campion; he's one heck of a lawyer. I know you're the reason he did my custody case pro-bono."

I tossed Grover a cookie. "Oh, for heaven's sake, Cruz can charge the next person double."

A while back, some troublemaker tenants of Gus Ivers began terrorizing Tolbert. I'd never met Mr. Ivers, but I called Slice and asked for same-day eviction of the renters. I wanted them off the property and asked that they be tossed from The Keys. Thrilled, Slice sent them running for the state line.

"I'll call Gus; he can be here in five, and he'll give you the details. He kicked a fuss, wanting a man for the job, but I reminded him you were instrumental in getting rid of his old tenant faster than the law would've done." Tolbert disappeared inside, the only person I knew who used a phone still hooked to the wall. It would only be interesting to me if I could listen in on a party line.

I felt bad for Grover, who fell asleep standing up with his head in my lap. I nudged him awake and slid over to the rocker couch. Grover jumped up and lay beside me, promptly closing his eyes. It took self-control not to stretch out beside him and nap.

When Tolbert reappeared, he had more iced tea and an extra glass. An eighties white Cadillac, with large steer horns on the hood, pulled into the driveway. Grover lifted his head, checked the car out, and went back to sleep.

As Tolbert introduced us, Gustav Ivers removed his Fedora. "The dog likes you, that's a start." He reached for a glass of tea, four sugars, and lemon slices, making himself comfortable across from me. "Call me Gus."

Unsure what to say, I kept the "What the hell?" comment to myself.

Gus looked me over. I clearly came up short. "How are you going to evict the drug dealers?"

The heck with good manners.

"I'll start with this," I said once I pulled my Glock from my thigh holster. I'd jump up and down later at how smoothly and impressively that went. "And why don't you call the sheriff to do your dirty work? They might point out that you like to rent to drug dealers since this isn't your first go-round."

Tolbert laughed and offered Gus a cookie.

Gus nodded, clicking his dentures. "The sheriff's part of the problem. They're putting together a case against Quirky and his sister Vanilla as we speak and by the time they're done shuffling through the process, I'll lose my car wash. I'd have evicted them long ago if it weren't for Quirky threatening to kick my old ass."

This ought to be good, I thought.

"Car wash, drugs, maybe you should start at the beginning," I said.

"Don't forget the raccoon meat side business," Gus added. "I hired the Poppins siblings to run my car wash, two doors down from Jake's bar. I did a little checking on you, heard you might be opening up the poker room. Still a ten percent buy-in? Give me a call. I can keep my mouth shut. I don't have any friends except Tolbert; the rest are dead."

The poker room was the worst kept secret; he's the fourth person who had mentioned it to me and asked why wasn't it open for play yet? He'd have to check out before getting an invitation.

"The car wash? Clean Bubbles?" That property had caught my interest since taking over Jake's. Transform that two-block strip and it wouldn't be a haven for late night entrepreneurs.

"Before Quirky took over, Clean Bubbles had never been what you'd call a money-maker, but it paid for itself and was all cash. Now it only makes him money. I have a soft spot for the property; it's my first investment. Now I own the block. In addition to the occasional wash and wax, Quirk-ass and Vanilla sell fresh raccoon meat out of coolers and the occasional assortment of other road kill." He downed his iced tea, pouring another glass.

"People actually eat that?" I suddenly felt nauseous. "Is that legal?"

"None of it is legal, including the home-grown hydro; Munger bragged he'd been supplying them for a hefty cut."

Munger, an old curmudgeon, lived in a shack in a woodsy area off the Overseas with a much younger hard-as-nails wife. He was one of the handfuls who boasted that their weed kicked ass. Someone should sponsor a weed-off so they could crown the true champion.

Tolbert spoke up. "Gus got word today

from a friend in the sheriff's office that they started staking the place out, waiting for a new shipment of evidence, and then they'll raid the place. Supposed to happen soon."

"I want Clean Bubbles cleaned out today; this week anyway. If you don't have the nuts to do the job, tell me now." Gus banged his glass on the table. "You get this done, I'll sweeten the pot."

I bribed Grover with another cookie to jump down. I stood, taking a business card out of my pocket. "I'll go check this out now."

"This is a cheesy business card." Gus stared at me.

"It's got the pertinent information you need to get a hold of me. Leave a message; I'll get back to you." I waved to them both. "Call you tomorrow. I'm on my way to get my car washed."

"Be careful!" Gus yelled. "Quirky Poppins is a mean bastard and Vanilla does what her brother tells her. My guess is that some inbreeding went on there."

"Miss Madison, if you think you're in danger, walk away. This old fart can hire someone else," Tolbert said.

Grover walked me to the Hummer. "Would you eat raccoon?" He sat patiently while I scratched his neck. "No, me neither."

* * *

I scanned the street before pulling into

Clean Bubbles and spotted Johnson and Kevin doing a stakeout half a block down. Two skinny, pale, six-foot bookends approached the Hummer. I'd bet money I was staring into the sullen faces of the Poppins siblings, Quirky and Vanilla.

"What do you want?" Quirky demanded. He'd written his name in black marker on the pocket of his dress shirt, rolled up his sleeves, and was wearing boxer shorts and flops.

Vanilla checked me over, yawned—running her fingers through her knotted hair—and disappeared inside the far stall.

"That's not very friendly." I stepped behind my Hummer, not wanting to be seen by the local sheriff. "I'm here with a friendly request for you to pack up and get the hell out tonight."

"Get out of here before I call the cops." Quirky stepped forward.

I whipped my Glock from my thigh holster. "Don't move or I'll shoot you. Just listen and then I'll leave," I hissed. "Put your hands down."

"I'm not going to forget this." Quirky glared.

"Sheriffs are across the street staking you out as we speak. Don't be stupid or you're going to end up in jail." I wanted to beat the snotty look off his face. "You have until midnight." I got into my SUV.

Quirky gave me the finger.

I rolled down the window and yelled, "How does a person know they're getting real raccoon meat?"

"We keep the feet and tail. Without them you can't tell the difference between coon and house cat; they taste the same."

"Let me guess. They both taste like chicken?"

Quirky snickered, "Come back tomorrow, me and Vanilla will still be here."

"You want to play hardball?" I winked at him. "You're on." I rolled up the window, happy the door was locked.

Another crap case.

As soon as I rounded the curve, the sheriff car pulled up behind me, lights flashing. "Get out of your car," Johnson yelled. "What were you doing at Clean Bubbles?"

I didn't know who was stupider, the Poppins for committing felonies while they knew the cops watched from across the street, or the sheriff for doing a stake-out in plain sight. Must be Johnson's idea; Kevin looked bored and irritated.

"Booking an appointment for a detail on the Hummer," I lied boldly.

Kevin circled the Hummer, looking in the windows. "The tint on this thing is too dark."

"It's a rental. You need to speak with Brick Famosa, you know, of Famosa Motors. I have the phone number."

"No one rents a Hummer," Johnson said with a tight, phony smile in place. "What's the daily fee?"

Out of the corner of my eye I saw Quirky pull a rope across the driveway, attach a homemade "closed" sign, and jump into a pickup with Vanilla at the wheel.

"My insurance company is paying the bill. Why was I pulled over?" I asked.

"Looked like expired plates, but I was wrong. You're free to go," Johnson said. "One more question, you didn't happen to pull a gun on Quirky back there, did you?"

"Why would I do that? I can pay for the wash and wax." My phone rang as soon as I opened the door.

"Bad news," Creole said. "Gabriel got released from custody."

"Thank you for all your help. We both owe you. I need to call Fab and warn her."

"Stay in touch," Creole warned. "I'll stop by tonight for an update." He hung up before I could answer.

I hit speed dial, but Fab's phone went straight to voicemail. "Call me as soon as you get this message. You don't, all promises are off."

* * *

Jazz started meowing the second I opened the front door. I picked him up and nuzzled his neck until he squirmed. He'd had enough.

I hit redial all the way home, getting Fab's voicemail every time. Now I had the Quirky situation to worry over. He's too stupid to pack and leave town, even with the sheriff watching and making a case for an eventual arrest. Aunt Elizabeth loved to collect IOUs from people and willed hers to me, along with instructions to get my own. I figured it was time to pull an Elizabeth IOU out of the drawer, since my favor was huge and last minute.

I sat at the kitchen island, laying my cheek on the cool countertop, mulling my choices. I could call Slice, but then Zach would find out. Slice and I had an unspoken agreement that he didn't hide things from his partner. Evicting coon-meat-selling drug dealers would definitely erupt into a fight. My only other choice was Jimmy Spoon, Mother's boyfriend; it felt sneaky but I knew Spoon would never rat me out. I met him dropping off Zach's 1957 convertible Thunderbird for maintenance, a car that circled the block a few times only to go right back to its parking space overlooking the water, behind locked gates. Spoon told me he could fix "anything." Time to put those skills to the test.

Spoon answered on the first ring. "You in trouble?"

"I need those 'fixer' skills you once boasted of, the sooner the better. I'm willing to part with one of my coveted Elizabeth IOUs." I reached in the junk drawer and took out the aspirin bottle; I had too much on my plate to entertain a banging headache.

"This ought to be good."

I related the entire story, ticked off the felonies, and gave him a heads up on the ever-vigilant Sheriff Johnson. I also mentioned Gus and Tolbert were friends, knowing that Spoon had a high regard for Tolbert Rich.

"Make it clear it would be bad for Quirky's health to bother Mr. Ivers ever again," I said.

"Problem taken care of. Give me a couple of days; I've got one favor ahead of yours. One day most of the people in this town will owe me." Spoon laughed. "The Poppins riffraff can go peddle their illegal meat and weed somewhere besides The Keys. You keep the IOU. This job is going to require my personal touch. I'm going to ask Quirky how he'd like to be skinned and served on someone's dinner plate. Call you when the job's done." He disconnected.

I shuddered at Spoon's words, happy to not be Quirky. I redialed Fab and got more voicemail.

I hit speed dial again. "Gabriel's out of jail and Fab's not answering her phone," I told Mother.

"I'm on my way, we can worry together."

Chapter 12

"I brought food!" Mother yelled, kicking the front door closed. "Heard from Fab?"

Mother rocked at to-go food. "Gabriel's got her, I know it." I went straight to the kitchen counter and lifted the lid on some great smelling grilled tilapia.

"What if Fab's out committing felonies?" Mother took out the shell dinner plates from the cupboard, and handed me one.

"If she's out setting fire to her life, we're not going to catch fire with her. Burglarizing houses and grand theft is a line I will not cross." I grabbed a pitcher of cold water that I'd filled earlier with oranges and strawberries to give it several hours to ferment.

Mother gave me a sympathetic smile.

"Why are you so calm? It's like you know more than you're saying." She'd better not say "Zach," or I'd flip.

"I have a little confession, since I got caught red-handed." Mother's cheeks turned pink. "Creole stopped by to take me to lunch. While he showered I snooped through his briefcase. He left it open and on the top lay a file about Gabriel and Fabiana. Before I got to the last page he snuck up on me."

My cheeks burned with embarrassment

for her. I gasped. "What did you say?"

"Can I at least read the last page? Pretty nervy, even for me." Mother shook her head. "He told me to read fast. Then he put his finger under my chin and forced me to look him in the face. He asked, 'Should I lock my briefcase in the future?'" Mother sipped her water before continuing. "I told him yes. How's that for honesty? I know it surprised him. He took my hand and we walked to that new bistro, Chez Nous. He never said another word, which actually made me feel worse."

"Aww." I pushed back the kitchen stool and hugged her. "I should call Creole and let him know what's up. I can't call Spoon; he's busy doing me a big favor." I told her about the Poppins siblings.

"I'll have to do something extra nice for him," Mother winked.

I crossed my fingers in an X to ward off any visual images. "No details, not even a hint. Fab would never forgive me if I called Zach. Their relationship is rocky at best. It's hard to believe they were once lovers." I called Creole; it went directly to voicemail, so I left a message.

"When the heck were those two doing it?" Mother fumed. "Why am I always the last to know?"

"It happened long before I met Zach and Fab. She once told me they had a better working relationship when they took sex out of the equation. Zach's problem is that he never meant for Fab and I to become friends and has never adjusted."

"How are you and Zach doing?" Mother smoothed my hair, pushing it behind my shoulders.

"He'd like it if, when he issued orders, I followed them no questions asked. We fight about stupid stuff. He wants me to commit to living together when we haven't even said 'I love you.' As much as I enjoyed being Jax's wife, let's face it—I sucked at it." I sighed and covered my face with my hands.

Mother patted my head. "Listen to me: Jackson Devereaux started out being a great husband and then one day decided his marriage no longer mattered to him. It takes two--and he checked out."

"I hear you, but I wanted so badly for it to work and it still feels like one of my biggest failures. I'm not interested in a second one."

"Come on." Mother took my hand and led me into the living room. "There must be some awful movie we can watch on television."

I took my Glock out of the desk drawer and put it under a magazine on the coffee table. "When you get tired you can sleep in my room; there's a gun in the bedside drawer. I'm going to sleep down here."

* * *

It felt like I only slept ten minutes, waking early the next morning to the smell of coffee brewing and Mother and Creole sitting at the island. Sitting on the counter was a pink box from my favorite place, The Bakery Café. Mother always over indulged so I knew it was chock-full of goodies.

"Gabriel's dead," Creole said.

Mother handed me a cup of coffee.

I gasped. "Where's Fab? Please tell me she isn't dead." I gripped the counter.

"Not one hundred percent sure, but my guess would be that Fab's in hiding," Creole said as he refilled his coffee. "She's been labeled a person of interest."

Creole shook his finger at me. "Don't get arrested trying to help Fab. This is a double-murder investigation."

"Double murder," I whispered. "Who's the other person?"

Mother sat next to Creole. I could tell by the look on her face that she already wormed the grisly details out of him.

"Gabriel was found dead on the back lawn of the estate of Maxwell and Chrissy Wright out on Fisher Island. Police found Maxwell face down in his study, both he and Gabriel with bullet wounds to the back of the head; twenty-five million dollars in art and jewelry stolen from the mansion. The security system was rendered ineffective, including the back-up systems, and the tapes from the cameras are missing," Creole told us. "It mirrors a couple of heists Fab and Gabriel pulled off in France, although the murder angle would be new."

"Fab would never kill anyone or Gabriel would've been dead a long time ago," I said.

Creole stared at me. "Do you happen to know where Fab is right now?"

I shook my head. "Don't take this the wrong way but I'm not helping you arrest Fab."

"Here's the deal. I won't use anything you tell me against her." Creole grabbed my arm. "But if I hear it from someone else then I have no choice. I'm on Fab's side until it's proven beyond any doubt to me that she's guilty."

"I agree with Madison, Fab's no killer." Mother stared at Creole, refilling her coffee. She pointed to his cup, he nodded and she topped his off.

"Why would Fab murder Maxwell Wright? I've never heard her mention his name." Anybody who didn't live under a rock had heard of the Wrights. The über-rich made headlines all the time, mostly on the covers of the local magazines that catered to the wealthy. "Is there one piece of evidence that leads to Fab?"

I leaped for my phone when it rang; disappointed it wasn't Fab's name on the screen, but Detective Harder's. I exploded at Creole, "I'm not helping the Miami police with anything to do with this case! You and your friend," I said pointing to my phone that just landed in the living room, "Can call my lawyer."

I stomped upstairs to shower.

* * *

I wiggled into my favorite jean skirt, which had two big pockets in the front for my cell phone and keys, and strapped on my thigh holster. In the shower, I had made a mental list of people I needed to call. I had no idea where to start looking, but I knew Fab would never come back here if she thought she were in trouble with the police.

Before I saw Zach, his voice boomed up the stairs and I groaned. His presence meant trouble. Coming down the stairs, I saw Creole hadn't left. He sat by Mother at the island, and they looked like such a united pair that it made me want to scream. Zach stood at the sink pouring coffee into his travel mug.

"What's new?" I stared at Zach.

"Looking for Fab, and your Mother assures me she's not here and hasn't been here." Zach flashed me his superior smile.

I fought to stay calm. "That sounds like you wouldn't take my word."

"I think you'd end up in a jail cell next to her if you thought you could help," Zach snorted. "If you'd listened to me when I told you she'd make a poor friend, you wouldn't be having cops sitting outside your house."

"What proof do you have that she committed any crime?" I asked. "And if she were here, would you arrest her?"

"We have her on video tape running from the Wright residence," Zach said.

"I thought all the tapes were missing," I said.

"Unprofessional of you to share information from a crime scene," he said, sneering at Creole.

Creole shoved his stool back and pulled up to his full six foot four stature, almost eye level with Zach.

Mother jumped up. "More coffee, anyone?"

To look at the testosterone stare-down, you wouldn't know that they had been childhood friends. I knew it annoyed Zach that Creole came and went from my house with increasing regularity.

"I'm sure you'll share anything you find out with Miami P.D., Detective Harder has been assigned to this case," Creole told him.

"I'll make a note," Zach said. "What's your interest? I thought you consorted with drug dealers all day."

"I have a personal interest," Creole smiled. "And what's yours?"

"The Wrights are clients of AZL," Zach said evenly. "We will retrieve the stolen art and jewelry." He turned to me. "Who are you anyway? Have you decided that stealing property and leaving behind two dead people is somehow romantic? That bother you any? You believe in Fab so much, and her innocence, then you need to tell her to come forward and turn herself into the police."

The doorbell rang, which meant more trouble. I raced to the door before anyone could move. "Kevin, what's up?" From the look on his face, he'd drawn the short straw.

"Here to speak to Fab," Kevin said, not quite making eye contact.

I opened the door wide. "Come on in, look around." Kevin walked into the kitchen. I grabbed my purse off the bench and scooted out the door. I cleared the driveway when Creole came running out the front door shaking his head. Two seconds later, my phone rang. The screen said "Mother," but my guess was that Creole would be on the phone. I pushed "ignore" and threw my phone on the passenger seat.

Looking in the mirror, I noticed Officer Johnson sitting on my bumper; guess he didn't know tailgating is illegal. I stuck to the speed limit, making a quick turn to drive along the beach. I needed to channel my inner Fab and figure out her hiding place. I led Johnson straight to The Cottages. I pulled up in front of the office; he skirted the lawn, which annoyed me. Who rolls their tires on someone else's green grass?

Hiring Mac turned out to be a stress reliever. Head phones on, she gyrated in the barbeque area to her latest workout routine, Zumba.

Mac whirled around and waved. "I see Mr. No Personality is back." She pointed to Johnson. "FYI, he stopped by earlier looking for Fab. I told him he could look around as long as he didn't touch anything."

I pulled my phone out of my pocket. Brick would help Fab and so might his brother Casio, if there were something in it for him. "Are you using your own phone?" Brick barked. "I don't know anything." He clicked off.

I didn't get a chance to hang up before my phone started ringing.

"Hi, Dickie." Dickie Vanderbilt co-owned Tropical Slumber Funeral Home with his partner, Raul. I'd met him at Aunt Elizabeth's funeral and we'd become friends.

Mac moved closer to listen. This was a bad habit she picked up from Fab.

"I'm cashing in one of those IOUs you gave me. I need you to escort a body to a funeral in Miami this afternoon. Raul and I need to arrive ahead of the deceased to make sure everything goes smoothly. This is a VIP burial and they are demanding all the bells. I had no one else to call."

A dead body! I wanted to pass out. "Dickie, I...uh...no!"

Mac made a face. "Eww," she whispered.

"You won't have any contact with the body, it's a ride along. I wouldn't ask you, but I have no one else I trust--and you did promise."

"I'm on way," I sighed.

My phone rang again and this time it was Creole. "Did you find her?" he asked.

"I'm being followed. Is my phone tapped?"

The long pause gave me my answer. "I don't know," he said.

I hung up on him. "Can I trade phones with you?" I asked Mac. "Before you answer, mine's being listened to, or whatever they do, by the cops."

"Follow me." Mac crooked her finger and headed to the office. She pulled open her desk drawer and handed me a phone and a charger cord. "This is an extra office phone I keep on hand since the jerk ran into the electrical pole and phone service was out for two days. I keep it charged so it's ready to use.

It's pay-by-the-minute and not registered to anyone."

"I'll see you later. Dickie's waiting for me." I reached in the drawer and put two aspirin in my pocket, just in case.

"Why do you get the dead people jobs?" Mac asked.

Good question.

I shook my head. "Just lucky I guess."

"I'll take an IOU and use it right now," Mac said. "You know Shirl, she broke up with her boyfriend. He kicked her out after telling her she could stay until her new place was ready, and that won't be for a few days." Shirl worked as a nurse at Tarpon Hospital, was a little crazy, and Mac's best friend. I liked her directness. You never had to wonder what was on her mind; she'd tell you.

"You know my rule—no more long-term tenants. Give me your word she'll be out in a few days and won't be fornicating in the pool."

"You'll never know she's here," Mac promised, holding up her hand.

As I drove out of the driveway, I noticed a brand new sheriff car parked half way down the block. The city had bought several unmarked Ford sedans, but the limo tint was the giveaway, the windows were totally blacked out.

I laughed. *Wait until he had to report back*

*about my next stop, Tropical Slumber Funeral
Home.*

Chapter 13

Unless you were a long time local, you wouldn't know that the funeral home got its start as a drive-through hot dog stand. It had three previous owners and each one added an addition to make it an architectural oddity. I parked opposite the front door in the vacant parking lot, and walked across the red carpet. At least I wouldn't be crashing someone's funeral.

Dickie opened the door and looked around before letting me in. "Were you followed?" He triple locked the door.

To say Dickie was odd would be an understatement. Today, he seemed downright paranoid. "What?"

Fab walked out of one of the slumber rooms disheveled and looking tired. "How's my cat?"

I rushed over and hugged her. "I'm so happy to see you. I gave Jazz bologna, but I think he likes it better when you feed him your meat surprises. You're hiding here?" I turned to Dickie. "Are you okay?"

"Miss Fabiana's a good guest," Dickie said.

Much to my surprise, he didn't look like the scared rabbit that he usually did when Fab came around. His usually pale face had a hint of color today.

Fab, hands on her hips, had a shocked look on her face. "Really, Madison, you're not the only one with party manners. Besides, who would look for me here?" Her laugh brittle, she sounded overwhelmed.

I looked around the main entry at its heavy ornate wood furniture and brocade fabrics on the chairs, slip covered in plastic. "This place never made my list."

"I'll leave you two to discuss her problems. If you need anything just ring the bell," Dickie pointed to a small writing desk.

"No dead body escort job?" I asked Dickie.

"I made it up to get you over here," Dickie preened. "I thought I did good for a last minute lie, no time to practice."

I wanted to yell, "Yes!" The whole idea of driving around with a dead body gave me an upset stomach. "Do you have any final send-offs tonight? We might borrow one of your hearses since the sheriff is parked over at the tattoo parlor."

"We have the night off," Dickie said.

He left, and Fab and I sat on a bench next to the front door. "What the heck happened?" I asked. "Did you shoot Gabriel or the rich guy?"

"Once we reached the island, the job

whiffed of a set-up. Gabriel went crazy when I told him I changed my mind and I tried to run. He tangled my hair in his fist and shoved me to the ground face first, planting his foot in the middle of my back and holding me down with his knee. He snarled at me, saying that if I tried to get away he'd break my arms and legs and let me swim back to The Keys. You and Madeline to follow."

"I'm going to call Cruz."

"I can't afford him," Fab said.

"We can work out something, short of sex." My luck, he'd want a refund since I'd lack the appropriate enthusiasm for indiscriminate banging.

"You can't run forever. Zach and Slice are looking for you. The Wrights are clients." I fished the burner phone out of my purse. "Since you didn't shoot anyone, then you need a lawyer and he can inform you of your next step."

Cruz Campion enjoyed the title of Best Criminal Defense Lawyer in South Miami; just ask him, he'll tell you about the cases he's won and his perfect track record, with not a single lost case. He wore his conceited I'm-better-than-you look like a badge of honor. What did he care? He was a winner. For some reason he liked me, so I tried not to abuse the relationship. I never said no to beachfront requests for his relatives.

His assistant, Susie, answered. "This is Madison Westin and it's urgent that I speak with Cruz."

Susie laughed. "Are you in jail again?"

Susie must think I'm a train wreck; it's always some emergency or another. The last time I talked to her, I'd been booked, photographed, and headed to the women's central jail. "This is for a friend who needs a lawyer. She's in desperate need of legal counsel; she's wanted for questioning in a double murder."

Susie put me on hold and came back in less than a minute. "You have five minutes and then he has an appointment." In their game of bad cop/good cop, I pictured her in black leather with a tasteful-sized whip in her hand. Susie relished her role; she laid down the rules and expected you to follow.

"Does this have anything to do with Fabiana?" Cruz asked.

"She needs a good lawyer and you're the best. She didn't kill anyone," I told him.

"You know I never ask that question. And I don't want to hear that you're hiding her from authorities either."

"Well, I'm not." Technically that's the truth. I crossed my fingers just in case. "What does she do now? Harder's lead investigator."

Fab groaned and covered her face with her hands. She and Harder had issues. She'd been a thorn in his side for quite some time. He itched to arrest her but never had any evidence.

"I want Fabiana in my office at 9:00 a.m. and not one second later. She doesn't speak to anyone about the case without me sitting beside her and that includes you," Cruz admonished. "You need to let me handle her legal problems. It would be a conflict for me to take you as a client in the same case, so don't get caught helping her."

Fab listened to the conversation.

"Can you stand to stay here one more night?" I rang the buzzer on the table. "If I don't leave soon, the sheriff outside might come in to investigate."

Dickie entered the room so quietly that if he hadn't cleared his voice, I wouldn't have known he stood in the doorway. "Fab can stay another night. No one will look for her here. If they do, we have good hiding places."

"One thing you two have in common," I said and nodded at Fab and Dickie, "you both eavesdrop. Loan me an empty urn so I can walk out the door with it in plain sight." Hiding a wanted person didn't faze Dickie; his cheeks flushed with excitement.

"In the morning, she can lie down in the back of the Cadillac and I can drive her into Miami," Dickie offered before leaving the room.

"I'll call in every favor that I have, including Aunt Elizabeth's, to help in any way." There were a few people that all I had to do was ask and they waved their favor-doer wand and poof, done!

Dickie came back, an ornate urn in his hands. I stared at Fab, silently communicating, "The things we do for friends."

Fab gave me a half smile. "I'll be waiting for your call. At least there's not a dead body in that thing."

"Fab and I both owe you and Raul." Dickie and Raul had been long-time partners, and I'd forged an interesting friendship with the two of them. I took the urn, thinking that with the lid off, it could pass as an ugly vase.

I didn't want to leave Tropical Slumber without my friend. At least I hadn't been there to make funeral arrangements. Out of the corner of my eye, I saw the sheriff car still parked at the tattoo parlor, the parking lot empty—his presence was bad for business. I made certain the officer could see the urn. I laid it on the floor behind the driver's seat.

Chapter 14

I slid into the last space in the beach parking lot not far from my house. My first call was to Famosa Motors, and Bitsy informed me Brick had left for the day but would be in his office early in the morning. Next, I called Creole. He answered on the first ring.

"What's new?" I asked.

"Where are you and whose phone is this?"

"What's going on at my house?"

"For someone without a rap sheet and no criminal record, well...sort of, you do think like a criminal. Madeline is there waiting for you. Heard you were at Tropical Slumber and left with a dead person, anyone we know?"

"A favor for Dickie," I lied, "a dead VIP who needs to be delivered to Miami tomorrow." I could hear in Creole's voice that he was about out of patience with me. "What's the latest on the Wright murder case?"

"Fab is a person of interest. Tell her she can't run forever and what she's doing now makes her look guilty. If you get caught with her, you'll go to jail," Creole said evenly. "Before you hang up on me, where are you?"

"I'm on my way home." I hung up and backed out, waving to the meter cop.

* * *

Mother stood in the front door waiting for me. "I'm glad you're back." She hugged me. "Is Fab okay?" she whispered in my ear.

"Yes and she didn't kill the rich guy and her ex," I whispered back. "Why are you whispering? Is my house bugged?"

"I wondered the same thing. Maybe I watch too much television. The sheriff stops by here every five minutes asking about her. The last time I didn't open the door."

"Everything is going to be fine." I didn't believe a single word of that but I'd keep repeating it to myself until I willed it to happen. I leaned forward. "Fab's lawyer is Cruz. Starting tomorrow he'll work his lawyerly charms and make her legal problems go away."

"Are you hungry? I cooked, it just needs reheating."

Mother never cooked anything, she ordered takeout and told people who didn't know better that she slaved over the stove. "Okay, I'm in the mood to pretend. What did you whip up?"

"One of your favorites—shrimp scampi pizza and a Caesar salad."

"Love you, and not just because you cooked my faves." The doorbell rang. "I'm not answering."

Mother tiptoed to the door. "I'll lookout

the peephole."

Then came a cop knock, equal to one of my own; mine sounded like six cops were knocking all at once.

"It's Creole." Mother opened the door.

I shook my head "no," but it was too late; he filled the entryway. If Mother hadn't been there, the look on his face told me he'd hurt me. I looked away and opened the pizza box, putting two slices on my plate and giving them a quick nuke.

"Looks like I'm in time for a home-cooked meal." Creole kissed Mother's cheek. He fit into our family, he adored Mother and the feeling was mutual.

"Do you have good news? If not, go get yourself a hamburger." I added salad to my plate and licked the Caesar dressing off my finger.

"Really, Madison," Mother scolded, and handed him a plate.

"You better leave me a piece for breakfast," I grumbled. Whoever didn't like pizza for breakfast had a genetic defect.

"Hey, whiney," Creole pointed out, "there are two pizza boxes and three people. Tell me what's happening with Fab. I already promised anything I learn from her or you won't be held against either of you."

The silence hung in the air. I trusted Creole but he was a cop, and he'd taken an oath. "Fab has a good lawyer, so I imagine you'll get to question her sooner rather than later."

"Interrogation is not in my job description, Harder will handle that. I'll review all the tapes. My expertise lies in undercover work, being every criminal's best friend. I asked to be assigned to this case. My focus now that the crime scene has been processed is to follow the trail of the missing art, and the possibility of a third person being involved."

"That's where Fab comes in?"

"I could see her shooting her ex-husband. Gabriel wasn't a nice guy––but why Maxwell? And both men were shot with the same gun. Zach told me about her past in France, and she has no arrest record here in the states—not a whisper of her being a thief. She seems to have left her criminal ways behind, for the most part anyway."

"We're agreed that Fab didn't shoot two people dead. Any ideas?" I asked.

"Gabriel was convicted for this same type of job. He'd steal what he wanted, no confrontation and no blood drawn. This time he ends up dead, which makes me think a third person double-crossed him."

"Isn't the first question you people ask, 'who stands to gain the most'?" I flashed a phony, insincere smile.

"You people?" Creole snorted. "Do I

have your permission to strangle her?"

"Ignore her," Mother said. "We're both worried about Fab."

"News flash," Creole said. "I'm not the enemy here. If Fab didn't do it, then there's a murderer running around feeling pretty confident right now." He shook his head. "Chrissy Wright, the widow, she's the one with the money and the social standing. Maxwell married out of his league. And she has an alibi."

"Anything linking Fab to the crime scene such as fingerprints, her spit, something?" I asked.

"Honey, saliva would be considered DNA." Mother looked proud of herself. She had cop shows on her television-viewing list.

Creole rummaged through the refrigerator, grabbing a bottle of water. "All we've got is security footage of her running down the back lawn, retrieved from outside cameras installed by Zach's boys. He's beating the bushes hard on this one; he has a lock on the security contract on Fisher Island and doesn't want any backlash."

"Doesn't Zach know he's wasting his time on Fab? He knows her better than any of us does; they had a relationship. The info he gave you on her background was learned while sharing the same pillow." I guess all bets were off when the relationship ended. Beware what you share.

"Isn't that a little messy, she bangs him and now you and her are friends?" Creole asked.

"'Bang,' Creole?" Mother stared him down.

I'd never seen Creole blush, and I was enjoying his discomfort. "I didn't know either one of them when they were 'banging,' as you so graciously put it. She told me she has no regrets and you men are not that emotionally deep."

"One of these days I'm going to shut you up, get the last word, and enjoy every second." Creole glared.

"Have you seen Didier?" Mother changed the subject. "They speak their own language, it's so cute to watch. Seems as though he gets her."

"It's called French, Mother. He left a few days ago for Europe, his calendar is booked with runway jobs, and then he'll be back."

"Smarty, you've seen them together," Mother said.

Yes, I'd seen them together. Saw plenty of ribbon on the door handle signaling hot sex. I never heard them argue or him tell her one time what to do. Just, "Cherie, be careful."

"I'm going to bed. I have to be up early, time's up on my turning in the Hummer. I'm going car shopping as soon as Fab can go and play hardball with the salesman." I put my plate in the dishwasher and kissed Mother's cheek, poking Creole's back on the way out of the kitchen.

* * *

This early in the morning there were no lookie loos at Famosa Motors. I envisioned Brick's criminal clients rolling a suitcase of cash through the front door, dumping it on his desk, and driving out in a Lamborghini or some other sexy sports car. Brick recently hired two new salesmen. They stood talking, an overdose of beach boy good looks, and both came up short in the brains department. One of the mechanics told me they were relatives of some sort and good with the ladies.

Brick's office encompassed the entire second floor and when I got out of the Hummer, I cupped my hands over my eyes and made out Brick sitting at his desk. It surprised me that Bitsy wasn't sitting at hers, her smile and big boobs firmly in place. I hopped up the stairs making a bunch of noise and a nuisance of myself.

"What the hell?" Brick glared. "You need to be announced."

"Bitsy wasn't at her desk. Did you want me to stand down there and yell for permission to come upstairs?" I leaned over and knocked on his desk. "Can I come in?"

Brick rolled his eyes, my charm lost on

him. "You didn't bring the cops with you, did you?"

"If Fab needs bail money, will you give me a good deal?"

"That depends on the amount." He scribbled on a notepad. "If it's reasonable, we can work something out. If they hit her with two counts of murder, she'll never get bail."

Brick didn't offer, so I sat in one of his uncomfortable chairs. "If that happens, I'll be asking you to use your connections to break her out."

He sat silent. "I can't remember the last time someone broke out of jail."

"Oh, I can. The last one took me hostage and almost beat me to death." After that, I started carrying a gun and took self-defense classes.

"You're a lot more resilient than you look. Do you really need a PI license? You've got enough on your plate. This is a crappy business."

I sensed a lecture coming and I wasn't in the mood. "Since you insist, you can have the Hummer back. Loan me something else for a couple of days to give me time to go buy a new car. My insurance check is in the mail."

"Change of plans. You keep the Hummer and when I want it back, I'll call and give you a heads up. I'll work you the same deal I do Fab."

My mouth dropped open, I snapped it shut. "You look like Brick, but who are you really? You've wanted the Hummer back from day one and now you've changed your mind. What's going on?"

He leaned forward. "Listen up, anyone asks, you bought the Hummer. You don't tell anyone any different. Got it?"

"Am I going to end up in jail?"

Brick sighed. "My sister, Margarite, wants the Hummer but let it slip my seventeen-year-old nephew would be driving it. She's out of her mind. That's not going to happen."

The only family member I'd met was his brother, Casio. I completely blocked out meeting his seven-year-old spawn. Casio, a decorated Miami police officer, dragged in the criminals one way or another. Gossip had it Casio made his own rules.

"He's not your favorite nephew?"

"He drag raced his last car down the Overseas, spun out into a 360, and flipped into the water. Stupid ass. He's lucky he didn't get hurt or worse, and the other guy took off without a look in the rearview mirror. I told Margarite it sold. If she sees it parked on the lot, she'll organize the rest of my sisters to gang up on me. You drive it until I find an interested buyer."

"How many sisters do you have?"

"Three and they're a pain in the ass." Brick tossed a key, and pushed papers across his desk. "I need a car picked up at the Fontainebleau Hotel. I trust you know where it's located."

"I can find it," I smirked.

"Why do you keep checking your watch?"

"Fab's in Cruz's office. Wish she'd call." Then reality set in that I'd never done one of these jobs without Fab. Now would not be the time to whine about that little issue.

"Check the VIP lot first. After 10:00 p.m. would be a good time," Brick said. "Don't screw this up."

I breathed a sigh of relief; I'd have picked Fab up by that time. "If the car's there, I'll have it back tonight."

"Katy announced to the family that she and lover boy had an amicable breakup. I knew you were the right one for the job."

I had worked up a good sob story for Ramsey Sinclair. Thank goodness he followed my advice and that drama was over with no broken bones.

Brick's phone rang; he answered in Spanish.

I waved and left Brick's office.

I plugged my phone into the cigarette lighter, pushed speed dial for Creole, and put him on speaker. "Have you heard anything?" I asked as soon as he answered.

Total silence. Then, "Not good news."

I didn't want to freak out, but it was too late. "What the hell are you talking about?"

"Fab's being arraigned for first degree murder," Creole said.

"You told me you didn't have any evidence against her!" I yelled.

"The District Attorney decided otherwise, did an end run around Harder, and had Fab arrested in his office, in front of Cruz. Harder was livid, the D.A. screwed him big time with Cruz."

"Why would he do that?" I asked.

"She! Ana Sigga thinks she has a case without needing any further investigation."

"What's the bail?" I asked. Murder One, the bail will be high.

"It's been set at ten million."

"Dollars?" The amount sucked the breath out of me. Even with ten percent, that's a million, cash, not to be refunded.

"Stay calm. Cruz is a kick ass lawyer. He demanded the case be fast-tracked and scheduled an evidentiary hearing to make the D.A. prove up her case. Fab won't be in jail long."

"Have you been to jail?" I demanded. "One hour is too long. Especially when you know you're innocent. The fear that you might not be able to prove your innocence fills your entire being. I need a favor."

"I can't and won't break her out," Creole said.

It seemed like the only people to slip out of lockout were hard-core criminals. "Get me a jail visit tomorrow or the next day. Anytime."

"I'll see what I can do and give you a call back."

I hung up feeling sick. Any bondsman, and that included Brick, would want upfront money in cash and the rest in assets. Brick might wave the assets, but I didn't have the million dollars. I knew that if you post through a bonding company that amount doesn't get refunded, it's considered their fee. The only way to get all your money back is to post the whole ten million with the court clerk.

Chapter 15

I turned onto my street; Brad's truck was parked in front of the house. Mother, as good as she is, would never be able to dance around all this drama and keep it to herself. If I were her, I'd just blurt everything out. Brad complains all the time about being left out. Dump every last bit of excruciating detail on him, maybe he won't ask in the future.

I tried to sneak a peek in the kitchen window where Mother and Brad sat at the island, but they saw me and both waved.

Brad beat me to the door. "How's tricks?" I knew by his tone of voice that Mother had come clean. The question was much she had revealed. We hugged.

"I hope Mother's cooking. Can I borrow some money?"

Brad's eyebrows shot up. "How much?"

"Ten million."

I actually rendered him speechless—his mouth fell open and I wanted to laugh.

Before Brad could respond, Mother asked, "Where's Fab?"

"Miami Jail." I told them everything Creole told me but in a tabloid headline style, my favorite way to relate bad news. I fished the ringing foghorn out of my pocket. I changed the ring tone again, the more annoying the better.

"Speak of the devil," I answered. "Good news this time?"

"Did you know that when an inmate gets booked, it takes about a week for the paperwork to make it over to the visitation unit?" Creole asked.

I counted to three. "You're telling me that you couldn't get me an appointment? Guess what?" I yelled. "I'll get my own appointment and I'll be seeing her tomorrow!" I threw the phone, bouncing it off the wall. I stopped counting, it only gave me time to get madder.

Brad leaned down, scooped up the pieces of the phone, and put it back together. "What was that all about?"

As soon as Brad turned the phone on, it rang again. He looked at the screen. "It's Creole again."

"Reject the call. Do you mind if I call your boyfriend?" I asked Mother.

"You told me you and Spoon were just friends." Brad glared at Mother, forcing her to look at him.

"Get over it. They're already friendly." I couldn't bring myself to say anything graphic. "We should all go out to dinner. You two should have a lot in common; you're about the same age."

"He's not that much younger than me," Mother sighed. "Get to know him before you decide to hate him. If you decide you really don't like him, I'll stop seeing him."

Brad might believe that lie, but no woman is going to walk away from a man who makes her happy and makes her laugh.

Mother's phone started ringing. She looked at the phone, then at me and answered. After a beat, she said, "Okay, hold on." Turning to me she relayed, "Creole says your appointment is at four tomorrow afternoon." She held her phone out.

"How did you make that happen so fast?"

"You cost me five bucks." I'd clearly stepped on Creole's last nerve. "Grow up, it's juvenile to hang up, and you did it before I could tell you about your appointment."

"You gave me some jive about waiting a week. What's up with the five dollars?"

"Harder got you the appointment and laughed his head off when you hung up on me. Bet me you'd call one of your criminal friends and get the appointment. And you were doing just that weren't you?"

I ignored his question. "I'll give you ten dollars for getting me the appointment."

"Don't ever hang up on me again," Creole replied.

"Yes, sir," I sighed. "I still don't

understand what happened today."

"My informant, who's on top of courtroom gossip, tells me Fab had an affair with the D.A.'s husband."

"If that's true, why is she on the case? Isn't that a conflict of interest?"

"Maybe someone ought to mention it to Cruz," Creole said.

"I know just the person."

Creole laughed. "I bet you do. Tell Fabiana that I have a friend or two at the woman's jail and I'll pull strings to get her an extra blanket or something."

"I would owe you big. Let me know if you hear anything." This time I said good-bye before hanging up.

"I get to see Fab tomorrow," I told Mother and Brad.

Mother looked at me suspiciously. "I thought you were turning in the Hummer."

"Brick had to choose between me and his seventeen-year-old nephew who recently drowned his last vehicle, and I won."

Brad asked, "Is that the moron who flew off the Overseas around Marathon Key, tying up traffic for hours?"

"Wait just a second. What do you have to do for Brick Famosa?" Mother asked.

"I get the same deal as Fab, but in the excitement of getting the Hummer I didn't ask about the fine print. I assume it's that I'll work for him with no pay."

"You tell him that if you get hurt or go to jail again, I'll shoot him," Mother said.

"Jail? Again?" Brad yelled. "I'm so sick of being treated like some slow-witted third cousin! You don't want me to know anything. I'm leaving."

I grabbed him by the back of his shirt. "You're not going anywhere. I could use help on a car retrieval I have to do tonight."

Brad smashed a soda can between his hands, slam dunking it into the trash. "You're repossessing cars? Why? Don't you have enough with those crazy asses at The Cottages, not to mention you're now the owner of a bar?"

"I need the hours to get my private investigator license."

"And you need that why?"

"I don't have a good reason other than I want to prove to myself that I can get one. There's going to come a time when you've had enough of commercial fishing. We could open a family detective agency—you, me, and Mother." I saw a spark of excitement as Brad mulled over the idea.

"We could make Jake's the main office," Mother suggested.

"I hardly recognized that rat hole. You've done a great job," Brad said. "I checked it out on the way over when a couple of my guys said they started drinking and shooting pool there again. What are you going to do when Jake comes back from being on the run from loan sharks and wants his bar back?"

"Buy him out. I paid all the past due food and liquor bills. A couple of collectors came by for gambling debts and I told them I was under the protection of Spoon. One called my bluff and got on the phone to verify. Whatever Spoon said, the guy turned and left without even a wave goodbye. The collection calls have stopped. I don't want to partner with Jake, he's too reckless."

"It's time for me to get to know Spoon. I'll invite him fishing. Good way to get to know the man," Brad said.

"When you two figure out which one of yours is bigger, you'll find out he's a man of his word and has a magic wand that makes problems disappear," I said.

"What's the plan to 'retrieve' this car?" Brad replied.

"I've got the paperwork and the key. You drop me off at the Fontainebleau Hotel; I get in the McLaren and drive away." I relayed all of Brick's directions. "Then you'll pick me up at Famosa Motors and give me a ride home."

"I'm driving." Brad plucked the keys out of my fingers.

* * *

Brad had two driving styles: one for when Mother sat in the passenger seat and the one for when she didn't. He didn't care if I screamed "slow down" from the back seat like the crazy woman I've been accused of being. I lay down, settling in for the long drive as Brad rocketed up Highway 1 just over the speed limit. What I didn't see couldn't scare me.

"We're supposed to drive through the parking lot, row by row," Brad grumbled. "What's the deal on this? What happens when security notices that on their cameras?"

"Brick said to start with VIP parking. How many McLaren MP4s could there be? I've got a picture. It's got a 230K sticker price on it. The problem with Brick is he rents his cars out to men of dubious character who show up holding a bag of cash. A few of them think he's stupid enough to rent to them, so why not screw him and keep the luxury auto?"

"Whatever happened to the Mercedes being guarded by the Dobermans?" Mother asked.

"Oh, this ought to be good," Brad snickered. "I'm so shocked this is the first time I'm hearing about this."

I tried to keep from laughing. "Sarcasm is not attractive on you, bro." No wonder he felt like the dumb one in the family, Mother and I hide stuff from him all the time. Our justification—we didn't want to worry him. "I didn't get the exact details, but I heard a few of Miami's finest showed up, guns drawn, threatened to shoot Porn Queen and arrest the guy's mother. The dude, being a coward, hid in the bedroom and mommy dearest said, 'screw it,' and opened the gates, and the Mercedes made the ride back to Famosa Motors on a flatbed."

"Who in the hell is Porn Queen?" Brad asked.

"Let me tell him," Mother said. "That's what the old lady named her dog, makes one wonder what she did back in her younger days."

Brad and I laughed. "Really, Mother, old lady?"

"See what comes from trolling the high school looking for a boyfriend? It boosts my self-esteem," Mother said.

"High school! That would make you a child molester. Thank goodness that Spoon character isn't younger than your children. I'd stop speaking to you." Brad banged the steering wheel. "Guess what girls, the VIP area is key card monitored, and the sign says to go see the front desk after hours."

Mother opened her purse and took out what resembled a credit card. "Here, try this."

Brad made an illegal U-turn and drove up to the gate, leaned out the window, and inserted the card, and the stick went up.

"Where the hell did you get this?" He looked at it closer. "I didn't know you hung out here."

He pulled into the open-air covered garage. During daytime hours, they ran a well-staffed garage and auto detail amenity for rich people who couldn't be seen in a car with a speck of dust on the exterior.

"I don't." Mother grabbed it out of his hand. "Madison and I got the cards from Fab. A friend of hers makes them and they open most of the gates in the city. I tried it out when Jean and I went joyriding around out on Aventura, it didn't open that gate, but I got in by driving in behind the car in front of me."

Jean Stewart is Mother's neighbor and new best friend since selling the family home in South Carolina and moving to Coral Gables. The drive between Mother and me is closer than Brad, who lives out in the Everglades.

I sat up and passed the picture of the car to Mother. "It's solid silver and the vanity license tag says, FAMM30."

"There it is," Mother squealed.

I tapped Brad's shoulder. "Pull up in front, I'll get in and drive it out, and meet you on the street."

"We're sitting right here until you're behind the wheel and ready to go," Brad said.

I jumped out. *Don't get nervous. Be quick and don't attract any unwanted attention.* The key would only go in half way; no way it could be the right key. "Damn you, Brick."

Mother rolled down the window. "What's wrong?" her voice a stage whisper.

Holding the key out, I whispered back, "Wrong one. I need to get this car back tonight."

"Brad said to get back in. We'll drive around the block and come up with another plan."

"Now what?" I asked climbing into the back seat.

Brad made two left turns and coasted out of the lot. He pulled over, parked, and adjusted the rearview to look at me. "You've got three choices: go get the right key, use a slim jim—which could screw up the wiring inside the door, and which you don't have—or break the window."

I pulled out my phone, exhaling loudly. "I'm not making this decision." Somehow, this whole fiasco would get blamed on my inexperience.

Brick actually picked up. "This better be good."

"You gave me the wrong key. Anybody at Famosa's who can give me the right one?"

The silence seemed never ending. "Bullshit, I didn't give you the wrong key. Bet you the bitch put in a new lock; he's the third dirt bag to try that trick. No one steals a quarter-million dollar car and drives it around right under my nose."

"My options will damage the car. There is no way I can get a tow truck in here without security crawling all over the car."

"This cash crap is not worth the aggravation. The cheapest fix, jimmy the lock. Last resort, break the window. And don't get fucking caught."

"I'll get it done." I hung up and crawled into the rear cargo space. Maybe Brick will get an attitude adjustment if I can get this car out of here. "I haven't practiced with this tool." I held up the slim jim.

Brad did a double take. "What the hell? Where did you get that?"

"Same place I got my lock pick set."

"Why doesn't he call the police? It's called grand theft auto not to return a rental car," Brad said.

"He'd need a court order and he's afraid he'll have to explain his cash business. He needs to start running background checks before he lets his pricey cars off the lot."

"Give that to me." Brad wiggled his fingers. "I can get us in but what if the ignition lock is different?"

"Mother can hotwire it, she's better and faster at it than me."

Brad turned on Mother, his face red. "Madeline Westin! Tell me your daughter's a liar!"

Mother picked up her purse and fished out her lock pick set. "Afraid not. Julie and I are star pupils, Madison needs tutoring."

"You're mean," I sulked. "I had a bad day, performance anxiety."

Brad took Mother's lock set. "Listen to you two. Madison, you drive the Hummer. I'll do the dirty illegal work. You better pay bail before they make me strip and assign me a cell. Follow me out. Where's the original key?" He snapped his fingers.

I fished the key out of my pocket. "Be careful."

Brad cut through the cars across the two aisles, came up on the passenger side, and had the door open in seconds. He leaned across the driver's side and opened the door. He walked around, and seconds later the engine hummed and he headed straight to the exit.

Mother said, impressed, "That was fast and, so far, we haven't run into a single person. Aren't you surprised not one security guard is out for a cigarette stroll?"

"If Brad had a criminal mindset he could make the big bucks jacking high-end sports cars," I said.

As I pulled out of the VIP lot, Brad fell in behind and followed us to Famosa Motors. After an attempted murder and a burst of stolen cars and vandalism, Brick hired two armed, beefy security guards to patrol the lot during non-business hours. They also took possession of middle-of-the-night returns and made sure they didn't disappear before morning. Brick recently told me he expanded his private detective firm to include personal body guarding services.

The two guards—dressed like twins in shorts, muscles bulging from their rolled-up dress shirts—stood at attention, hands on their side arms, when the Hummer drove on the lot followed by the McLaren. I retrieved the keys from Brad and handed them over.

Brad opened the back door for me. "I'm driving."

I stuck out my tongue and climbed over the driver's seat.

"Fasten your seatbelt, ladies." Brad squealed out of the parking lot. "The valet left the passenger door unlocked, key worked in the ignition. Someone took a screwdriver or something to the driver's side lock, rendering it mutilated. Wait until Brick sees the inside, full of trash, smells like rotten food, interior is stained and has burn holes."

"Why would someone do that?" Mother asked.

Brad shook his head. "Because they could. If I were Famosa, I'd hunt the asshole down, kick their balls into their tonsils, and retrieve another bag of cash for damages." He stopped at the red light, checking out the blonde in the convertible.

"Take us back to my house; I've had enough drama for today. I've got a full schedule of it tomorrow." I leaned back against the seat, my feet propped up behind Brad's head.

"I'm spending the night," Brad told me. "I'm taking Julie and Liam to the boat races up in Ft. Lauderdale tomorrow."

"One of us needs to get up early and go to The Bakery Café and get breakfast." I nudged Mother's shoulder. "Or I could cook."

Chapter 16

I couldn't believe I overslept. I jumped out of bed and into the shower, letting the water rain down on me. Note to self: Get visiting days with Fab every day she sits in jail. I stepped into a jean skirt, reached for a long sleeve T-shirt, and pulled my long red hair into a ponytail. That would pass the dress code at the jail, which was basically to cover yourself; nothing provocative, and no open-toed shoes. The house was eerily quiet as I went down the stairs. Walking into the kitchen, I saw the note on top of the pink bakery box. *I went with Brad, Julie, and Liam to the boat races. See you later. Got your favorites.* Mother drew an arrow to the bottom of the page.

I hopped in the Hummer with my coffee mug and a pecan roll, and headed to Clean Bubbles to see if the Poppins had packed up and left. It had to make them nervous, the local sheriff watching their every move.

I called Cruz Campion's office wanting an update as to when he'd get Fab sprung from jail. He needed to know about Fab and the District Attorney's husband. The D.A. can hate her guts, but she doesn't get to over-prosecute the case to get back at Fab. No one talked to Cruz without going through Susie. Lately, my success rate for getting my call put through to Cruz ran under fifty percent.

"Hi, Susie, this is Madison Westin. I'd like to know when Fab's next court date is?"

"You're not our client and we don't discuss other client's cases," Susie scolded.

I got privacy, but I wasn't in the mood. "I'll just go to the courthouse and wait for Cruz to come out of the courtroom and ask him."

"You've got a big pair of balls," Susie said, not amused by my blackmail attempt.

Be nice. "Fab's my best friend and I'd like to have some good news for her when I see her later today."

"Another bail hearing is calendared for the end of the week. Mr. Campion is applying pressure on the prosecutor's office. How did you get a jail appointment so quickly?"

I ignored her question. "Thank you, Susie, I appreciate the info. Have a great day." I hung up before she could ask any more questions, and besides, I had an incoming call.

I parked the Hummer around the corner from Clean Bubbles so I could observe street traffic.

Brick's name popped up on the screen. "What the hell happened to my car?" he demanded when I answered.

"The guy you rented it to is a pig. What did he do to the driver's side door lock?"

"Asshole smeared glue on a file, stuck it

in the lock and broke it off. Any problems I should know about?"

"Went smoothly for a change." Thank goodness.

"I'm guessing you didn't call about bail since it's ten mill. Anything else I can do let me know."

"Don't hang up," I said loudly, in case the next sound I heard was dead air. "There is something I want. Fab's next court hearing is at the end of the week. Can you get me on the jail visitation schedule every day? I'm not picky on the time."

"Done. Bitsy will call you later with the info. Don't worry about Fab, Casio has connections, made some calls, now she's got friends."

I got all teary eyed. "Thank you." Then I realized he'd already hung up on me in typical Brick fashion. Fab had worked for him for a long time, and there was mutual respect there. Brick called her first on every job, except for dead people and animals, those jobs went to me.

I'd been watching the sheriff car at the other end of the block; from my vantage point, it was impossible to make out who sat behind the wheel. I drove past the car and looked in the window, checking to see if I knew the driver on a first name basis. I didn't recognize the sheriff; he must've drawn the short straw. I made a U-turn and drove back to the car wash.

The Poppins had zero sense. Clean Bubbles showed no signs that they'd paid attention to one word I said. Vanilla sunned herself in a lawn chair in the front.

Vanilla sat up and took off her sunglasses when I drove in the driveway. "I thought Quirky told you to take a hike," she told me when I got out of the Hummer.

"Where is Quirky?" I'd run out of patience for the day.

Vanilla's eyes darted toward their make shift office, which was basically a large storage room. She drew herself up out of the rickety chair. "He's, uh, not here. Now hit the road, before I kick your ass."

I didn't take out my Glock. Instead, I hiked my skirt. "You take one boney step in my direction and I'll shoot you and the sheriff sitting across the street can corroborate my story, you made the first move." I watched Vanilla's body movements. I'd be ready for her, a couple of short kicks would have her lying on the ground looking up.

Vanilla pulled her unwashed hair back, tying it with a piece of a rag. "I'm going to get the sheriff."

"Go ahead, that would give them probable cause to ransack your illegal operation and arrest you two for the scams you're running."

Vanilla grabbed her beach chair. "You don't know what you're talking about."

"You tell Quirky time's run out. Jimmy Spoon and his boys will be here to kick your asses to Georgia. If you've never heard of Spoon, I suggest you ask around."

"We know Spoon." Vanilla gave me the finger and disappeared into the storage room.

Not interested in going home to an empty house, I headed to The Cottages. I planned to sneak out onto the beach and let it work its magic on my frustration before heading to the jail.

I drove alongside the white sandy beach with the windows rolled down and a cool breeze blowing across my face. The first stop I made after the Tahoe got stolen was the Shell Shack, for large, old-fashioned, metal-themed buckets, perfect for picking up shells. Besides being inexpensive therapy, I used them for mulch in the potted flowers around my house. The waves looked tame today and the beach was not overly crowded.

The Cottages looked quiet, but that could be deceiving. We hadn't had any problems for a while and the sheriff stopped coming around every day for nuisance calls. As I pulled into the driveway, I groaned out loud. *Could there be any bigger spectacle than those two sunning in the barbeque area?* Mac and her friend, Shirl, two overly-endowed middle-aged women, were lying in chaise lounges with either their underwear on, or really short shorts, and tight low-cut tops.

"You have the best boss that you can sit outside and work on your tan," I told Mac and waved to Shirl.

"I got the phone between my legs," Mac said as she pointed, "and we've got four eyes on the property."

The barbeque area, located at the front, was the first thing you saw when you drove in the driveway. If you positioned your chair just right, you could see every cottage and watch the comings and goings from everyone's front door.

"It's all quiet around here, well almost, with the exception of him." Mac crooked her head.

Joseph lay sacked out in a lounge chair that he pulled into his parking space, sound asleep. "What's up with him?" I asked.

"Drama Queen came screaming, drunk, out of his cottage, yelling, 'I cut my finger off.' He doesn't fool me, he just wanted Shirl to bandage his paper cut so he could look down her top. Men act like they've never seen a pair of boobs before. Wait until Svetlana finds out he's cheating on her."

"I'm a little disappointed," Shirl said. "All the stories I've heard, and so far no real drama."

Chapter 17

I arrived at the jail visiting center in time to snag a bench in front of the door. The sheriff stood, ready to yell the rules to everyone. Next stop, the metal detectors. I had nothing on me but a key, which I dropped in the box and then I gave them my name in exchange for a booth number. Television screens were lit up and I could see down the row that no inmates had shown up yet. Fab came through the door first; once she sat down we picked up our phones, which started the clock on our twenty-minute visit.

I waved at the screen. "The blue uniforms look better than the ugly orange ones on the men's side. Can you take the shoes with you when you check out? I'll put them with the orange pair and get a collection going."

Fab looked tired, her scary face firmly in place. "Miss you, too. How's my cat?"

"He's my cat and he misses you. Jazz's wondering where his treats are. You have a faint shiner what's up with that?"

Fab touched her eye. "One of the girls singled me out for a friendly welcome."

"And your response?" I knew I wouldn't get a blow-by-blow of the butt-kicking the girl got because we both knew all calls were recorded. Two signs posted in every aisle gave you a heads-up warning.

"I welcomed her back and let her know I had one friend and didn't want anymore." Fab flashed me an evil smile.

"How's the food?" I'd heard stories from previous visits on the men's side that it was pretty disgusting.

"Don't know. The wannabe friend, Bertha, didn't understand my one-friend policy and I accidentally dropped the runny meat and beans in her lap. She yelped to the guard and I had to hand over my apple. Before handing it over, I licked it and then spit on it so it would be nice and clean."

"Bertha? I thought that name was only on television shows." She would do well to find someone else to torment.

"I don't give a damn what her name is, I'll call her whatever I want."

"You have any roommates?"

Fab knew she had to be careful and not get any additional charges. "Cuban girl, quiet, and she shared crackers and some mystery sausage with me after lunch. We're both in for murders we didn't commit. You got any news?"

"You're getting a field trip at the end of the week, another bail hearing. I have it on good authority that they don't have squat."

"I wanted to jump out the window

146

when two Miami police officers barged into Harder's office and arrested me."

"Is it true about you and Ana Sigga's husband?"

"Bastard never mentioned a wife until she walked in on us and introduced herself. Now I have a policy, call me when the ink is dry on the decree. I fell hard once for a man who was separated, supposedly getting a divorce. He used me to get his wife to let him wear the pants in the relationship. And it worked."

"I had a couple of friends fall for that tired line, never a happy ending. Don't get comfortable," I said. "Creole and Brick both sent you friends, whatever that means."

Fab half smiled. "A few things make sense now."

"I got appointments to visit you every day this week and every day after that until you get out of here. Bitsy texted me the times."

Fab raised her eyebrow. "What's the catch?"

"Brick has a soft spot for you. He felt generous after I went and picked up a rental for him. The Westin family did the retrieval. Brad turned out to be the star. He's got career options after fishing."

"I'm missing the good stuff," Fab sniffed.

"Next time, you and I will ditch them

and sneak out the French doors for our own adventure."

The light flashed on the screen, giving the one-minute warning, signaling the end of the visit.

"I'll be back tomorrow. You want anything; I'll get it for you. And when you're in court, I'll be there with my party face to give you a ride home."

"Thanks for making this happen; it's nice to see a face of someone I actually trust. Call Gunz. Tell him there's a slight delay in his case, contact info in my day planner."

We hung up as the screen went black.

* * *

I grabbed my purse out from under the front seat and retrieved my cell phone. One morning while Fab showered, I co-opted a few numbers off her phone. Her "what's yours is mine to snoop through" policy had worn off on me.

I sat waiting for the visitor center parking lot to empty. Gunz answered his phone but didn't say anything.

"Who's this?" he demanded.

"This is Madison Westin. I visited Fab today, she wanted me to call and get started working on your case." So what if none of that was truthful. "We didn't discuss details, since conversations are taped."

Gunz made a choking noise. "Yeah, no

thanks. You're not qualified."

"You should've stopped at, 'no thanks.' You're forgetting that I know you're a criminal." I stopped from ending with, 'you bastard'. "If this job was on the up, you would've called someone else by now."

"You keep your mouth shut about what you know and don't know."

This conversation had degenerated rapidly. "You need a reference, call Spoon." I hung up on him. Reminding him of my friendship with Spoon might keep him from doing something stupid.

* * *

"Hi, Susie, this is Madison Westin, is Mr. Campion in?" I could've sworn she groaned. "I have something to tell him about Fab's case."

"He's in court today. I'll take a detailed message and pass it along."

"Hello, are you there?" I asked.

"Go ahead, I can hear you." Susie sounded exasperated.

"Hello?" I paused. "Damn." I hung up hoping I did a good job at letting her think we got cut off. It wouldn't surprise me if Susie blocked my calls.

The criminal courts were about five minutes away from the jail. Cruz would be easy to find, the court clerk posted a calendar of every case being heard that day and in which courtroom.

My lucky day, I had my pick of metered parking in front of the courthouse. I ran up the stairs hoping he wasn't in trial. Hopefully, I'd have no reason to call his office in the near future because when Susie heard about this, she'd be livid. I cleared the metal detector and went in search of the list that got posted on the bulletin board by the elevators.

I lacked the appropriate business attire, but looked better than most defendants who show up to plead their case. I hoped to run into Cruz in the hallway and pretend, "Isn't this a coincidence?" His current case was assigned to the last courtroom on the third floor. The benches were empty, which either meant court was in session or everyone had left for the day. I looked through the small window in the door; Cruz sat at the defense table. A man and woman sat on the prosecution side, the guard and two people were seated in the front row. The judge and clerk were apparently on break.

I pushed the door open. No one turned around. I walked to the railing behind the defense table. "Mr. Campion," I whispered.

He turned and stared at me. "Are you in trouble?"

"No, I have some information about Fab's case that might be important."

Cruz looked slightly amused. "How did you know I was in court? Oh, never mind. This better be good." He straightened his tie.

"I'm only telling you because I want Fab to be treated fairly. She slept with the D.A.'s husband." I tossed my head in Ana Sigga's direction. "At the very least, it's a conflict of interest."

A dark-haired woman walked from the prosecution table and dropped files in front of Cruz. "Here's the rest of the discovery."

"Ana, don't you think you should recuse yourself from the Merceau case since she had an affair with your husband?" Cruz asked.

Ana's jaw dropped, but she recovered in an instant. "Who told you that?" she hissed.

"I did," I spoke up.

Ana turned on me, her eyes flared. "You're a liar and you better not repeat one word of that fabricated bullshit."

Cruz looked at her. "I don't care one way or another. Just hand the files over to someone else."

"Go to hell." Her high heels clicked as she flew out of the courtroom. Any hint and the gossip would run rampant and the headlines would be lurid.

The pain on Ana Sigga's face gave me a stomachache knowing I put it there. "It seemed like something you should know," I said to Cruz.

"Susie will be calling you." Cruz had a

slick air about him. "My aunt and uncle are coming for another visit and requested to stay at The Cottages. The highlight of their last trip, a fight broke out and a man and woman got arrested." His eyebrows arched. "I don't remember getting a referral."

"No money for your hourly fee."

"Unless you have photographic proof that Fab slept with the judge, I need to look over these files."

"Thank you," I said and left.

A hand grabbed my arm and yanked me back as the elevator doors opened. "Are you going to tell anyone else?" Ana glared, her lips pulled tight.

"Fabiana is my best friend and I want her to get fair treatment. I promise you, I'll never repeat one word of gossip about you and I always keep my word." Even though she looked at me as if she'd stepped in something smelly, I appreciated the opportunity to apologize.

"You're a better friend than she deserves." She turned her back on me.

I admired her six-inch red-soled Louboutin heels as she walked back into the courtroom.

Chapter 18

Fisher Island boasts the wealthiest inhabitants in the U.S. It is home to obscenely rich people who owned elegant mansions and reassured their neighbors they all held the same social standing. How often do I find myself in Miami with free time? It wouldn't hurt to drive by the murder scene. A few turns later, I found myself on the causeway that would take me out to Biscayne Bay.

Ever since Liam paired my cell phone with the dashboard, it made talking on the phone so much easier, not to mention my driving sucked with a phone in one hand. The dash started to ring, the only drawback—no call-screening ability.

"What are you doing?" Creole asked.

"Just finished my visit with Fab, and heading home. Anything new on getting Fab out of jail?"

The noisy background told me Creole was cruising the streets in his pickup truck. "Word is charges will get dropped before the court hearing. Tests are coming back and nothing's linking Fab. The backyard video is being heavily scrutinized because it didn't go through the correct chain of command. You got anything for me after your visit?"

"We didn't talk about the case. We talked about her new friends and how yummy the food is. I have another call, I'll talk to you later." I clicked off. If we talked any longer, I knew I'd blurt out my destination.

To my surprise, the only mode of transportation over to Fisher Island was a ferry. The incoming one had just docked and there were half a dozen cars in line for the return trip. I came to a stop in front of a guard with an official looking clipboard and rolled down my window.

"Your name?" he asked.

That surprised me. "Madison Westin."

He flipped the page on his clipboard. "Who are you here to see? I'll need to call and confirm to give your access."

Who knew that private island meant private? I laughed with embarrassment, my cheeks burning red. "I'm joyriding. I planned to drive around the island, grab a coffee, and come right back."

"That's not allowed. One hundred feet ahead, you can make a U-turn."

Before I could put the Hummer in gear, Creole stood staring at me through my driver's side window. "How's it going, Stan?" he said to the guard. He yanked on one of my red curls. "You do realize that you're sixty miles in the opposite direction of your house? Park over there next to my truck." He pointed to a small parking lot that held about ten cars.

I parked next to his truck. Creole jerked my door open. "You're such a liar." The corners of his mouth turned up. "You need to pay attention to your rearview; then you might have known I'd been following you since you got on the causeway."

I knew some of my antics amused Creole but for how long? Where Creole laughed and warned me that I'd be in big trouble if I got hurt, Zach would get mad and stomp away.

"I didn't feel the need to detail every stop I made on my way home."

"Let me guess, once you got over to the island you'd cruise the murder scene? Or worse, get out of your car and sneak around the property?"

I decided to pull my favorite and answer with another question: "How did Fab and Gabriel get on the coveted guest list?"

"Gabriel jacked a speed boat; Fab used it as her ride off the island. We found the boat tied up right where Fab said it would be at the guest dock of a yacht club. Turned out to be stolen out of Lauderdale by a man fitting Gabriel's description."

I flashed him a flirty smile. "You're a cop; you have access. Take me for a murder tour. You could narrate it like an overpriced bus tour, 'and this happened here.'"

He traced my lips with his fingers. "Careful. Don't flirt with me unless you're willing to accept the consequences." Our eyes locked. Damn. There was that electric jolt of chemistry again. "It's against department rules."

I stuck my chin out, letting him know I'd make an end run around him and get over there on my own. "Have a nice day."

Creole grabbed my arm. "It's just a house; the yellow police tape hasn't been removed." He gave me a shake. "How long before you're back here?"

"Tomorrow. And I'll be a legitimate guest of someone, so don't worry about me breaking the law."

"I don't have all day. We'll take one of the police speedboats." He motioned to follow him over to the dock, stopping at the dock master's office, flashing his badge and filling out a form.

Creole reached into a storage box and tossed me a life jacket. "Put it on. I'm going to drive so fast that you'll get sea sick and want to turn around and come right back."

I loved boats, but the thought of wave jumping, the bottom of the boat hitting the water hard every few seconds, made me nauseous before I even set foot aboard. I looked him straight in the eye. "And you can explain to Mother why I'm green and puking."

He and I knew that was a well-played trump card. If I hadn't seen the flicker in his eye, I would've backed down and not gotten on board. I'd been seasick once and it had been gruesome and lasted long after I set foot on solid ground.

He held out his hand, holding tight, while I stepped across from the dock and into the boat. "How do we get around if we arrive by boat?"

"We have two police trucks and two golf carts on the other side, which is the preferred mode of transportation. Going by boat cuts down on the waiting time for the ferry. There are private boat marinas on both sides for island residents. Some boat over or walk on the ferry. It's convenient for them to leave a car on this side."

"The golf cart sounds like fun. Can I drive?"

Creole's blue eyes were blazing. "Ground rules: I'll drive you by the house, you can hang out the window all you want, and then we leave. Agreed?"

"What if I have to go to the bathroom? Or I need something to drink?"

He narrowed his eyes. "Can you swim?"

"No, I can't."

Creole smirked and turned the key. I stood in the front on the port side, feeling the water spray in my face. I grabbed hold of the railing to keep from falling when he first took off, none too smoothly. A perfect day for a boat ride, I loved the blue-green waters of Florida getting deeper blue the closer we got to the Atlantic. If this had been a planned trip, I'd drop anchor and spend the rest of the afternoon reading and napping.

All too soon, Creole pulled into a visitor slip. He helped me off the boat, grabbing my arm. "You stay by my side. If you even try to wander off I'll handcuff you."

The golf carts had all been assigned out by the time we got to the island, so we climbed into the last pickup instead.

"When I told you that you could hang out the window, I hoped that you'd just roll down the window and stay inside the truck," Creole snapped and jerked my top.

I poked my head back inside and pointed through the open gates to the inside courtyard that could easily park ten cars. "That's Zach's truck up there in the driveway."

Creole squinted. "You don't know that, you can't see the tags from here. There are a lot of overpriced SUVs on this island. Could even belong to Chrissy Wright."

"Well, does it? You're investigating the case, you should know every car licensed to the Wrights."

He turned into the driveway, his look

letting me know that what ever happened I deserved it. "What ridiculous lie are you going to tell?"

"Zach's my boyfriend! Can't a girlfriend stop and say hello?"

"You must drive him crazy. He's such a control freak and you're a wild card!" Creole shook his head.

Creole hung back and leaned against the truck, arms crossed, as I walked up the walkway. Zach shut the front door behind him and started down the steps.

He blinked, looking surprised and not in a good way. "What are you doing here?"

It didn't matter what I said, he'd be mad. "How about a tour?"

Zach fixed me with a glare. "Our client doesn't wish to have any visitors, her husband was murdered in case you hadn't heard, and you're trespassing. You've been ducking my calls and you show up with here with him." He pointed to Creole. "What does she have on you?"

"Hey, pal," Creole yelled back, "don't be mad at me! I only drove to keep her from being arrested."

"You can get over being mad at me," Zach said to me. "I didn't have anything to do with Fab being arrested. I called to tell you I pulled strings and got you an early jail visit."

"Thanks, I saw her earlier. She's making

friends."

"Who did you use to get a next-day visit?" Zach held up his hand. "Never mind, I don't want to know. You have to leave. I have to do some hand-holding and assuring the client she has nothing to fear. I'll come by later."

I waved and started to walk back to the truck. No kiss, no hug, nothing.

"Zach," a blonde called, coming out the front door. "I thought you'd left." She ran to his side. "Who's she?" She looked me up and down and dismissed me in one glance. I felt dowdy in comparison.

The widow, Chrissy Wright, was a curvaceous blonde who screamed money; complete with a gigantic diamond on her left hand, designer sundress, and strappy shoes.

Zach put his arm around Chrissy, whispering in her ear as they walked back inside.

"That's the high-maintenance widow," Creole said, shoving the truck in reverse. "Methinks the clingy act is just that, and it's draining how much attention she demands."

"Is she the sole heir? How much money are we talking?" I asked.

"It's all Chrissy's money, every last million. Maxwell came into the marriage with nothing but his good looks and some dubious pedigree lineage."

I looked out the window at the well-manicured lawns. "When was the last time someone got murdered on this island?"

"A few years back, one of the residents was shot to death over in Miami, drug deal gone bad, does that count?"

"This island is only accessible by boat or ferry. How does someone murder two people and skip off with twenty-five million in goodies and no one sees or hears squat? Notice the cameras at every single stop light? Did you check those?"

"Are you insinuating I don't know how to do my job?" Creole slammed on the brakes. "You can get out and walk."

"I'm not walking anywhere. Thanks for bringing me here, the boat ride was the best part." I leaned my head back against the seat.

"Then you're going to do what I tell you?" Creole put the truck in gear.

"I hope you solve this case just so Fab isn't the subject of a whisper campaign for years to come or worse, moves away."

"I'll call and see if I can get you a visitation appointment for tomorrow."

"That's nice of you, but I have appointments for the rest of the week."

"Inmates are only allowed two visits a week and you get five?" Creole looked at me.

I knew he had a question but when he didn't ask, I let the moment pass.

Creole called ahead to the dock master's office and let them know we were on our way since the ferry was getting ready to leave. He flashed his police badge and we made our way to the front, where we'd be first off.

My phone rang from inside my pocket. "Hi, Mother. Are you having a good time at the races?" "We're headed to Brad's for dinner. Can you meet us and then we'll spend the night at his house?"

I poked Creole and put a finger to my lips. "I'm feeling sick," I lied. "I'm headed home to lie down. Zach's supposed to come by later."

"Are you sure?"

"Yes, have a great time." I threw my phone in my purse. "Before you start, it was easier to say I didn't feel good than I'm never setting foot in the Everglades again or at least anytime soon."

Creole raised his brow. "Brad invited me out to see his place, he made it sound nice."

"He bought an old run down shack, sticking to the original footprint. He restored it into a nice house. It's environmentally friendly, solar paneled, entirely off the grid, did all the work himself."

"And the problem?"

I pushed down ugly memories. "It's creepy out there; the bugs are the size of small animals. At night it's eerily quiet, except for the sounds of nature, which are magnified and scary."

Creole walked me back to my SUV. "Promise to call me before you do something stupid?" He kissed my cheek and flexed his muscles. "You won't like my reaction if you get hurt."

Chapter 19

"What are you doing here?" I asked, walking into the kitchen. I came home and fell on my bed for a nap from all that fresh air. Boating across the Biscayne tired me out, not to mention the sunburn.

"Tonight we're going to kiss and makeup." Zach stood at the island prepping vegetables in a bathing suit and apron.

"I feel overdressed. I'm going to change." I poured myself a margarita from the pitcher sitting on the counter and headed upstairs. I wasn't in the mood, but he'd already assembled fish and shrimp skewers and had them ready to grill. I knew for a fact that tequila had a mellowing effect on a bad mood.

I exchanged my jean skirt and T-shirt for a two-piece royal blue bathing suit, pulling on a skirt cover-up and twisting my hair into a clip.

I wanted to drink, have banging sex, and sneak in a couple of questions. I wondered if we could do all three without getting into a fight. I downed the rest of the margarita and headed back downstairs.

Zach eyed my empty glass and picked up the pitcher. He jerked me to him, kissing me. "Come tell me what to do." He picked up a platter of vegetables and fish, threw his other arm around me, and we went out to the barbeque on the patio.

"Let's eat out here." I opened a cupboard and pulled out a tablecloth, three conch shell candles, and a lantern with a large candle. I flipped the melon-colored chair cushions and pulled some colorful throw pillows out of the storage bin. The pool lighting had been set on a timer and would come on in a few minutes. The tall palm tree trunks were wrapped in white Christmas lights. Every flower pot had a solar stake or two. I set the table with flowery napkins and bamboo silverware.

"Where's your mother?" Zach crooked his finger.

"She's spending the night in the Glades with Brad. I can't guarantee complete privacy; anyone could walk in with no notice and no knocking." My family knocked on the front door; friends followed the path between my house and the neighbor and entered through the side gate.

Zach took the skewers off the fire, put one on each dinner plate, and added the fresh asparagus. I followed him carrying a pitcher of margaritas for me and a European beer for him.

"This is yummy." I picked a shrimp off the platter.

"I'm going to see to it that we spend more time together." Zach rubbed the corner of my mouth. "Why are you looking at me like that?"

Because he wants to be with me or check up on me? That question would ruin the mood. "I haven't been complaining."

"We'd have more time together if you'd move in with me," Zach said.

"Why don't we try a vacation or something before making address changes?" I downed my second margarita. "What happened to the pool of blood where I shot that guy who died face down?"

"A crime scene cleaning service got most of the blood cleaned up, and then I refinished the concrete floor." Zach had completely renovated the upstairs floor of an old warehouse into ultra-modern living quarters with glass, chrome, and leather furniture; but it had no swimming pool, not even a hot tub.

I hadn't worked up the nerve to tell him that if anyone was moving it would be him and that was a big "if." He'd never tolerate the steady stream of people who came and went; my fear was that he'd scare everyone away. He'd succeed in getting rid of Fab.

"Why don't you like Fab?" I managed to ask calmly.

Zach's face tightened. "We're talking

about living together, not Fab. Dinner's almost over so now's not the time to fight."

"No fighting. I do have a couple of easy questions for you." I devoured the fish and decided enough with the vegetables.

"I like Fab just fine. As a PI, she's as good as any of my men." He finished off his beer. "She has a reckless side. Since the two of you have become best friends, you take unnecessary chances every day. And you end up paying the price. One of these times you might not walk away alive."

I wanted to tell him that I'm happy I'd toughened up since arriving in The Cove, no longer anyone's doormat. I held out my glass for a margarita refill. He'd be lucky to get sex; I might just pass out drunk first. I reminded myself, *no fighting*. I asked, "Why do you think Fab murdered two people?"

"I don't. It's not a stretch that she'd shoot her ex-husband, there is a fine line between hating him and wanting him dead. But I don't think she'd kill a total stranger. Since I've known her she's scared more than a few men out of their shoes but hasn't killed a single one of them."

"In Fab's mind, she thought she could do this one job and he'd be gone."

"Never happen. They'd be looting mansions until they both ended up in prison."

Zach's face turned hard and edgy. He

believed the right woman sat behind bars. His main concern was the art and jewelry, he wanted it back for his client and he didn't want to tarnish AZL's perfect track record.

"Do I think she partnered on this heist and things went horribly wrong? This job mirrored the last one she pulled with Gabriel, and like the other, the valuables are nowhere to be found. How is it that Fab's the one left standing and doesn't know a damn thing?" Zach asked.

"In all the time that you worked with her, did she ever steal anything?"

"She's retrieved a few things and returned them to their rightful owners, but no, she's never stolen anything. When I first hired her she came clean about her past, convinced me it was all behind her." Zach's eyes narrowed. "Why would she get involved with Gabriel again?"

"Gabriel threatened to kill me and my family. He came to town, stalked her, and learned her routine. One morning Gabriel stopped by for a friendly chat, sat at my kitchen table, and pointed a gun at me, demanding her appearance."

Zach's fist hit the table hard, toppling my glass and the last of my drink. "Why didn't you tell me any of this?"

"I thought the problem solved itself when, shortly after, he got arrested. I hoped for deportation."

"What did he get arrested for?" Zach closely scrutinized my face in that official way when trying to spot lies.

"I honestly don't know what the charges were." No need to mention Creole's involvement now that those two were getting along. The best thing that could be said, they were friendlier. The odds on best friends again were unlikely.

I stacked the dishes on a bamboo tray and carried them into the house. One night I lazily left a couple of dishes behind and, the next morning, I had big palmetto bugs walking on the table. The three-inch bugs were cousins in the cockroach family. Soon after, I found a nest in some red-bark mulch nearby. I forcibly evicted them, replacing the mulch with seashells.

All the talk about Fab put Zach in a distant mood he seemed determined to hold onto. He moved from the table to a chair at the side of the pool, staring into the water.

If he had plans for an early exit, he was about to have his mind changed. I walked up behind him, running my fingernails across his neck, and leaned down to kiss his cheek. I stepped in front of him and he looked up at me, his blue eyes hot with frustration. I untied my cover-up and let it drop to the ground. "Are you ready for a swim?"

"Not in the mood for a swim. Maybe later," he said.

Unhooking my bathing suit top, I let it fall on top of the sarong. I pushed my bathing suit bottoms down and kicked them off. I grabbed his face in my hands, kissing his lips hard. Hooking my fingers inside his trunks, and tugged slightly. He lifted his hips off the chair and I pulled them off, running my nails from his waist down his legs, tossing the trunks to the growing pile. I held out my hand for him to stand up, and then shoved him onto his back on the double chaise, which was slightly smaller than a double bed. I straddled him, pushing him flat against the cushion.

"Would you cook naked for me sometime?" I asked.

* * *

"Dude you need to put some pants on. Grandmother's here," I heard someone whisper. I opened my eyes; I lay stretched across Zach's body, my head in the middle of his chest, a beach towel draped across my butt. Zach and I had fallen asleep by the pool, both of us naked. Liam stood over us.

Zach tightened his grip, holding me down so I wouldn't jump up and share too much.

My brain was liquor soaked, and I still felt a little drunk. "What's going on? How did you get here?"

"Grandmother didn't want you to spend the night by yourself, because you're upset about Fab being in prison." Liam stared at us like a disapproving father. "We drove back from The Glades in the middle of the night."

Liam had to be exaggerating but if he's here, then Mother is in the house. "Where is she now?"

"Upstairs checking on you."

"Go stall her." As soon as Liam cleared the patio doors, I jumped up. "Grab your suit and get in the pool," I told Zach. "She'll think we were swimming." I grabbed my suit off the ground, going down the steps into the pool as Zach jumped in.

"Why do I think you've done this before?" Zach pulled on his trunks.

"Aren't you glad we didn't go up to my bedroom? We might not have heard her." I turned around so that Zach could hook my bathing suit top.

"You're a grown woman. She has to know we...umm...whatever."

"We don't talk about sex and we're not going to start." I kissed him.

Mother and Liam walked through the French doors; I heard them talking about a video game. Liam had changed into his swim trunks and jumped into the deep end.

Mother sat at the top of the pool steps

and pushed up her Capri pants to put her feet in the pool. "How's Fab?"

"She's got another bond hearing this week, hopefully they'll lower it to something reasonable," I replied.

Zach dragged the basketball hoop into the water, and he and Liam started shooting Styrofoam balls, yelling out their score.

Chapter 20

I needed to stay busy until my next jail visit later in the afternoon, so it was a good time to check up on The Cottages. Not paying attention—busy staring at Carly and Miss January walking down the driveway together—I barely missed the front planter.

Those two were a most unlikely duo. Carly, a neighborhood drunk, lived several streets over in a house nicknamed "the drunk house." The several women who lived there had a history with the law and, when they weren't in jail, they got into fist fights and scared the neighbors.

My over-protective instincts of Miss January snapped into overdrive. She didn't have an arrest record and hanging out with Carly was a bad idea. I pulled into the space in front of the office. The sign on the door read, "At the pool," along with an arrow down the walkway.

Mac and Shirl lay on recliners by the pool. "You've got a cushy job," I said to Mac, nodding at Shirl and pulling up a chair.

Mac rolled on her side, one boob a breath away from freedom. "It's quiet here; the sheriff hasn't been around in a while. Do you suppose they miss us?" Mac shoved her boobs back in place, giving them a reassuring pat, and adjusted her bathing suit top, if that's what you call two pieces of string.

It's hard not to stare, both women were large breasted, and curvy, both struggled to control their girls. "Why is Carly, the drunk, visiting Miss January?"

"I asked her, she mumbled something about pee," Mac said.

"As in vegetables?" I asked.

Shirl giggled. "Urine. She didn't want to talk about it and shuffled off to her cottage, slamming the door."

"You," I said, looking at Mac, "need to find out what the hell is going on. If she gets arrested you will be her ride home."

Mac threw her arms out. "Why me? Besides, Miss J and Carly never leave the property together. Carly comes to visit once or twice a week, stays about ten minutes, and shuffles her way to a waiting car."

"Yesterday, Miss January stood out at the curb and I asked her if she needed help." Shirl stuck her leg in the air and rubbed lotion on one and then the other. "Last time the liquor store delivered her cigarettes she sat down to smoke a couple and needed help getting up. I helped her into the chair on the front porch. She asked me to go get Kitty, the cat liked the sun; told her I was allergic."

"You deal with dead people," I

reminded her.

Shirl made a face. "They're not hard and lumpy, with one eye staring at an odd angle."

"Find out what you can or I'll go pay Miss Carly an unfriendly visit," I said.

"Fab getting sprung anytime soon?" Mac asked.

"I've got a visit later. How's work?" I asked Shirl.

"Last night we had a little excitement. Old Man Henry was back with a dildo stuck in his butt, and it was still turned on."

"The last time I ran into the Henrys at Custer's, the wife told me they still had sex every night and they're eighty. I chalked it up to too many beers," Mac said.

"They were both drunk last night, the missus sobbing by his side; started to tell me about their adventurous lifestyle and I walked away. You'd have thought he would've learned from the two previous times things went awry with their so-called adventures."

Shirl's story had my butt cheeks clenching. "Anything else I need to know?" I asked.

"I met Svetlana when I checked on Joseph--his ankles looked more swollen than usual. Do you think they make rubber boyfriends?"

"Take the new boyfriend to Custer's and you'll be the hot gossip by morning," I said.

Custer's is a popular local hangout for the beer and screw top wine crowd. No food allowed, the health department told them. It was too dirty. Almost every night fists fly in the alley and most manage to connect a punch before the sheriff shows up.

Mac rolled her eyes. "Shirl, I know you've had crappy boyfriends, but a rubber one? I hear NA and AA are good places to meet people, and you being a nurse, that might work out."

I knew a girl back home who went boyfriend shopping at Narcotics Anonymous. She said the trick to score someone "good" was to go to meetings in rich neighborhoods. "I have a number for a great matchmaker. She'd love to fix you up." Keep my mother busy fixing up other people and she would stay out of my love life.

Chapter 21

I hung up the phone and called the jail to see if inmates could get visits today. Yesterday when I showed up, the jail was locked down due to—what I weaseled out of Brick—a fight over drugs. An inmate who had trash duty along one of Florida's scenic highways decided to erase all that work time credit by taping contraband under her overly large breasts and sneaking it back inside. Prisoners knew they had to strip off their uniforms when coming back from work detail, though most guards were lax about body searches.

I wanted to throw a fit, but decided I didn't want to end up getting arrested. Instead, I took myself home, gave my nerves a nap, and spent the day by the pool ignoring phone calls.

My finger hovered on speed dial for Cruz. I wanted to scream, "Get Fab out of jail already!" As nervy as I could be, I didn't dare continue to make a nuisance of myself. Besides, I'd get the lecture about attorney/client privilege and a not-so-nice reminder to stay out of his case. I hadn't talked to Susie since ambushing Cruz at the courthouse. I planned to ignore her until she forgot.

Jazz sat on the floor, rubbing his face on

my leg. I picked him up and put him on the counter, which I had to constantly remind Fab was not allowed. He stuck his face in mine and meowed as loud as he could.

"I didn't hear a please." I scratched him behind his ears, forcing a kiss on him.

I opened the refrigerator door, taking out a butcher-paper wrapped package. Whoever said humans were servants to cats couldn't be more right. We had run out of mystery meat, so I substituted the sliced turkey Fab bought before getting arrested.

Jazz and I sat at the island and I fed him a piece at a time, fidgeting, kicking my foot. Jazz stopped after a couple of bites, not impressed, time for a nap. He looked at me and meowed, a reminder that he was too old to jump off the counter. Hearing the roar of a motorcycle outside my kitchen window, I picked Jazz up, held on tight and slid open the kitchen drawer where I kept a handgun amongst the rarely used utensils.

Big, burly Gunz walked by the kitchen window, his hair sticking up. It surprised me it didn't blow off if he'd been riding without a helmet. Jazz licked my face to remind me he wanted down. I set him on the floor, and pushed the drawer closed. I started for the front door when it opened.

"You need to knock, dude." Gunz had never been to my house before and my open door policy didn't extend to everyone. I remembered locking the door behind Mother, which meant he could pick a lock every bit as fast as Fab.

Fab walked in looking like she could sleep for a week. "Gunz can't pick locks."

"So happy to see you." I ran and hugged her. "Cops after you?"

"Charges were dropped for now. Tests came back and neither my fingerprints nor my DNA were on the gun or anywhere in the damned house. Cruz said the clincher, a video tape from a security camera several houses down, showed me driving away in the boat around the same time of the shooting." She pulled my hair. "Don't you dare cry. If I'm not doing it then you sure as hell aren't either."

"You got any beer in here?" Gunz had the refrigerator door open, his head halfway in, rooting around.

"Bottom shelf, help yourself." I shook my head at Fab. Gunz, a triple-X-sized man, experimented with hair concoctions; today he decided against his au natural bald and donned a black wig that he'd trimmed with pinking shears. I would've bet money that nothing could look worse than the faux hair paint he favored, but today was a jump ball.

Gunz took the bottle opener I had in my hand. "Sorry about telling you to mind your own business. Did that sound nice?" He looked at Fab. "Let me know what you find out." He left, sat on his bike and downed his beer, then sent the bottle flying into the recycle bin.

"Why didn't you call me, I'd have picked you up?" I asked.

"I had no idea I'd be getting released until they called my name. I wanted out fast in case they made a mistake. Gunz rode past me while I stood in front of the jail, he'd just finished posting bail for a client. I bummed a ride. Good thing. I didn't have any money or my phone. I'd have had to walk or stick my finger out."

"What does Gunz want?"

"A personal item got stolen, he needs it retrieved. It's currently being held for ransom, but he sniffs a double cross. He's running out of time, this job needs to be done tonight. I need you to come along and create a distraction if needed."

"You look dreadful. Don't you need a night off? Besides, you have calls to make, letting people know you got sprung."

"I'm showering. And a double latte, espresso, whipped cream is all I need." Fab disappeared up the stairs.

I picked up my phone and called Mother. "This is your prodigal daughter. Fab's out; the charges got dropped."

"I'll drive down and take the two of you to dinner."

"We'll take a rain check. She's got a job tonight she committed to before going to jail and needs to get it done," I told Mother. "It will be an early night. She looks dreadful and needs a good night's sleep. Jail isn't conducive to sleep with twenty-four hour noise."

Mother sighed. "Have you two thought about keeping a low profile?"

I went upstairs to my bedroom and strapped on a thigh holster. My knee-length tropical-print skirt covered it. I changed into a long sleeve T-shirt and grabbed my jean jacket. It would be sheer stupidity not to be prepared on a job with Fab.

Chapter 22

Fab rocketed up the Overseas Highway to Miami. "What do you know about Mango?"

I pulled my seatbelt tight. "You would've thought when Mango tried to amputate Gunz's nose with her teeth that would've put an end to that happy relationship."

"They did call it quits. On her way out the door she lifted his book of contacts and wants a half-million to buy it back, or she sells it to the highest bidder."

I gasped. "Does Gunz have that kind of money?"

"In assets, but not cash."

Never judge a person's bank account by their looks.

Fab cut over to the toll road. "Mango strips nights at Brick's place out on the Tamiami Trail. I bought information from Bitsy before getting arrested. She told me Mango just moved into a condo in South Beach. She's working tonight, so we'll search her place."

"We need to verify that Mango showed up for work before we barge in uninvited. What makes you think she's keeping the black book in her condo? She hasn't quit her job so she must not be one hundred percent about her extortion skills."

Fab cut around another driver and received a horn and a finger wave out the window. "The doorman at the club told me he knew for sure she hadn't moved from her old place. My guess is she knows Gunz is going to come retrieve the book or send someone else to do it and what better place than the address no one knows anything about?"

"How does Bitsy fit into this story? I bet you cash Brick doesn't know about her side business, selling info on his other employees." I gripped the hand rest; our exit to the expressway coming up next.

"Mango needed a reference, so she paid Bitsy to pretend to be her current landlord. Apparently, it's well known that Bitsy's favors come at a price. She keeps her mouth shut unless paid more."

To my surprise, Fab turned on her blinker while exiting the toll road, not forcing anyone behind us to slam on their brakes.

We pulled up in front of a boldly painted pink, blue, and yellow 1920s art deco apartment building; ultra-modern, sleek lines. We circled the block four times before finding a parking place.

"You're lookout," Fab informed me.

"For what? I don't know what Mango looks like. Do not open the car door without a plan."

"Mango is a six-foot tall bleach-blonde, good-sized, has huge boobs, and never goes anywhere without her six-inch stilettos." Fab jumped out. "My plan is to find unit 3B, search it quickly, and get out. Don't leave without me." She slid a lock pick out of the back of her jeans before reaching the security door.

The sidewalk was crowded with tourists and locals making their way over to Collins Avenue, where all the action happened. South Beach came alive at night, the bars and restaurants filling with partiers, lasting into the early hours of the morning. Two street vendors passed me, both loaded up with colorful neon flashing beads around their necks. One carried a sign with an assortment of pins, lit-up and blinking. The other had a pole stacked with baseball caps, hanging precariously. My favorite: "I threw up in South Beach."

Two beefy men slithered out from between the buildings, wearing shorts and way too tight T-shirts to emphasize their muscles. They stopped under a spotlight at the door to Mango's building and accessed the security pad; the door buzzed, allowing them entry.

A minute later, my phone rang. "What's up?" I answered.

"Two guys just walked in," Fab whispered. "Get me out of here. Don't shoot them."

"Last resort, a bullet to their leg will

slow them down."

I dug through the junk in my purse to find my lock pick set. I removed a pick and shoved it into my skirt pocket. I took a breath to calm my nerves. Although I'd been practicing, my skill level would be considered pitifully slow. "Thank you," I said when the security door opened. A dark-haired young woman with huge dark glasses blew by me. I slipped in after her, and she never looked my way.

The elevator doors opened immediately. Punching the button for the third floor, I tried not to freak out.

Think. You're good at outrageous lies.

When I stepped off the elevator and came face to face with the fire alarm, I pulled my shirt up, wrapped the material around my hands, opened the clear cover, and jerked the alarm. The screaming noise reverberating through the building would freak out the residents, but they could consider it a practice run like grade school. The noise would wake the dead. I ran down the hall and banged on 3B, yelling, "Fire alarm!"

Both men pushed their way out the door. "What the hell's going on?"

"Fire on the second floor, you need to get out." I ran toward the exit sign. Both men hit the stairwell right behind me. I let them go by and followed them down the stairs. Several owners of the units had already gathered on the sidewalk, talking, pointing upward. I heard one say, "I hope the fire department gets here before the building burns down." Neighbors across the street had their windows open, hanging out, some on their balconies.

I had the engine of the Hummer started before the door closed. I couldn't risk getting blocked in by a fire truck, which I knew had been alerted. I could hear the sirens in the distance as they screamed up Washington Street. I lucked out, finding metered parking around the corner. Checking the sign, time had expired, so no need to scrounge for change. The ashtray served as a spare change holder for meters and toll roads. I held my boobs in place and ran to the corner, relieved to see Fab casually walking in my direction.

"Good job. First for the alarm, then for banging on the door; I was happy to hear your voice. When I didn't hear any commotion in the hallway, I looked out the peephole in time to see you disappear into the stairwell. I went in the opposite direction."

I looked at Fab, wondering why she climbed into the passenger seat without a complaint. "Where's the book? And who were those two?"

"Bitsy sold me bad info. There's no woman living there, no clothes, no personal items. Two lacey G-strings were displayed as souvenirs. Total upscale dude place—chrome, glass, pool table. I searched the living room, went into the master, and only men's clothing hung in the closet. When the front door opened I slid into the second bedroom and hid."

"You need to pay Bits a special visit and demand a refund or, better yet, you want correct information and you want it now."

Fab grabbed the dashboard. "What the hell did you stop for?"

I bit my lip so that I wouldn't laugh. "The light turned yellow."

"Pull the hell over. Smokin' hot Hummer and you drive it like an old woman."

I looked out the driver side window and smiled big. "I didn't coerce you into the passenger seat. You went willingly, and now you're stuck."

"I won't make that mistake again," Fab grumbled. "Thank you, by the way. This partner thing worked out well tonight. Without you, I would've had to pull my gun and muscle my way out the door and, with two of them, if either had a gun, it would've been messy. I have to wait to shoot someone, or they'll charge me with Gabriel's murder for sure."

"Finally, I get partner appreciation."

Fab pointed. "Keep your eyes on the road. We need that book. Now what?"

"Where's Mango's old place? You said

she's working tonight, we'll do a drive by, check it out and see if she moved."

Fab picked her phone off the console. "I'm calling Gunz."

Good luck with that, he rarely answered his phone.

"Call me," Fab growled into the phone.

I pulled to the side of the road, not saying one word to Fab. I got out and walked around to the passenger side. She'd already climbed into the driver's seat. She put her hands together in prayer and whispered, "Thank you."

Fab's phone rang. "That address in South Beach was a waste of your money. Give me the other address."

I input the new one into the GPS. Neither of us had a clue where we were going.

Chapter 23

"Bitsy and I are going to have a chat. She should be more selective in who she screws," Fab huffed. "Brick won't be able to ignore her side job if it's pushed in his face."

"I'll go with you and remind you not to shoot her."

"I'm only going to scare the hell out of her and let her know she owes me."

As we traversed our way across town the areas got worse until we ended up in The Heights — a designated historical neighborhood. The city poured money into the area, sending investors flocking to purchase and renovate old homes and open new businesses. The Heights was one of those areas that changed street by street. Mango's street had seen partial renovation and her building had recently undergone a facelift. A six-unit townhouse complex was under construction next door. It faced five worn-down, dilapidated homes on the other side of the street, two with Keep Out signs. People milled around in front of the houses, visible by their lit cigarettes.

"I'm not getting out, and if you do you're on your own," I said. "We've already attracted a ton of attention." Being in an SUV with dark tinted windows made us look like drug dealers. "I'll bet you there's no fire alarm in that building." Fab drove slowly, checking over every structure on the street, now circling the block.

Red lights and a siren blaring rolled up behind us. "You want to see if I can outrun them?" Fab asked.

"Just pull over," I hissed. "I'm not in the mood for a chase. Did you know that's mandatory jail time?"

Fab didn't immediately pull over, which agitated me. Finally, after turning another corner, she pulled into the parking lot of a closed pawnshop. The liquor store's sign still flashed open, and two people stopped to gawk.

"Roll your window down," I motioned.

"You sound like your mother," Fab said.

"You just keep Mother in mind. If you get us both arrested, you'll be the one to tell her you were the smartass."

The officer shined his flashlight in the window and throughout the interior. "License and registration."

Fab already had her license in hand. I got the registration from the glove box.

"You don't live around here." He looked at Fab's license. "Says here the SUV is registered to a dealer. Do you have paperwork that shows you have the right to drive this car?"

I leaned across Fab. "Famosa Motors rented this to me because my other SUV got wrecked."

"I'll need to see the rental contract." He flashed his light in my face.

Damn.

"I work for Mr. Famosa and we have an informal arrangement."

"I'll bet," he snickered. "Don't go anywhere." He walked to the back of the Hummer, exchanged words with his partner, and then got in the patrol car.

"Get your concealed permit out just in case we're ordered out, hands up. We should've already disclosed; I'd like to avoid a gravel sandwich if it can be avoided." I hiked my skirt up and turned in my seat, as the officer sat talking on his phone. "This is a sign telling us to go home," I told Fab. "It's best to conduct business in this neighborhood in the early morning hours. We'll come back when everyone's sleeping off the alcohol/drug induced state from the night before."

Fab checked her rearview mirror. "What's he doing?"

"Still on the phone, his sidekick's leaning in through the passenger window. Good news is that neither of them has a gun pointed at us. By this time they've found out we're not wanted anywhere."

"That may change when they see my

191

recent mug shot for murder."

"Talk to Cruz and see if it can be erased from your record. Doesn't seem right or fair, you get wrongly arrested and it follows you around forever."

Fab pulled her hair into a ponytail. "I don't expect fair, so I'm never disappointed."

"Cop dude just opened his door." I looked at the clock on the dash. "What was he doing for fifteen minutes?"

The officer handed Fab's ID back through the window. "What are you doing in this neighborhood?"

"Took a wrong turn or two," Fab said.

The officer looked at me. "The tint on the windows is illegal. Get it fixed or get yourself another rental. I'm letting you off with a warning, but next time I'll ticket you and you'll be forced to have it removed.

"Where are you headed? I'll give you directions," the officer said to Fab. "This isn't a neighborhood for two women at night."

Fab started the engine. "Thank you, we're headed home." She raised the window.

"You're so rude," I sighed. "Let's get out of here before he changes his mind about a ticket."

Fab picked up her phone. "New plan. You need to make sure Mango's not in her apartment at daylight." She hit the speaker button.

Gunz's voice boomed through the phone. "I'm here at the club. She gets off at 3:00 a.m. I told her I'm ready to negotiate. Since it's been awhile for the both of us, I can get her over to my place for some bear lovin'. You've got a couple of hours and you'd better be the hell out of there."

"Call me when Mango leaves your place and call if you don't score." Fab hung up.

"Hours of bear lovin'? I want to wash my ears out."

"Gunz is a kinky bastard. He likes it hard and rough. His women are willing and one step short of certifiable. We had a meeting one day and he didn't show, so I went to his place. His big naked body, handcuffed to the bed, bruises all over him. Apparently his latest girlfriend took a riding crop to him when she found out he'd been cheating. I uncuffed him. He sighed like a girl, smiled, and said he'd be sending her flowers."

"I don't believe you," I laughed. "I thought he lived out in one of those middle-of-nowhere Keys with his sisters?"

"That's the family home; comes and goes as he pleases. His sex palace is in Coconut Grove. He's got a really big—you know—just in case you wanted to know."

I clinched my eyes closed, forbidding the image. "I'll get you back."

"You're no fun."

193

* * *

We arrived back at Mango's just before daylight, having spent the night in the parking lot of Famosa Motors. The streets deserted, Fab parked illegally in front of the ongoing townhome construction.

"Another good idea of yours," Fab said.

"I'm well-acquainted with the habits of riff-raff. This early in the morning they're either passed out or strung out in front of the television watching cartoons and jumping with paranoia."

"If you were hiding what looks like an address book where would you put it?" Fab asked.

"I'd hide it in plain sight. Stuff it in a vase sitting on a cabinet, inside of an appliance I don't use. Not taped to the underside of the desk or in my underwear drawer."

Fab whipped out her lock pick and pushed open the door.

"Show off," I whispered. "This is too easy." I pulled my Glock from my back holster, the door closed quietly. We quickly checked out the three rooms for any surprises and then split up.

Fab ransacked the large open space, living room, dining room, kitchen combination, searching like a cop under and behind all the furniture, removing the drawers of the end tables, and behind the pictures.

I headed straight for her bedroom, looking around to see if a possible hiding place stood out. *Where would I hide the book?* As obvious as the mattress is, I picked up each side for a quick look, running my hands underneath. Nothing. She had several display racks of costume jewelry and a coat rack used for purses; I went through every one of them. The small walk-in closet was typical of an older apartment building. I went through every piece of clothing, thinking possibly one had a pocket large enough for the book. A shelf display held several boxes too small to hold a book, and various knick-knacks. I almost missed the black quilted Chanel clutch on the top shelf next to a framed charcoal drawing of a young girl.

Hiding something valuable on a display would be what I'd do. I grabbed a hanger off the bed, stood on my tiptoes, and hooked the clutch chain, catching it in my hands. I admired the purse, knowing it to be vintage. I unsnapped it and gasped, withdrawing a dog-eared black leather address book. I flipped through the pages. First names only, each one had its own page, filled with a series of numbers and abbreviations which meant nothing to me.

"You found it," Fab shrieked from the doorway.

I handed the book to her. "Does this

mean Gunz has to be nice to me?"

"Gunz breaks your gray-line rule; his dealings are criminal in nature." The black book disappeared inside the waistband of her jeans.

"What we're doing right now could get us charged with a felony, so let's get the hell out of here." I got to the front door before Fab, sticking my head out to make sure the hallway was clear. "If you wake anyone up, I'll shoot you," I told her.

We played push and shove on the stairwell to see who could get out the door first. Fab slammed the bar and shoved the door open; we stood on the sidewalk out of breath, laughing.

Chapter 24

I lay face down on my outstretched arms across the bar at Jake's.

Fab slid onto the stool next to me. "You look like crap."

"I'd like to toss down a shot of tequila but I'm afraid if I start drinking in the morning, I'll like it so much I'll do it every day."

Fab walked around the bar and helped herself to a cup of coffee clearly not up to her usual standards, but she didn't complain.

"Where the hell did you go so early?" I snapped at her.

"I met Gunz and handed over his criminal diary in exchange for an envelope of cash."

I hit my head on the bar and flinched from the pain. "I wanted to go."

She ignored my grumpy attitude. "Can we use your boat?"

"Not without my brother finding out. I know what you're up to and it's one heck of a long ride. Can you read a water map? I can't. Don't you have a connection where we ride over on the ferry, our names magically appearing on the list of approved guests?"

Fab spit out her coffee and helped

herself to a bottle of cold water, sliding one down the bar in my direction. "I thought we'd boat over and dock close by the Wrights."

"Now that there's been a double murder, every single resident will be on the lookout. Your plan needs serious work."

"You pull this off and I'll owe you," Fab said.

"As in an IOU?" I'd never been able to wiggle one out of Fab.

"Don't be gloaty. It's unattractive."

"I'm going to pull this off so that neither of us ends up in jail. And you, my dear, will owe me two." I flashed a smile that I knew she'd hate.

Fab squinted her eyes. "What millionaire do you know living out there?"

"I think I'll surprise you."

Fab groaned, "I hate your surprises."

"What is your hot plan for when we arrive? Knock on the door and ask the grieving widow for a look-see around the property?"

"I'll have a plan before we get there."

"What are you hoping to accomplish?" I asked.

"I've racked my brain as to what went wrong that night. Gabriel planned his jobs; he excelled as a thief. How did he end up with a bullet in the back? Gabriel's drug of choice was the high he got from stealing priceless objects. I'll never believe he shot Maxwell Wright."

"Creole could answer your questions. I'd suggest Zach, but we both know he'd tell me to stay out of it. Speak of the devil." I nodded my head toward the door.

Zach and Slice walked in. "Morning, ladies," Slice said.

"No time like the present," I whispered to Fab.

Zach kissed me. "You look sick." He slid onto a stool.

I shook my head. "Late night. Fab's bartending."

Fab put soda in front of them. Slice picked up the glass from the corner of the bar and nodded to Fab.

I put my hands on Zach's thighs and slid forward, wrapping one leg around his waist, and leaned in for a kiss. "How about an update on the case?"

"There really is nothing new; I'm not blowing you off. We're hoping someone does something stupid, boasts to a friend, or fences a painting or piece of jewelry. What was Gabriel's connection to Maxwell?" Zach wrapped his fingers in my hair and pulled my face to his.

"Fab told me she didn't think Gabriel knew anyone in Florida. She swears she had no prior knowledge of the theft and was not in on the planning of the heist and I believe her." I also added, "She didn't know why he chose the Wright mansion."

"There was clearly a third person involved and I hope for your sake it doesn't turn out that Fab is a big liar." He kissed me again.

Slice walked around the bar and helped himself to a bottle of water. "Fab got a call and went outside to talk. Guess she thought I'd listen in."

"Do either of you know what Gabriel did with his free time in Florida before he made his presence known?" I asked.

"We're still checking to see how he got into this country; he's not on any flight lists or in the customs data base," Slice said.

Zach leaned in and whispered, "Are you done using your lips to coerce information out of me?"

I blushed. I had several more questions but kept them to myself--we'd only fight. "I've got a job and could use some scary muscle. Would you mind if I asked Slice?" I left out the part where I had Spoon lined up but he called with an out-of-town emergency.

"What kind of case this time?" Zach shook his head.

Slice rubbed his massive hands together. "I don't care what kind of case it is, I'm in. Yours are far more entertaining than anything we get at AZL. Besides, I've kept track and I have a nice stack of IOUs with your name on them."

Not quite a whisper, but almost: "A middle-of-the-night eviction at the car wash."

They both stared at me for a second and burst out laughing.

Fab returned to the bar. "What's so funny?"

"Asking Slice to flex his biceps and expedite the Poppins to the curb along with their grubby possessions," I told her.

"Is Slice getting paid in coon meat?" Fab asked.

Both Slice and Zach shocked at the same time was a rare sight. I glared at Fab. "Slice asked for an IOU from you and I told him you'd be happy to step up anytime."

"Where do you find these people?" Zach slid off the barstool. He ran his hand under my shirt and up my back. "We'll talk later about your use of under-handed tactics for information."

"Have a nice day, honey." My face was beet red.

"Try and stay out of trouble." Zach kissed me.

"Call me with the when and where," Slice called over his shoulder.

Before they hit the exit, Zach said something to Slice and they both laughed.

I looked at Fab. "I saw Slice nudge you and give you a tasty morsel look-over."

"Slice has always been a good friend to me. He loves women. Have you noticed he's less intense since he got rid of that ice cube of a wife?"

"I met Jade once. I didn't measure up to her standards. She mentioned doing the girlfriend lunch thing; frankly, I was happy I never heard from her again."

"Didier and I ran into Slice and Ana Sigga at the trendy El Lago in South Beach. I saw her lick his fingers, smiling and hanging on his every word."

"The prosecutor? She's more high profile than Cruz. Wait until she finds out you and I are friends with her lover boy."

"Hey, boss." Phil, the bartender, a leggy blonde, in a very short jean skirt that just barely hit the bottom of her butt cheeks, showing the occasional flash of black lace panties, came through the kitchen doors. She'd taken scissors to her tight Jake's T-shirt and turned it into a crop-top. She stored her large bag behind the bar.

"It's all yours." I slid off the barstool. "All the shipments for today have been unloaded and checked in. The bar is stocked."

Phil waved from behind the jukebox; she overrode the system, music filling the bar.

I tossed the car keys to Fab. "I'll tell you what I learned on the way to the car wash." I related what Zach told me.

"Gabriel used several aliases in France. He had money socked away so he didn't come out of prison a poor man."

"What about the Beemer he was driving?" I asked.

"Gunz ran the plates. Turns out it's registered to a scurvy rent/buy-here lot, filled with high-end cars in a ratty neighborhood— clearly a front for something else. I stopped by for a look through their records and could've bypassed the alarm, but not the two Rottweilers inside."

"On one of your insomniac nights, you thought you'd go toss a business?" I glared. "Try walking in the front door during business hours and blackmail them. We, as in you and me, take pictures of the Beemer, trade location for info."

Occasionally Fab surprised me by obeying all the traffic laws; this was one of those days. "The Beemer's still sitting in the same parking space at the Yacht Club where he parked it before we launched from their dock."

"Did you sleep at all last night or just busy yourself driving around without me?"

Fab pointed to the black Ford. Tarpon Cove had acquired several new unmarked sheriff cars. "Looks like Kevin drew the short straw and he's on stake out."

I rubbed my temples. "This is what I don't get about Quirky. He knows he's attracted the attention of law enforcement, yet he doesn't pack his guns, meat, and whatever else, and set up shop someplace else."

Fab pulled into one of the wash bays. Vanilla came sauntering around the corner in cutoffs that showed off the longest pair of legs and a white T-shirt accentuating her pancake chest.

"You don't listen very well." Vanilla glared at me. "Quirky will hurt you. He'll make you wish you listened the first time he told you not to come back."

Fab pulled her Walther from her waistband, opened the door, and pointed the gun at Vanilla. "Listen to me, skinny bitch. Get Quirk-ass out here now."

"You're not going to shoot him, are you?" Vanilla sneezed, wiping her nose with her hand and then dragging it into her matted hair. She looked like she'd had several dye jobs, the latest one being pinkish-blonde.

"We're going to have a one-sided conversation and then we'll be on our way." Fab motioned her up against the wall. "Don't make me shoot you."

"Quir-keeey!" she hollered. "Get out here."

Quirky lumbered from the back of the building, wiping his hands on his already stained white shorts. "What the hell do you want?"

Fab shook her gun at him. "Stand next to your sister and shut up."

Quirky looked at me. "I told you to never come back here," he snarled.

"Listen up, Einstein," Fab said.

"Who's that?" Vanilla whispered, her face drained of color.

"You're not much of a thinker, neither of you." Fab pointed her gun at one and then the other. "The sheriff is sitting across the street, staking the place out. It's only a matter of time until they put you in jail. Pack your crap and be gone by sundown. This is a friendly warning; tonight you're gone one way or the other."

"You coming back tonight for a piece of Quirky?" he snickered.

"Can I shoot him?" Fab asked me.

"No one needs to get hurt here unless Quirky insists. You and your sister have over-stayed your welcome, now get out. No more friendly requests." I stared back at Quirky's angry face, never flinching.

"Quirky, I don't want to go to jail again." Vanilla started crying. "I'm leaving."

Quirky grabbed a fist full of Vanilla's hair, jerking her off her feet. She clearly feared Quirky more than Fab and I.

"Where the hell you going? You don't have a job!" he screamed in her face.

"You're always hurting me." Vanilla

stepped back, hitting the wall. "I can dance," she said with a tiny bit of defiance.

"Guys aren't shelling out money to see women with no tits work the pole." He slapped her face with his open hand.

Fab kicked Quirky in the upper thigh. He let go of Vanilla, who almost tripped running away. She took off down the street.

"No more warnings." I motioned Fab back to the Hummer. "Play time's over."

Quirky furiously rubbed at his thigh, shifting one foot to the other. "Bitches," he spit, limping back into the office, slamming the door, and throwing the bolt.

"That was fun," Fab said. "Quirky's not going anywhere. He's too stupid or he'd have been gone the first time he saw the sheriff sitting down the street. Better call Slice. If we do it, we'll have to shoot him and then have the dilemma of what to do with his body."

Fab backed out of the wash bay, pulled into the street next to Kevin, honked and waved.

"Kevin only sort-of tolerates me and you doing stuff like that won't help." I hit her arm. "Which way did Vanilla go?"

"Toward the trailer park. Stay out of it," Fab warned. "Let brother and sister kiss and make up on their own."

"If she's willing to get naked and shimmy on a pole, why not do it for Brick?

He'd make sure she never got abused."

"Have you seen Brick's dancers?" Fab put her hands under her boobs like a platter.

I pulled out a business card from the console and scribbled Brick's number on the back, then added some cash I always had stashed. You never knew when you'd be starving for a hamburger and out of money.

"What the hell are you doing?" Fab asked.

"A phone number and a little cash gives her options that she apparently doesn't have at this moment." I pointed up ahead. "There she is sitting on the abandoned bus bench." There was no bus service in Tarpon Cove. If you didn't have a car or a bicycle, you walked or begged your neighbor for a ride.

Fab pulled to the side and I lowered my window, sticking my arm out. "Vanilla, if you're interested in dancing, call the number on the back of this card and tell Brick you got the number from me."

Her eyes were red and swollen, round as saucers, and filled with fear, which matched her cheek. "I don't want to go back there. Please don't hurt Quirky; he won't leave on his own. We're making more money here than any other place we've been."

"Good luck to you," I said.

"Thanks for the cash." Vanilla counted the money as we drove away.

Fab handed me my phone. "You better call Brick with a heads up."

I lucked out when it went to voicemail. "Brick, it's Madison. Sending a girl named Vanilla your way, wants to be a dancer or something, needs to stay out of The Cove." I looked at Fab. "I should've had Mother call, she makes him nervous."

"What are you planning now?" Fab asked.

"Let's go to the Yacht Club, then the car lot to exchange friendly hellos."

Chapter 25

"This might not have been one of my better ideas," I said. "They're not doing business with the locals, wonder why they picked this neighborhood?"

"Let's stay outside. We don't step foot inside the office and we do our dealing in the parking lot, in plain sight of the street. My guess is if we screamed, no one around here would call the cops. You have your Glock on you?"

"I never leave home without my other best friend." I flipped my skirt up. "I'm giving us some added insurance." I hit speed dial.

"Who are you calling? Put the call on speaker."

Creole answered on the second ring. "What's up?"

"If I don't call you back in ten minutes, we need help. Or if I do call back and tell you to feed the dog, I'm in big trouble."

Dead silence. "Where the hell are you?" Creole yelled.

I gave him the address. "We're at the car lot where Gabriel got his Beemer."

"Leave there now, that's a drug- and crime-infested neighborhood."

"Remember: ten minutes." I hung up.

"One of these days, I fear there will be a price to pay for always hanging up on him, like strangulation."

"Look they're waiting for us." Fab pointed to two men who slithered out of the office.

"Nice ride, ladies," said the one in neck-to-ankle tattoos. They were both dressed in linen shorts and tropical shirts, leather loafers and blingy watches. The gaudy diamond rings could easily put an eye out. "I recognize you." He pointed to Fab. "We have you on tape trying to break-in last night."

The other one whipped out his gun. "Come on in the office."

Fab's Walther came out the same instant his did. "We'll stay right here."

"We're not here for a gunfight," I said. "We'd like to trade some mutually beneficial information and be on our way. In the interest of disclosure, I have to make a call in," I looked at my watch, "eight minutes, or cops will arrive."

"What kind of information?" The other one, the color of watered-down milk, must be from one of those abnormally cold Northern states; he'd never seen a day of sun, ever.

"Wouldn't you like to have your Beemer back, license number SOUMIA?" I held up my cell phone in one hand. "Here's a picture."

The two men exchanged a look. "And

you want what?"

"A look at the rental application." Sweat trickled down my back, more from fear than the humidity.

"I'm not showing you crap. You tell me where my fucking car is and Oren here won't shoot you."

"You look smarter than that," I said as I looked at my watch.

A black sedan with dark tinted windows blew into the driveway. In the moment of distraction, Fab shot the guy holding the gun in the shoulder, dropping him to the pavement. Two men stepped out of the car, looking fresh off a stakeout, bone-tired with beard stubble, guns drawn, and law enforcement badges hanging from the front of their jeans.

"Let's play nice here," one of the officers called out. "Carlos, your associate need an ambulance?"

"The hell with him, she's got my Beemer and I want it back." Carlos pointed to me. "Oren, pick your sorry ass up. If you're bleeding, clean it up."

"Or I'll take the Hummer," Carlos pointed to my ride.

"I never had your car and that wasn't the deal. Information trade, remember?" I reminded Carlos. "Nice meeting you." I backed my way to the Hummer.

My phone rang. "Get the hell out of here," the cop said. "Just drive away, no one is going to stop the two of you."

We slammed the doors of the SUV; Fab revved the engine, blew around the cop car, and out into the street.

My phone rang again. "Where's the Beemer?" Creole demanded. "I've had enough of you two."

Fab spoke up. "This is your other sister. Here's the trade, tell me where Gabriel was living."

"The end of South Pointe, in the tallest of the twin tower condos."

Fab pointed to the GPS. "Beemer's parked at the Miami Yacht Club, over by the launch ramp, right where we left it the night of...you know."

"Tell me that when we dust the inside for prints, Madison's won't come back as a match?" Creole asked.

"They're not anywhere on that car, inside or out," I said.

"Forget about going to South Pointe. It's part of a crime scene and hasn't been released. Now go home."

Fab made a U-turn to take us to the expressway.

"Do you think they have a guard posted?" I asked Fab.

"One way to find out." Fab cut around a

slow driver, the driver laying on the horn. "The last stop was a terrible idea." She smirked. "Do you suppose this next stop will see more gun action?"

* * *

We cruised into the Guest Parking lot. The Tower and its distinctive architecture sat on the Government Cut waterway across from Fisher Island. There was an adjacent park and each unit had an amazing view of the ocean. The sign boasted twenty-five floors, yet not a single person was milling around.

Fab pounded on the glass door.

"You can't manage a polite knock? I only turned my back for a second."

"This way we'll find out if there's a security guard on duty. One could be around the corner."

"I'm still nauseous over the last stop. Pick the lock," I said.

Fab stepped in front of me, taking her pick from the back pocket of her jeans. "One of these days you're going to wish you'd been practicing."

I stuck my tongue out behind her back, but she was right. She popped the front entrance door in seconds and I would've flailed around until Fab pushed me aside and did it herself. Much easier this way.

The lobby looked freshly renovated, everything in marble. No name directory. In the mailroom off to the side, three walls held oversized mailboxes for each tenant. They were big enough to fit a medium-sized box, the room had a barred door, the kind you see inside a bank vault. It required a keycard. The only identifier a number. My guess they didn't match unit numbers.

"Now what?" I asked when we reached the twin elevators. It also required a keycard to ride.

"This kind of setup was probably a source of amusement for Gabriel. He was snobby about his skills and he became more confident after being released from prison. Bragged he honed his skills from other artisans he'd been housed with." Fab, always prepared, pulled two keycards out of her pocket. "One of these better work or I want a refund."

"I highly doubt that people who engage in criminal activity give refunds."

"You sure get cranky when the guns come out." The first card opened the elevator.

The doors closed, and I held my breath while Fab inserted her trusty card again and pushed the penthouse button. I let out a small sigh when the car rose, relieved we weren't trapped inside an elevator.

"Don't you think a building that costs an easy million to live in would have security cameras and/or a guard? And there's neither."

"Not if criminals live here."

The elevator ride made my stomach jump. When the car stopped, the doors didn't open. I thought I'd be sick. "What now?"

"Don't freak out, we're not stuck yet. This next part is easy." She inserted her pick into the lock next to the Penthouse button and the door opened.

I hadn't noticed when we got on the elevator that each floor required a key to exit.

The doors opened into a small hallway. There were two doors, one at each end, and the front door opened into a one hundred eighty-degree beachfront view of the waters that connect the Biscayne Bay to the Atlantic Ocean.

"Gabriel has good taste," I said. From the walls to the furniture, everything was stark white and reeked of expensive—a designer showcase.

Fab looked around, assessing the pricey objects. "There's no way Gabriel could afford to buy or rent here. My guess is that there is a very wealthy partner involved. I'm checking the master bedroom first." She headed for the glass staircase and stopped at the top. "You wait here and let me know if anyone shows up."

"How am I supposed to do that? Yell? This place is so big; you'd never hear me while you're poking around in the closet. You're acting like a jealous girlfriend."

"Just because I don't want him doesn't

mean he gets to be happy with someone else. You look around down here. No one's coming in anyway; if the cops were going to stop by they'd do it after their morning donut."

I wanted to be what I thought would be the first person to sit in one of the white buttery leather chairs, placed to enjoy the view. This condo belonged on the cover of Miami Digest, a look-but-don't-touch-or-sit-on-anything feel. The door to the office just off the living room stood open. A glass top desk and oversized leather desk chair dominated the room. Not a single picture or personal item was on display. Two black and white drawings of the backside of a naked woman hung on the walls. Her face not exposed.

I pulled a pair of latex gloves from my pocket and opened the drawers, most were empty. The top one held a couple of expensive pens and a leather notepad that didn't contain a single entry. No trash can. Maybe if rich people decreed there'd be no trash then it would magically disappear.

I wandered into the kitchen and pulled open the drawers where there were only the barest of cooking utensils. The overhead cupboard held china for four and various sizes of crystal; nothing was in the refrigerator except a bottle of champagne and coconut water. I opened the trash compactor, but it held only a clean bag. I was beginning to believe that the condo had been purchased as an addition to an already overflowing real estate portfolio. I'd bet no one had ever lived here.

A search of the living room yielded nothing, not even a single speck of dust, the half bath unused. I slid onto the piano bench of the baby grand, head in my hands, elbows on the keyboard cover, staring out at the water. Wondering what I could spy over on Fisher Island with a telescope.

The lock on the front door clicked and brought me back to reality. My heart pounding hard against my chest, I flew off the bench and crouched behind the curtain panels bunched together at the end of the rod. I fumbled in my pocket to extract my phone, hurriedly pushing Fab's number on speed dial, waiting a second, and disconnecting.

The door slammed shut. "I know you two are in here, your damned Hummer is parked out front," Creole yelled. "Get out here!"

I held up my hands in surrender. "Look, latex gloves, no fingerprints."

Creole's face was red with anger, his blue eyes hard. A vein I never noticed before stuck out on his neck. "Where's Fab? And how did you get past locks and card readers?"

"I'm up here." Fab stood at the railing overlooking the first floor. "We got lucky and followed people in."

"And if I strip search you?" Creole glared.

"This ought to be fun," Fab flashed her special mean dog smile.

"You two can't just drive by like a couple of high school girls checking up on some guy who doesn't know you exist."

"You're making my ears hurt," I covered them.

Creole fixed me with a stare. "Get down here," he jabbed his finger at Fab. "Did you find anything?"

Fab threw one leg over the banister and slid down. "What did you bag as evidence when you were here?"

That looked fun, but with my luck I'd fall and actually break something.

"You answer my questions; not the other way around," Creole said. "I can arrest you," he flipped a pair of cuffs out of his pocket.

"How will you explain *that* to Madeline?" Fab said, hands on her hips. To her credit, she didn't smirk or do anything stupid.

Well played.

She had him now. The two of us knew he adored Mother. "Stop, you two. What did you find?" I asked Fab.

"Gabriel's personal items, clothes, and shoes. Did you pick up his laptop? What about a briefcase and what did it look like?" Fab fired her questions.

Creole closed the space between him and Fab. "We got his laptop. It was wiped clean, not even a social media profile. The black leather briefcase had a designer monogram on the clasp, nothing in it except a map of Miami Beach and ten thousand—in hundreds. I suppose that was spending money?" Creole towered over Fab, staring down. The look on his face daring her to do anything so that he could use the cuffs he twirled on his finger.

Fab straightened up and looked directly at him. "Gabriel had a second briefcase, a Presidential Louis Vuitton, which held all the good stuff."

"Where do you suppose it is?" Creole's tone suggested his anger had abated, but his eyes told another story.

"What is this place anyway? Who's the owner?" Fab asked.

"Owned by a corporation out of Belize. This place, according to the realtor, has been up for sale for about six months, with no bites at twelve and a half million. Back to the briefcase: where is it?"

"Does it look like I have it stuffed in my jeans?" Fab spun around. "Gabriel never had one hiding place. He always had a backup plan."

"Get out of here and don't come back." Creole waved the cuffs in her face. "Next time I will arrest you."

Creole followed us to the elevator.

"You want us to leave you need to open the elevator." Fab smiled at him.

"You need to get a better story than following residents through several layers of security. Obviously, you didn't run your story by Madison first or I suspect it might have been believable."

I refrained from a curtsey, but I'd remind Fab of this moment later. I couldn't believe that there hadn't been a knock down fight where one or both of them ended up maimed.

"Remember my warning," Creole told Fab. "Where are you two going now?"

"The Cove," I said. Who knew where we were actually headed, but telling him we were going home would stop another fresh round of yelling. "What alias did Gabriel use?"

Creole escorted us to the Hummer as reassurance that we wouldn't detour anywhere else inside the building.

"Henri Ricard. Sound familiar to you?" he asked Fab.

"Dead uncle on his mother's side, a first-class forger. Gabriel idolized him. He never used that name for criminal activity because it was a favorite identity he never wanted to retire."

Creole stood in the driveway, arms across his chest.

"Interesting family your ex has." Once we were back cruising the beach, I thought briefly about hanging my head out the window like a dog sucking up the sea air.

"You don't know the half of his familial lineage. His mother, days away from being forced into a convent by her father, was kidnapped by her high school boyfriend and persuaded into marriage. There are many other colorful members on his side of the family, not a bland personality in the bunch; another reason for my family to be horrified."

"Did you find any women's clothing?" I asked. "You couldn't possibly have searched the entire upstairs for the elusive briefcase."

"In the bathroom there was an expensive La Perla lace thong and a fifty dollar tube of Guerlain lipstick. The woman either had money or was an expert in spending other people's."

"When are we coming back?" I asked.

Fab ignored me. "The briefcase has to be there. Where else? Even if Gabriel had another accomplice, he didn't trust anyone and he never played nice. Are you working on our ride to the island?"

"Tomorrow I'm going to go see Brick."

Fab glared at me. "Why does he like you

more than me? He would never agree if I asked and I never pointed a gun at him."

Chapter 26

My eyes flew open, the morning sun flooding through the window. I'd gotten up in the middle of the night and Fab's bed hadn't been slept in; her Mercedes was not in the driveway. My bet she'd driven back to the condo. It irked me that she didn't wake me up and take me with her.

If she wasn't awake she would be in a minute because I'd drag her butt out of bed. Hanging from her doorknob a pair of men's black bikinis—her subtle message that Didier was back and they were having sex. Maybe I'd been wrong and she'd been out with him.

I lingered under the warm water enjoying my new showerhead, a flashy square rain model that had five jets. I checked my phone while stepping into a lime green flowery skirt with pockets—a useful place to put my keys. I'd gotten a text in the middle of the night saying, "moved out." One more thing to cross off my to-do list. I need to call Mr. Ivers and let him know he could go back to business as usual.

I picked up Jazz and nuzzled his neck; he looked at me and meowed as if saying, "Hug me once if you have to. Anything more irritates me." I needed to refresh his food and water bowl. If not up to his standards, he'd be howling the house down. I needed an injection of coffee.

After feeding Jazz, my first stop would be The Bakery Café. Instead of my own home brew, I needed something stronger with caramel and whipped cream to jump start the day. My phone rang as I climbed into the Hummer. I groaned when I looked at the screen. Slice never called to say hi, how are you?

"Is this a friendly chat?"

"I apologize in advance," Slice started. "We moved Quirky and his crap out, even loaded it onto his truck. Disgusting doesn't quite cover the mess he left behind. One of my men followed him to the turnpike and waved good-bye."

I sat in the driveway, happy for the good news.

"It just came over the scanner, Clean Bubbles fully engulfed in flames. I tore over there to check out the situation. Quirky must've doubled back on us and set the place on fire."

My shoulders sagged. "What the hell am I going to tell Mr. Ivers?"

"There is good news. The concrete walls are charred but still standing, burned the roof off, destroyed plumbing and electrical and all the equipment."

"That's some crappy good news." I felt responsible. "What else?"

"The old weirdo at the trailer park, out on his nightly rounds of snooping through people's trash, investigated and saw Quirky lurking, and a short time after, flames leaped through the roof. Quirky's nowhere to be found now."

"What about Vanilla? Did she leave with him?"

"When Quirky left the first time, he left his sister's belongings in a couple of boxes outside the office. But when he went back, he threw them inside and they burned in the fire."

"The owner is an old man...."

"Tell him the truth. At least no one got hurt or worse. Honestly didn't see this coming. My guess? Quirky had this planned."

"Thanks for the heads up." I stared out the windshield wondering what to say to Mr. Ivers. I called and left a message, telling him we needed to get together.

* * *

I pulled into the driveway of The Cottages thinking about my trip to Clean Bubbles. I sat at the curb and surveyed the damage, feeling guilty. I'd learned a lot in my previous life with my ex-husband, Jax. He'd been a contractor and used me as an errand girl more than a few times. I spent a lot of time at the hardware store. After a while, I began to take on my own projects and my first one, a flip-house, made a big profit. Even having to replace the entire electrical and plumbing, the wash bays could see action soon.

As I sat in a daze, the Hummer jerked forward. Looking in my rearview, a two-door pickup slammed into my rear end, pushing my front bumper up against a pair of twenty-foot palm trees. The truck roared back in reverse and burned rubber, banging into me again.

I threw the door open and jumped out. "What the hell?" I screamed. The Hummer was thoroughly smooshed in, courtesy of the steel bars across the woman's front grill.

Damn, another crazy one with a license. The woman, not satisfied with her handiwork thus far, revved her engine again.

A gunshot rang out and the front tire of the pickup went flat. Mac stood in the driveway, Smith and Wesson in her hand; Shirl behind her with a Berretta.

"Get out of that piece of shit truck!" Mac yelled and waved her gun. "Now."

A six foot tall bleach blonde slinked out with legs for days, which were displayed in cutoff jeans that barely covered her lady parts, and red stilettos. She was wearing the tightest T-shirt ever pulled over a pair of double Ds.

"Are you drunk?" I yelled.

"You bitch." She kicked off her heels, flipping them into the truck bed. "Where's your crappy little friend?" Spit flew from her mouth.

I pulled my Glock from its thigh holster. "Forget about her." I pointed to Mac. "You take one step in my direction and I'll shoot you. I have a proven track record."

A taxi pulled up in front and Joseph struggled to get out, reaching back to grab a couple bags of groceries.

Shirl holstered her gun and hustled to help.

"I wouldn't shoot one of Brick's top dancers if I was you," Joseph said, and spit into the bushes. "I want a rent credit for that good advice. Hey, Mango," He nodded to the blonde, "Be careful, she shoots people." He pointed at me, giving the two bags in his hands to Shirl and shuffling up the driveway.

I looked at the back of the Hummer and really wanted to shoot her. So this is Mango, Gunz's psycho, nose-biting, black-mailing girlfriend.

"Just so you know, Mango, you just dented one of Brick's autos. Good luck explaining that one. Now what do you want?"

"I want what you and your bitch friend stole from me," she screeched. "Don't bother lying from those puny lips of yours. Bitsy told me."

"First of all, you stole the book to begin with and held it hostage, you greedy bitch. The only reason you're not dead is because you-know-who likes to bang you."

Two men from the rental house across the street came outside, sat in a couple of rickety chairs, and put their feet up, smoking and sucking down a beer. One gave me a thumbs up.

"I'm calling the cops." Mango deliberately sent a stream of spit in my direction.

"Dare you. Do you want to use my phone?" I pulled my phone from my pocket, holding it up.

Mac laughed. "I'll call for you. I think handcuffs would look good on you."

Mango regarded me with an unflinching stare. "That was my retirement and ticket to the good life."

"Consider yourself lucky that the disgruntled party got his book back, because at some point he'd stop thinking with his dick and you'd disappear—never enjoying one day of 'the good life.' Get out of here and don't come back," I warned her.

Mango looked at my gun and then Mac's. "This isn't over," she said, and got back in her truck.

"If you're planning on a long life, it better be!" I yelled.

Mango flipped me the double finger through the windshield, screaming every variation of the 'F' word she could think of out the window. She ground her gears in reverse, and, with steel-on-concrete scraping noises, made a dramatic exit, running on the rim of the bad tire. She rolled into the planter across the street and sparks flew all the way to the corner.

The two men across the street wolf whistled and clapped their hands over their heads.

"What the hell was that all about?" Mac holstered her gun.

"Backlash from a little job. Fab retrieved some stolen property and returned it to its rightful owner. Anything new going on? What's going on with Shirl and Joseph?" I tossed my head in the direction of his cottage.

"It's the nurse thing. She looks out for Joseph and Miss January. Oh and by the way, Miss January confessed she's selling her urine for cash."

"Who buys urine?" I rolled my eyes. "She was probably drunk."

"She sells fresh pee to Carly, who's on probation and subject to random testing. She takes clean pee to every appointment to pass her drug tests."

I knew Carly by reputation as a neighborhood drunk, and I knew it would be bad news for her to be hanging around here. "Let me guess, you put a bag of pee in your pocket and no one notices?"

"Sometimes you have your Dorothy in the cornfield moments." Mac shook her head at me in disbelief.

"Don't make me shoot you."

"You're so ungrateful after I saved you from that long-legged Amazon." Mac held up her skirt, admiring her legs.

Who ties their flip-flops around their ankles? I snapped my fingers. "Educate me about clean pee."

"Miss J pees in a bucket. Carly has already stopped at the gas station, bought a small energy bottle and washed it out, turns out it's the exact number of ounces you need. Give it a quick nuke and secure it in your underwear to keep it warm. Fresh is a cheaper buy than synthetic, which you can get online but costs fifty dollars."

"I'm so glad I don't do drugs. What if you get caught?" I grabbed my water bottle off the seat and finished it off.

"Carly violates her probation, gets arrested, and gets extra jail time."

"What happens to Miss January if stupid Carly rolls on her for leniency or just because she's having a bad day?" I asked.

"The sheriff will issue an arrest warrant. Most likely gets probation because she doesn't have a record." Mac pulled a chewed piece of gum out of her pocket. "I can't shoot and chew at the same time and I wasn't done yet."

I bit my lip and looked down. Laughing would only encourage her. "Does Miss January need the money?"

"Told Shirl she always wants a cigarette in her mouth; calms her nerves. She had to cut back when the prices sky-rocketed."

"That's great, and when she's drunk and one of them falls out of her mouth and sets her muumuu on fire, then what? Carly's banned from the property. I'll deliver the message." I made a mental note to talk to that dumb drunk. A threatening conversation might save me bail money.

"Carly used to buy it from her mother, but when dear old mom raised her prices she looked for a cheaper alternative. Once she eliminated her drug-addicted friends, her choices were slim."

I couldn't imagine asking Mother to provide clean pee so I could pass a drug test. Much to Mother's relief, I'm sure, neither Brad nor I took a liking to drugs.

"You know how I'm always doing nice things for you, showing up to work on time, that kind of thing?" Mac asked.

"Yes. Now what do you want? Before you ask, I reserve the right to say no."

"Can Shirl stay as a regular?" Mac blurted. "She had movers lined up for the weekend but her ex, Ronnie, went over to the new place and started a fight with the landlord and he rented the unit to someone else. Besides, she likes it here. She can pay. Her nursing skills have already come in handy. The other night when Miss J passed out on the porch, Shirl knew she wasn't dead."

Hmm…a nurse!

Shirl kicked the office door open but caught the knob before it hit the wall. "Did you ask her?" She looked at Mac.

"There is one other thing," Mac continued. "When Shirl moved out, she stored her boxes in the ex's garage with his permission and now he won't give them back. Says he's going through them and what he can't sell, he'll give away. Maybe you and Fab could retrieve them?"

Wait until Fab heard about this job, I thought. "Allowing you to move in violates my no-more-full-time-renter rule, but I'll make an exception as long as you follow the rules."

"What rules?" Mac looked suspicious.

"No drugs, second time the sheriff pays you a visit, you move with no whining. No sex in the pool. You stop paying and I'll have you forcibly moved out."

"The sex part sounds fun, but I can follow those rules." Shirl stuck out her knuckles. "I called the sheriff on Ronnie about my boxes, and they questioned him. He lied and said I took everything with me. He opened the garage and told them everything in there belonged to him," Shirl said.

"Text me Ronnie's address; make room for a delivery at your cottage." I reached for the doorknob. "We have two half-dead people who live here; if you'd keep an eye out, I'd appreciate it. See you two later."

"Can I call for bail money?" Shirl giggled.

"If you can pay me back." I stopped at my front bumper and took a couple of pics with my phone, and then went around the back and did the same. Wait until Brick sees the damage.

* * *

I blew through the doors of Famosa Motors, and when Bitsy looked up, her "I love everyone" smile disappeared. The caged look in her eyes told me she knew her business deal blew up in her overly made-up face.

"Your double-crossing greed is the reason the Hummer's all smashed up." I crossed to the reception desk.

"Get away from me," Bitsy scrambled for her purse and pulled out a gun.

"You're not your usual friendly self," I leaned across the desk, grabbed a fistful of her hair, and yanked her off her chair, which rolled out from under her. She dropped her gun and it slid under the filing cabinet. Bitsy jerked against the hold I had on her, and I was left clutching a wig.

"Give that back," Bitsy yelled, swiping at the hairpiece and coming up with air.

I twirled around the mess of fake blond hair and flung it at her, wiping my hands on my skirt. "You think you're going to get away with selling bad information? Watch your back." I walked to the staircase.

"You bitch," Bitsy screeched.

"You better talk some sense into your friend Mango or you're both going to end up hurt or worse." I raced up the stairs.

Brick sat in his chair, feet up on the desk. "I didn't hear gun shots, I suppose that's good."

I ignored his mocking smile. "I have bad news and I need a favor."

"You're ballsy, Red." Brick's feet hit the floor. "What the hell now? Bad news first!"

"The back end of the Hummer is all smashed in courtesy of your dancer, Mango. You might check to see if she has insurance. You want me to file a police report? I have witnesses."

"Mango's easily excitable; she just needs a firm hand. I'll take care of everything. Since when did you start pissing off my strippers?" Brick looked me up and down.

"A case didn't go to her liking." I pulled my hair off my neck, repositioning the clip. "Two favors: I got my insurance check for the Tahoe. Make me a deal on an SUV. Or since the

Hummer's old and has been in an accident, fix it and discount it to where I can afford the payments. Do you finance?" I smiled.

"Do you have one breath of appreciation for the fact they are no longer manufactured, making it a collectible?"

Proud of myself that I didn't roll my eyes, I said, "Yes, I do." In my opinion, that sounded sincere.

"The damn vehicle is becoming a headache; my sniveling nephew is still whining that he wants the Hummer. You let me know what kind of car you want and I'll hook you up on a good deal. In the interim, choose a car from the rental side and get the keys from Bitsy."

"That was too easy. How about a boat ride over to Fisher?"

"Did you see the sign out front — Luxury autos, not a boat on the lot?" Brick stared me down. "I know what the two of you are up to; you'll get arrested sneaking over there on a boat. I'll hook you up with a pass; drive on and sneak around, or whatever you two do. Once you get on the island no one will bother you."

"You're the best." I jumped up, momentarily thinking about giving him a hug. "How soon can we get the passes?"

Brick leaned back in his chair, a smug smile on his face. "You remember that the next time I call." He wagged his finger. "Stop by tomorrow and I'll have a car ready. It will have an electronic box that will get you past security. Ernesto in service will have the key."

I fingered the candy bowl on his desk, helping myself to two chocolate bars. "I'll take a bottle of cold water."

Brick had a small refrigerator that held soda, water, and his favorite chilled vodka.

"Nothing happens to Bitsy. You get her and your crazy girlfriend to kiss and make up." Brick's cell phone rang; he picked it up and waved me off.

The side lot had limited choices. I slid behind the wheel of an Escalade. It looked exactly like Zach's, only newer. I asked once if I could drive his and he laughed.

Chapter 27

Fab had gotten better at sharing the driveway, so parking the Escalade wasn't a problem. I reached for my Glock when I noticed the kitchen blinds were down. I slowly opened the front door and it was all quiet; not even Jazz came to meow.

"Are you alone?" Fab called from the living room.

I holstered my gun. "You must be doing something illegal."

"I don't think so, but some people might not agree." Fab sat cross-legged on the couch, Jazz asleep next to her.

"I hope those people aren't the police." I dumped my purse at the bottom of the stairs. "I've had enough excitement for today."

Fab sat, knife in hand, cutting out the bottom of a briefcase. "Look what I found."

"Gabriel's?" I narrowed my eyes. "Since it probably didn't drop out of the sky, you must have gone back to the condo and broke in for the second time. Where was my invitation?"

"Don't yell, you'll wake Jazz," Fab ran her hand down Jazz's back.

"No need for both of us to go to jail. Besides," Fab explained, "along with everyone else in town, you're my first call for bail money and a jail pick up."

"Where did you find it?" I sat opposite her, excited to see the contents.

"In the guest bedroom closet, behind a shelf unit, tucked inside the wall. My last place to look, I'd been through every room. The duct system had been my first stop. I thought for sure he'd hidden it in there, especially when I saw it had a not easily-seen space between the bedroom and bathroom."

"Are those bundles of hundreds? Is it real?" I did some mental math. Unsure of the exact number of bundles, I estimated about one hundred thousand. "What else besides the cash?"

"A nice Ruger and Sig Sauer." Fab pulled the guns out, setting them on the coffee table. "Untraceable, I'm sure." She pulled out two large manila envelopes and rifled through the contents, yielding three complete sets of identities.

"Lookie: a bank account in the Cayman Islands, and even one in the last of the tax havens, Belize. And my favorite, complete floor plans for the Wright mansion," Fab said, and she held them up. "Here's a list of the items to be stolen, their value, and a map where each item was located in the house. He had codes to the outside gate and house."

I sat there in opened-mouth awe,

impressed by the organization. "Having never been a professional thief, are you always this detailed?"

"I'm convinced Gabriel and Maxwell were partners in crime and that they had a third partner who lacked sharing skills and killed them both. What else makes any sense?"

Thoughts of the dead Gabriel sent a shiver up my spine. If he hadn't died that night, he would never have let Fab out of his control. I'm certain he would have sought retribution for running. "I'm happy you ditched him that night, you might have ended up dead."

Fab looked fearful. "Gabriel didn't like the newest version of me; in fact, it angered him. He told me I'd gone soft and he didn't find it attractive. I read between the lines. I'd outlived my usefulness. After a pain-filled lecture, he dragged me out to that island to take the fall and end up in prison; or he'd shoot me himself and I'd still take the blame in death."

"Did he hurt you?"

"I couldn't believe it, but that night he used the same hands which had brought me hours of breathless pleasure, to inflict unspeakable pain." Fab's face clouded over, lost in the ugly memory.

Fab held up an expensive black leather journal. "He kept track of all of his jobs, like a scrapbook. Kept detailed lists of what he stole, the worth, what he netted, and a South Florida to-do list. He left behind an interesting address book, too. He had two more high-profile thefts in the planning stage, more floor plans, and a list of what he would be stealing. In the back is a list of several more mansions on his wish list. He had plans for another heist on Fisher Island and their neighbor, Star Island."

"You never did tell me how you ended up on Fisher Island that night."

"Gabriel called and wanted to broker a truce. Said I'd be happy, he was going back to France. Americans got on his nerves."

"Can you imagine if he'd stayed at The Cottages?"

We both laughed.

"I underestimated him. He held out his arms for a hug, then flipped me around and pushed my face into the ground. He cuffed my hands behind my back and pulled them tight, using the cuffs to jerk me off the ground. I thought he'd break my wrists. He slammed his hand over my mouth, but I struggled and bit him," she said and then choked back tears.

Grabbing her water bottle, she downed it and screwed the cap back on. "He dropped his hands long enough for me to scream, and then slapped me hard across the face, almost giving me whiplash," she paused to take a breath.

I didn't say a word, afraid she'd stop talking and I'd never get the whole story. I did put my bottle of water in front of her.

"He dug his fingers in my neck and squeezed," she said, "telling me if I used my feet other than to walk, he'd break both my legs. He then warned me not to speak without his permission or he'd gag me."

"You survived, that's what I care about." As her best friend, I needed to distract her. "Good news, but in exchange I need a promise."

Fab arched her brow. "I'll listen, but the answer is no."

I channeled Madeline in a quick second, hands on my hips. "You listen to me. I've had a crappy day." I mimicked Mother's no-nonsense voice. "Mango bashed in the back end of the Hummer, looking for you. You will promise." I wagged my finger.

"How the hell did Mango find out about us?" Fab huffed, sticking her chest out. "Okay, whatever, what? I went to Catholic school, if I can stare down the nuns, I can out stare you."

"I got us a ride to the island and some credentials. It all goes down tomorrow. In exchange, no retaliation against Bitsy."

"Let me guess, Brick's sleeping with that dumb-ass blonde?"

"Gee, I forgot to ask," I snapped my fingers. "Your promise, please."

"Sure." Fab held up her right hand. "No Hummer, huh? What are you driving now?"

"A big Escalade that's newer than Zach's," I was so pleased, I wanted to drive by his house, honk, and make him ask, "Where did you get that?"

I continued. "You're making a promise to your best friend who would get out of bed in the middle of the night to bail you out of jail."

"You're so whiney you're making my head hurt." Fab packed everything back in the briefcase and snapped the locks down.

"What are you going to do with the briefcase? Someone's going to figure out the condo got tossed. If it's Creole he might just strangle you. Or if it's Harder who comes banging on the door he could put you in jail. Make sure no one can find the damn thing. Creole will wait until we're not here and snoop around on his own. He's good, girlfriend."

"Got any ideas?"

"I want deniability," I motioned for her to get up off her butt and follow me. "Besides, you know this house better than I do."

* * *

I tossed the Escalade keys to Fab. It irritated me that she got behind the wheel and took off smoothly down the Overseas, unlike me, who had it jerking and jumping until I got used it. If she ever found out I'd never hear the last of the comments.

"What are you getting paid for this job and why do I have to come along?" Fab pouted.

She blew down to Pigeon Key going just over the speed limit. Gazing out at the blue-green water reminded me I needed to get to walking on the beach again every day.

"I don't trust you not to get in trouble. I'm terrible at the money issue. I'll deal with the clients, but you need to quote the job and explain terms."

Fab hit the steering wheel; another driver cut her off and she had to slow down. "A carwash eviction? How are we going to have any credibility when you take these weird jobs? And the place burned down?"

"Only the roof burned off, and a few minor issues like plumbing and electrical, and all the equipment. Surely, Mr. Ivers must have insurance. Even you, hotshot, wouldn't have known Quirky would double back and torch the place."

"We need to advertise our eviction services. Our slogan: We'll evict the crappy tenants no one else will."

"You post, I'll be back up. Or I'll post and you shoot."

Fab slowed for the exit, and this time when she hit the gravel, we didn't weave sending dirt and gravel flying. We drove under the arch into the driveway of the Wild Bird Farm. The colorful parrots that crowded the cement overhang had doubled in number since the last visit.

"Tolbert will be happy to see you. You're clearly his favorite," I said.

"He reminds me of my grandfather; no judgment, doesn't harp on wanting me to change into something I don't want to be."

Grover stood guard at the top of the steps when we pulled into the driveway. Once we got out, he cleared the steps in a leap, bounding over to give me a lick hello. I missed walking on the beach with him. I remembered the new box of dog treats before I left the house, pulling out two and putting them in my pocket. Grover wolfed down the treats and moved between me and Fab to get petted.

Mr. Ivers and Tolbert sat on the porch. "Today I have iced tea or orange water." Tolbert motioned to the tray on the table. As usual, he thought of everything. Fab and I chose orange water. Fresh slices of oranges in ice-cold water.

I smiled at Mr. Ivers and grabbed two pillows, throwing them in a chair before sitting. "The Poppins are gone, but you probably know that there was a fire. I have a friend, Jimmy Spoon, and his crew can have the car wash running in a few weeks."

"Everyone around here knows that

Spoon character is a criminal. And I'm tired of his ilk," Mr. Ivers growled.

I squared my shoulders and glared. "Spoon is reformed. No other local will do the work without screwing you. It's your choice. Or go with someone your insurance company recommends and see how that works out."

"Mr. Ivers is it?" Fab stopped pacing the porch and settled into a chair next to Tolbert. "We accept cash."

Uh-oh, Fab's narrowed eyes meant trouble. She looked Mr. Ivers over with outright suspicion.

"The deal was to evict those crazy inbreds, not leave me with a burned-out building. Job's not done. The only people who deal in cash are criminals."

"Don't run some crazy old man story, they only work on her." Fab pointed to me. "The job was for an eviction. Period. You need to pay up."

Tolbert laughed, winked at Fab, and reached across to refill her water.

I gave Fab the eye. "Of course, we want a happy customer." In the future, I'd be handling all customer service issues.

"You need to get Clean Bubbles up and running again. I'm an old man and not up to the stress." Mr. Ivers put his hand on his chest.

"I'll be happy to handle the contracting responsibilities. We'll have to negotiate a new contract," I said.

The job excited me; a flashback to the old days. I could do this on time and on budget.

"My insurance is getting back to me today on what they're paying and that's your budget. You can hire all the criminals you want; you'll be responsible." Mr. Ivers turned steely eyes on Fab. "My deal was with her," he said, and pointed to me. "Weren't you in jail when the heavy lifting got done?"

"And after the car wash reopens, then what?" Fab glared back.

"Get the car wash up and running, you two can run it, and it will keep you both out of trouble."

"You're senile," Fab snorted. "Why would you think either of us would agree to that?"

"More tea, anyone?" Tolbert asked, a big smile on his face.

"I'll sign over half the car wash to you," Mr. Ivers said to me. "You can hire her, although I wouldn't. She seems unstable."

"She'd be my employee, I could tell her what to do and she'd do it?" I bit my lip so I wouldn't laugh.

"You're senile too." Fab glared.

"Let's get this straight. I oversee the repairs and, in exchange, I get half interest in the property and can run it without any interference by you?"

"I'd expect my half of the profits deposited into my account each month." Mr. Ivers sat back satisfied with his part in the negotiations.

"Put it in writing with a little notary stamp, and repairs will start right away," I said. "And don't forget the silent partner clause."

"You're better at negotiations than you think," Fab whispered.

"Why do girls whisper? I can't hear with my hearing aid turned up." Mr. Ivers fiddled with his earpiece. "What'd she say?" He looked at Tolbert.

"I told her to dump your ass," Fab said. "Blow up that stinking carwash and make an example out of non-payers."

"If I was younger, I'd ask you out on a date." Mr. Ivers winked at Fab.

"We have another appointment," Fab lied. "Not one thing gets done until you send a signed contract and the insurance check. Madison isn't fronting money for you with your poor track record."

"You'll hear from me this afternoon," Gus told me.

Tolbert and Fab walked back to the SUV, Grover and I trailing behind.

I waved through the windshield as Fab backed out onto the road. "I'll sign half of my half over to you," I told her.

"I'm not carwash material. That old man scammed you."

"It would give you a tie to Tarpon Cove. Harder for you to pack and leave town on a whim," I said.

"I thought about that in jail. Being part of the Westin family means I won't be running off anytime soon. What's that noise?" Fab looked at my phone.

"I downloaded a new 'Hey' ringtone, lets me know I have a text." I scrolled down and read. "Our ride and credentials await our trip to the island. Ready?"

"Driving over is a way better idea than my idea or riding over on a boat."

"Remember when we get to Brick's, no harassing Bitsy."

Chapter 28

Fab and I walked into Famosa Motors; I pinched her arm as a reminder to play nice. Bitsy didn't look surprised. "Brick's not here. He left this for you." She pushed a manila envelope across the counter. "He says to take the Mercedes GL63." She passed me the keys.

Fab leaned across the desk. "You think it was a good idea to make an enemy out of me? Watch your back."

"You worked Mango up, you call her off," I said to Bitsy.

"Fab, catch." I tossed her the keys. The prospect of driving a new car would dissuade her from administering an ass kicking.

The black Mercedes SUV sat waiting, not a speck of dust and with a full tank of gas; a bit intimidating with three rows and seating for eight.

Fab circled the SUV, kicking the tires. She got on her hands and knees and checked the underside. "Least he's not tracking us."

"Notice the sticker. No one will question that we belong out there." I opened the console box and pulled out the paperwork.

"You're so nerdy. The owner's manual?" Fab laughed.

"Says here big engine, lots of horses,

and the best part: good, low-end torque."

Fab pushed all the buttons, checking out the dashboard. "There's a screen here, I can watch myself back up."

"When we get to the island, do not do anything to attract attention--and that includes driving fast." I opened the envelope that Brick left. "According to the notes, the window sticker will get us on the island, no questions. Here's a gate card and an address where we can park and go snoop around." I put it in her outstretched hand. "It's four big mansions away, so we'll have to walk. Got a plan yet?"

"I want to retrace my steps the night of the shooting, before and after." Fab was on a roll, hitting every green traffic light. We hit the expressway in record time.

"Don't you think the widow probably has extra security? Can you do this reenacting from the street? Trespassing on millionaires' properties is a good way to get arrested, or if the widow has a security guard, we might get shot."

"I'll do the sneaking around, you stick to the street; you see security guards or cops, call me. Then double back and I'll meet you at the car. At least we know it's a safe rendezvous point."

"Promise me, word of honor, you're not going to break into the widow's house?"

"I've thought about it, but I'm not prepared, and it would be a bad decision."

I didn't believe a word she said; Fab was more prepared than any Girl Scout.

* * *

A quick look at the tag in the window and the guard waved us onto the ferry. Fab and I decided not to attract any unwanted attention and agreed to stay in the SUV for the ride across the Biscayne Bay. I breathed a sigh of relief when we drove away from the dock. I kept looking out the side mirror; everything had gone so smoothly. It wouldn't surprise me to see lights flashing and hear sirens behind us. Brick had put directions in the envelope, but we ignored them in favor of GPS. Fab pulled into the driveway when we got to the address Brick gave us. She inserted the card and the electric gates that surrounded the perimeter of the property opened. It didn't look like anyone was home, but all the houses looked like that. No one opened the door and waved to us.

My first choice would've been to sit by the pool with my feet in the water. Instead, I struggled to look inconspicuous, walking down the street in front of the murder mansion. Before they noticed me, I saw bike riders coming around the curve, a young couple laughing. Creole raised his sunglasses, blue eyes rock hard. Smile vanishing, he shifted his attention back to his friend.

Curiosity killing me, I turned and watched them pedal away. Creole looked good in a pair of white shorts and a golf shirt, his creamy caramel-colored skin reddened by the sun.

They turned their bikes into the Wright's driveway. I recognized the woman as Chrissy Wright, and she, too, was dressed in total white. She didn't look so sad, and apparently had cut her grieving short. Chrissy and Creole made a striking couple. He turned and shook his finger before disappearing up the driveway.

I pulled my cell phone out of my pocket and called Fab. When I got no answer, I texted her to let her know trouble just got back to the manse. Creole and the widow looked comfortable together. Were they dating? Had they known each other before the murder?

I ran back down the street to the house where we parked the SUV. Six turns later, I had the Mercedes turned around in the driveway, awaiting Fab for a fast getaway. If I crossed my fingers hard enough, would it keep her from getting caught? I slumped behind the wheel, waiting, checking my watch every few seconds.

The electric gate opened and Fab appeared out of nowhere and hopped into the passenger side. "This wasn't the worst idea I've ever had, but damned close."

"Did you get caught inside?" Not hearing sirens, I put my foot on the gas and lurched out of the driveway.

Fab rolled her eyes but refrained from a snotty comment. "The widow has some impressive security; spent my time trying not to get my face on camera. Thank goodness I was standing outside the patio doors when the lovers came riding up on their bicycles. Didn't take Creole long to move in there. The widow looked at him like a delicious morsel. Her husband's been buried; time to move on."

"That was going to be my bad news. Creole saw me hanging out in the street, he knew you were at the house. I think we need to hide from him for a few days."

"The widow looked down her snooty nose and pretended to be afraid, pressing her body against Creole, who asked me, 'What are you doing here?' I decided to channel a Madison Westin story. What would you say? Then I told her I came to offer my condolences, sad for her loss, and although I had been married to Gabriel at one time, I had nothing to do with what happened at her house that night. Then I wiped the non-existent tears from the corner of my eyes."

"I'm so proud. And tears, too? That's proof you do listen to me." I gave her a big smile.

"The widow then said she hoped the

police knew what they were doing when they released me from jail. She asked how I got on the island, and did I check in with security. Creole interrupted her, thanked me, and told me I should leave and not to come back. He put his arm around her, whispered something in her ear, and they went into the house. I walked to the road and, when out of sight, ran the rest of the way."

"She gives new meaning to the term, 'grieving widow.'" I got in line behind several cars waiting for the ferry. "I'll be glad when we get off the island."

"I'm more convinced than ever that there's a third man involved. Gabriel was in cahoots with Maxwell Wright, and the third one got away. He didn't leave a single clue in his briefcase as to who that might be."

"Now what?" I drove onto the ferry, shut off the engine, and ran around to the passenger side. "We need to return this car. I'm going to tell Brick to get me a deal on a new Tahoe. I'm going to miss the Hummer, but I'm tired of not having my own ride."

"You could trade sexual favors for info with Zach?" Fab climbed over the seat.

"I tried that and he figured it out in a second. We swapped spit and not a lot of information. If you want to trade favors, the man in the power seat is Detective Harder."

"Are you suggesting he and I...?" Fab

choked. "We can't stand one another."

"Even if you could stand one another, I wasn't suggesting you tie him to one of my light fixtures and rock his world. I'm suggesting a professional favor. An info exchange."

"Hmm.... That's where a best friend comes in, a really good friend, one who could set up a meeting. He at least likes you," Fab said.

"Best-friend promise that you keep whatever agreement that the two of you make and if you can't, don't swear upfront. You are not to screw him over. If I vouch for you, you damn well better keep your word."

"When can you make it happen?" Fab held out her pinky finger.

"I'll put it on my list."

Chapter 29

Fab and I sat by the edge of the pool, occasionally kicking water on the other, laughing, enjoying ourselves.

"Got your car. Get down here and pick it up," Brick barked through the phone when I answered.

"What was that about?" Fab asked over the rim of her coffee cup.

"Brick's short on social skills but good on his word. He'd said he'd have my new Tahoe in a week and it's been delivered."

"What's it costing you?" Fab didn't concern herself with the cost of cars; she worked a super-secret deal that let her trade-in her cars when she got bored.

"I told Brick he better beat the sticker price. I reminded him that I wouldn't be like the rest of his clients who showed up with a bag of cash. He agreed to accept a cashier's check from my insurance payoff and to finance the rest. I made it clear I wasn't interested in being in the loaner program. There were too many strings attached. I want the luxury of saying no."

"I'll go with you, I like new cars." Fab jumped up, but not before kicking more water on me.

"I'm going to be the first one to drive my car, not you," I sighed. "You don't need to go anyway. Why start trouble with Bitsy?"

"I didn't tell you? Must have slipped my mind. Paid her a late night visit and negotiated new terms. Oh, don't look so horrified, I didn't hurt her."

"Forget, my ass," I fumed. "She probably went straight to Brick."

"Don't think so. I explained to her the benefits of my not being an enemy. Told her I better not ever hear that my name crossed her lips. We parted friends, no hard feelings."

We grabbed our bags from the entry bench. Once inside the front door, everything ended up there unless it went in the refrigerator.

Fab, in one of her possessed moods, decided to set a record of how fast she could get to Brick's. I pulled my seat belt tight and closed my eyes.

"Where was your Glock?"

"You know I pack a Walther PPK. I'm offended you think I can't carry on a persuasive conversation without a gun."

"Your stories need work. You could stand some tutoring. Call Mother. Teach her something illegal and she'll teach you to lie better."

Fab laid on the horn; the driver of the other car, not amused, hung her finger out the window and cut around a little close to the front bumper. "Your mother scares me a little. I've never seen anyone hold their own with the likes of Spoon and she has him wrapped. And what if she gets arrested because of something I taught her?"

"And when Brad finds out we're dead. We'll need to pack and leave town."

Fab ran the yellow light and zipped into Famosa Motors.

I looked around for my new ride. The only Tahoe was a white one, and I'd seen it parked there before. The Hummer sat at the front, detailed to perfection. The auto body shop had worked its magic, and you'd never know it had its back end bashed.

"You deal with Brick. I have a snitch who works here. I need to remind him of our special relationship." Fab adjusted her gun at the small of her back.

Bitsy's smile never faltered when I walked in the door. "Brick said you could go straight up, he's not in a very good mood."

If she wanted to pretend nothing ever happened that was fine with me.

I walked into Brick's office; he was on the phone arguing with someone in Spanish. He motioned me to one of the uncomfortable chairs in front of his desk. It was a big joke with him that they were horrible, he didn't have to sit in them. I decided to stand at the window and scan the lot for my new ride.

Brick slammed the phone down. "Sit," he pointed. "This is your lucky day; I'm in the mood to negotiate. Show me your check."

I had my insurance settlement for days, turning it into a cashier's check. "I'm preapproved to finance the rest with Tarpon Bank."

"Here's the deal, take it or leave it. I'll take this," he said, and took the check out of my hand, "and you get the Hummer."

I shook my head. "Hummer? The check is a whole lot less than what you say the used car is worth. What's the catch?" When something appears too good to be true, my little voice told me, *Beware. Don't jump across the desk all gushy.*

"Women!" he yelled. "It's a damn classic. You'd be doing me a favor. I need it off the lot now and I don't have another buyer."

"Are there strings besides the check?"

"Hell yes. Here's the story and you don't change a single word. You bought the car back when you first started driving it. The reason it took so long for the title transfer, paperwork glitches, it's now all worked out, legal like."

I stood up. "I'm going to pass. I'm not getting pulled over and the title doesn't pass muster, then I need bail money at your interest rates."

Brick slammed the desk with his fist. "There's not a single car on this lot that's not legit. Sit back down."

I refrained from using sign language and sat, reaching into his candy dish and taking a fistful of chocolates, throwing them in my purse.

"The problem is my nephew, Bruno. While it was in for repairs, he stole it, taking it for a joyride. He found the title and saw that it was still registered to Famosa Motors. I got a screaming phone call from my sister, how disappointed she was in me because I knew she wanted the car. She even called my wife, crying. My wife, sick of the phone calls, told me to give it to her. I told them both our newly concocted story. I gave my sister two choices: either I'd send a couple of collectors to retrieve the car, but I couldn't guarantee Bruno's safety, or I'd call in a felony stolen car report."

"Bruno brought it back?" Damned kid had more nerve than sense.

"He called and told me to "F" myself; said his mother already gifted it to him. Did I mention he totaled two cars in the last six months? He has two reckless driving tickets, court hearings pending. If he doesn't get his license revoked, at the very least it will be suspended for a long time. And I'm the bastard in the family," Brick fumed.

"How did you get it back?" I didn't feel

the least bit bad asking questions that were none of my business.

"Casio spotted it parked in front of a sleazy strip joint in the hood. He used his connections, moved the tow request to the front of the line, and got it back here without having to bash in his smug face." Brick clenched and unclenched his fists, taking one of those stress balls out of his drawer. "The interior was trashed, clothes, condoms, and liquor bottles in the back."

"I'll take good care of it and bring it by for visits." I tried to make him smile but it didn't work. "I'm good with the story if anyone asks."

"I'd rather sell it to you than dump it on another dealer out of state. It's been detailed inside and out and is ready to go, service up to date. The repair and paint an A+ job." He shoved papers across the desk. "Sign by the Xs."

"What happened when Bruno came out and found the Hummer missing?" I asked as I signed.

"Little shit assumed it got stolen, but didn't tell anyone. He finally fessed up to his mother. She called screaming, worrying over that grown brat's psyche. I suggested she stick both her feet up Bruno's ass and we haven't spoken since. The good thing to come out of it, I gave my wife an ultimatum: my sister or me.

That ended the conversation and we haven't had a single fight since. Wish I'd thought of that sooner."

"Based on personal experience, if Bruno had the big ones to come here and steal a car off your lot, he'll be back."

"I'm one step ahead of you. That little bastard has been banned from here." Brick's eyes were black and hard.

I finished signing, double-checked, and handed back the contract.

Brick opened a side drawer and pulled out an 8x10 photograph. "Can you believe what a makeover can do?"

"Vanilla?" The knockout statuesque, now brunette, in a string bikini and heels, long tan legs, smiled back at me. Her hair was pulled into a ponytail, and she wore minimal makeup.

"Vanilla became an overnight club sensation. Turns out the combination of her small boobs and long legs are quite the turn-on. Gone is the frightened-deer look, a little confidence and she's quite charming. There's a fragility about her that sets her apart from my hardened pros. I told her no pole for her, she hostesses and makes as much as the dancers."

"You have a little crush?" I asked.

"Maybe a little. I'd never act on it. We sat and had a long talk. She needed someone to give her a chance at a life, not be on the run from her psycho brother who sells road kill. Vanilla is under my protection as long as she works for me, just like the rest of my girls. She doesn't know this, but Quirky's been relocated to Mississippi. My guys gave him a choice and he left town." Brick handed me the keys.

"If you hadn't hired her, she'd have been out of options and forced into life on the street or to go back to Quirky."

"Who names their kid Quirky?" Brick snorted.

"Stoners." I stood up, keys in hand. "Thank you."

Brick winked. "I didn't lose money on the deal."

I laughed. "Of course you didn't." I wore a silly smile all the way downstairs.

Fab sat on a concrete bench, babbling in French. I unlocked the passenger door of the Hummer, leaving it open, and went around to the driver's side to start the engine.

Before Fab got in I said, "Not one word about how awful my driving is, get in and close your eyes like I do." I pointed to the passenger seat.

"Do you have pictures of Brick with farm animals?"

"A straight-up business deal." I refrained from squealing the tires out of Famosa Motors and screaming out the window, "It's really mine!"

Chapter 30

My bedroom door opened, and I rolled over. It must be morning, since sunshine streamed through the window.

"Wake up, sunshine, I don't have all day." Creole didn't look happy. Filling the doorway with a black T-shirt stretched over his abs, I thought to myself that he certainly knew how to fill out a pair of jeans.

"How did you get in?" I wished I could have this confrontation after coffee.

Creole's blue eyes were angry, his hands behind his back to stay in control, perhaps. "You think Trouble across the hall is the only one who knows how to pick a lock?"

Fab's bedroom door banged against the wall; she wasn't happy. "Keep your voice down."

Creole turned to Fab. "Oh good, you're awake. Saves me from the special wake-up call I had in mind." He turned to me. "Coffee's ready downstairs. Five minutes."

"Fifteen!" I yelled after him. A quick shower and I'd be ready with evasive answers to his questions.

One good thing about living at the beach: pulling on a skirt and a top, sliding my feet into flip-flops, and tying my hair back in a ponytail, and I had my uniform ready for the day.

* * *

"Did you bring breakfast from The Bakery Café?" I asked as I walked into the kitchen.

"Where's your friend?" Creole growled.

"I'm right here." Fab walked in and headed to the coffee pot. She took a sniff and put it back down.

"Your favorite is in its usual place in the refrigerator," I said, knowing she'd be out the front door in a second and leave me to answer to Creole.

"I feel like a latte and I'll get you a pecan roll," Fab said to me, heading to the door.

Creole cut her off and pointed to a chair at the island. "Sit down." Not quite a yell, but damn close.

"Stop yelling or...," I hesitated, not being able to think of anything. "I'll tell Mother."

I glanced at Fab and gave her a stern look; more antics would push him over the edge. Fab couldn't care less. I thought she would laugh.

Creole fished his phone out of his pocket. "Catch." He tossed me his phone. "I dare you to tell Madeline the two of you snuck onto a private island where you could've been arrested."

"Mother will only be mad she wasn't invited. And arrested for what? We were invited guests," I said.

"Give me their name and number," Creole demanded.

Fab stood up. "What do you want? I have a busy day!" she yelled back at him.

Creole looked like he wanted to strangle us, Fab first. "What were the two of you doing out on the island?"

"I wanted to check out the scene again. You'd do the same thing. How did a simple grand theft turn into murder with no suspects except for me?" Fab flipped her hair, and then stuck her nose in the air. "Where was the widow that night? Surely, you got around to asking her. You seem like the kind of guy who would ask after sex."

I tried hard to choke back a laugh and, instead, a weird sound came out of my mouth. They both stared.

Creole stepped in front of Fab, inches from her face. He stood close, towering over her with his over six-foot frame, his body wound tight. Fab straightened and glared right back at him. "I'd bet my left...uh, that you found that damn briefcase of Gabriel's. Tell me now what was in it and anything you else you found. Don't bother with one of your suck-ass lies. We have you on hidden camera entering his condo. You know, the other crime scene, the same one I told you explicitly to stay away from. Then you rigged the system and went through the place, not leaving a clue behind as to what you did. You're good, I'll give you that."

"Next time you break into my house, bring breakfast," I said to Creole, in an attempt to lighten the mood.

Creole whipped his cuffs from the back of his jeans. "You're both under arrest. I'll hold you," he said, and pointed to me, "until Fab tells what she knows. Fab wouldn't save herself. But you? In a minute," Creole said.

"And we could shoot you, too," I threatened and took a couple of steps back.

"Are you threatening a law enforcement officer?" Creole's arm snaked out, pulling him to me, feeling my lower back.

"My Glock's upstairs so don't go looking anywhere else," I snapped and jerked away. "You broke in without a warrant. Shooting you would be self-defense." I'd been to jail once and had no desire for a return visit; but Creole would get a taste of how a girl fights before I let him cuff me.

His mouth twitched slightly. "You two are interfering with a damned murder investigation."

Fab stuck her chin out. "Is banging the widow part of your investigation?" Her voice dripped in sarcasm.

If Fab got us arrested, I'd force her to deal with Mother.

Creole leaned across the counter. "Did it ever occur to you that your friend here is hiding what she knows even from you?"

Fab gave a quick nod behind his back.

I leaned in so that we were nose to nose. "No, it hasn't," I said, knowing chances were she was doing exactly that.

We stared at one another, a snap of chemistry, and he pulled away. "Damn you." He turned. "Where did Fab go?"

I stood and carried my coffee mug to the dishwasher, looking out the kitchen window. "Fab just drove out. Zach would've parked behind her." I turned and faced him with a smirky smile.

"Listen very carefully, Madison." Creole's hands gripped me tight.

My heart raced as I stared into Creole's angry face. I wanted to step back but I had nowhere to go.

"You set me up, knowing I'd be distracted by your lips." Creole pushed my back against the sink, forcing me to look at him.

Creole grabbed the back of my neck, slamming his mouth against mine. Erotic need rushed through me with every flick of his tongue. His lips ravished mine, unmercifully. I moaned in his mouth, which increased the assault.

He broke the kiss, pushing me away. "I'm going to get the info I need. Keep in mind, there's a double murderer walking around," he said, slamming the front door.

Chapter 31

My cheeks burned, lips swollen. I had surrendered willingly to his lips, letting his hands roam over my body in an intimate way. I enjoyed being trapped by his feral body, his mouth clamped on mine. Much to my embarrassment, the more his lips lashed mine, the more I moaned in his mouth.

I jerked up my briefcase and keys, pushing Fab's number on the speed dial. It went straight to voicemail. I waited to unlock the door when I heard a car pull into the driveway.

Peeking outside, I saw that Slice had his arm around Zach's shoulder, hauling him out of his pickup truck, Zach's face black and blue, his right arm in a sling.

"Good, you're home. He's all yours." Slice rolled his eyes, looking ready to run.

I held the front door open for him. Zach shuffled past me and made himself comfortable on the couch.

"Doctor says I need someone to keep an eye on me for the next couple of days," Zach said, "make sure I don't develop any symptoms. I'm supposed to avoid anything that requires concentration or complicated thinking. I promised the doctor I would stay with someone while I'm still seeing double."

"What the heck happened?" I looked at Slice; he stood ramrod straight, arms across his chest. His face told me he'd like to strangle Zach.

"In a hurry to get to a meeting, I cut some guy off, didn't pay attention when he maneuvered in behind me and slammed my left quarter panel, sending the Escalade into a spin. The guardrail was the only thing stopping me from a nosedive into the water. The SUV came to rest on its side. The bastard drove off, but another driver saw the whole thing, stopped, and helped me out."

"And you didn't bother with your seatbelt," Slice said.

"Did you go to the hospital?" I asked.

"The paramedics insisted I go to be checked out. The double vision factored into my decision to cooperate. You don't mind my coming here do you?" Zach asked.

"Of course not." I gave him a lame smile. "At least you're not bleeding this time." Last time he'd been a terrible patient and he'd been shot. Prescribed to just rest, he'd be a pain in the butt.

"Can I get a couple of real pillows?" He jerked one of the couch pillows out from under his head.

I could run out like Fab, forcing Slice to play nurse. Aunt Elizabeth left me with a well-stocked linen closet, full of towels and sheets. It took me awhile to clean and organize, and I'd replaced all of the lumpy flat pillows. The hardest part had been getting rid of the mothball smell. I washed every single item and if it retained the hideous odor, out it went.

Halfway down the stairs, Zach called out, "Can I get a blanket?"

"Anything else while I'm upstairs?" Who in the hell wanted a blanket when it was hot outside?

I came back with a blanket and pillows. The first thing I noticed, was that Slice had bailed. "Where did Slice go?"

"He had to go back to the office to do my job and his." Zach's cell phone pinged a couple of times, letting him know he had messages. "I'm not supposed to be left alone." He wiggled his fingers, motioning me to hand him his phone.

If he were really sick, he'd be quiet and want to be left alone. No wonder Slice raced out of the driveway. "I have an electrical inspection that demands my appearance. I'll get Mac to come and stay with you."

Unless I decided to run away from home.

"You're always complaining that we don't spend enough time together. Besides, Mac's nuts."

"One hour tops, well, maybe two. Take a nap and you'll never know Mac's here." I couldn't miss this appointment. It's my job to sign off on every last detail.

The front door opened. "Honey, it's your mother!" she yelled.

"We're in the living room," I said.

"I'm ready for some fun." Mother walked into the living room and tossed her purse onto the chair. "Who kicked the crap out of you?" She smiled at Zach.

I hugged her and whispered, "Be nice."

"Car accident. Slight concussion. Madison's nursing me back to health." Zach didn't look happy.

"Can you stay with him for an hour while I go to an electrical inspection?" I asked Mother. "He might be your pretend son-in-law if we move in together. You two can use the time to bond."

"Can you get me a bottle of water?" Zach asked. "Where are you going? When will you be back?"

I ignored Zach's questions and walked into the kitchen. I knew they were just beginning.

Mother, hot on my heels, whispered, "He's going to drive you crazy because he's not sick and will make a nuisance of himself."

"This carwash project is important to me; I gave my word it would come in on time. Then I'll hurry home." I unscrewed the cap on the bottle and took it to Zach.

"What the hell are you talking about? What carwash project?" Zach demanded. "I thought it burned down."

Mother smirked, reveling in the fact that she wasn't the last person to know this time.

"You know the carwash got torched on my watch, so to speak. I agreed to oversee the renovations, making sure everything is up to code. My budget doesn't allow for my guys to sit around and do nothing. If there's downtime, I'll have to let them go; they'll move onto other jobs and I'm left to find another crew."

"Why would Ivers hire you? You're not qualified," Zach snorted.

Creole's kiss left my nerves stretched tight. "I am, too, damn it," I blew out a loud breath of frustration. "I juggled the paperwork on all of Jax's projects and was good at it, and everyone made money. Take a nap or something."

"How long are you staying?" Mother asked Zach, sitting in a chair across from him.

"A few days." Zach smirked at Mother. "We may make it permanent and live together. I'd like Madison to move into the warehouse."

The front door banged open. "Anyone home?" Brad called.

Now what? I looked at my watch. I hated it when people were late and I didn't tolerate it in myself.

"Doesn't anyone call first?" Zach asked.

"You don't, and neither does anyone else. And that's my brother."

Brad set a big cooler on the kitchen island. "We're having fresh grouper for dinner. Fresh out of the Gulf this morning." After every trip, Brad always shared fish with the family; you'd think we'd get tired of it. There were perks to having a commercial fisherman in the family.

Julie followed in behind, setting down a large salad bowl and shopping bag. Liam had a pink dessert box.

Liam ran over and hugged me. "I like family dinners."

"Madison," Brad said, "I called the cook at your dive bar and he's delivering that rice everyone likes and vegetables on skewers for barbequing."

Liam threw himself on the end of the couch and stared at Zach. "Who beat you up?"

"Car accident," Zach grumbled.

If Liam noticed Zach glare at him, he didn't let on. He clearly wasn't impressed with Zach's explanation.

"He's so modest." I stood protectively behind Liam. "Six guys jumped him in an alley, he beat them all off and they're in the hospital."

"Way cool," Liam laughed. "I'd tell everybody Madison's version of it if it was me."

Julie and Brad sat in the oversized chair together, my most favorite piece of furniture. Aunt Elizabeth had purchased the chair in an upscale beach store and I'd had it re-covered.

"Dude, you look like crap," Brad said to Zach.

Mother piped up. "Zach and Madison are moving in together."

Brad slapped his knee and laughed. "Twenty bucks says you don't last a week."

Liam grabbed my ringing phone off the island and handed it to me when I came into the kitchen. "I'm on my way," I answered, then asked Julie, "Will you look after Zach while I'm gone? I'll hurry back."

Zach pointed to my phone, hand up; he wanted me to tell him about the call. "I'll go with you," he said.

Mother, hot on my heels, opened the refrigerator door and stuck her head in, then laughed. She knew questioning me drove me crazy. "I'll hurry," I told Zach. I rushed out the door before one more person could say a word.

Zach needed to understand, there'd be a snowstorm in hell before I moved into his warehouse. I'd only gone back to his loft once since I shot someone in the living room. If there were to be any house playing, it would have to be at my house. He would need to get used to the fact that people came and went and that wouldn't change. It only bothered me when someone pointed a gun.

* * *

I pulled up to Clean Bubbles and the city pickup truck sat in one of the wash bays. It surprised me to see one of my aunt's friends, whom I hadn't seen since the funeral, leaning against the wall.

"Hi, Quatro," I said. He'd earned the nickname because he had four fingers on each hand.

I nodded to Ben, the project manager. The first time I met him he fidgeted around, a tall string bean, just out of prison. Long hours in the sun had been good for him; he filled out, had a dark tan, and carried himself with confidence. One of Spoon's boys. Ben had driven the getaway car in a bank robbery. His words: "I was young and stupid, looking for a free ride, and thankfully no one died."

Ben proved his skills at Jake's. He managed the men, followed my directions, and refrained from telling me I didn't know what I was talking about. We worked well together.

Quatro handed me his business card. "I don't think I told you, but Elizabeth's funeral was the best I've ever been to." He had trimmed his beer gut to fit into his city uniform of jean shorts and a city-monogrammed golf shirt.

"I didn't know you worked for the

county." I looked at his card.

"I drive around all day, post the appropriate stickers, and schmooze my ass off. Lunch with the guys at Roscoe's every day. Now there's a cheap bastard. Good hamburgers, but we have to bring our own chairs."

Roscoe's served the best burgers in The Keys. But after a couple of fights broke out, he discouraged loitering. His policy: Take your food and go home.

"Did we pass inspection?" I asked.

"The electrical reports came across my desk; I got my butt over here quick. Must have cost a pretty penny to update from knob and tube." Quatro tapped his clipboard, hooking his pen inside his shirt. "You're all signed off and legal."

"Appreciate your speed. Stop by Jake's anytime and have a beer on me." I had tucked a couple of business cards in my pocket and handed him one.

"Surprised old man Ivers didn't bulldoze. Who washes their own car? They're usually a front for money laundering."

"Another week for paint and we'll be done here," Ben told me.

"Got two more inspections. You need anything expedited, give me call." Quatro shook hands with Ben.

Ben checked out Quatro's hand with a

look of surprise. "Dude, what happened to your fingers?"

I wanted to ask the same question but hadn't figured a way to work it into the conversation. The funeral didn't seem appropriate.

"An old girlfriend hacked off one during a fight. The other got cut off in a snow blower." Quatro flexed his remaining fingers.

Why did it take a missing finger or other appendage for some men to realize the girlfriend's unstable? My guess is in the pursuit of hot sex, the littler brain thinks it's worth the chance. "Snow blower? In Florida?"

"Picked it up in a garage sale. Thought I could fix it and sell it to a snowbird. Can you believe the doctors couldn't sew either finger back on? I kept them, but eventually the dog ate them both."

There was a moment of silence. I didn't dare look at Ben; I might start laughing.

"What happened to the dog?" Ben asked.

"Pinto died from old age; a collie, the best dog ever." Quatro pulled out his keys. "Now I've got two Saint Bernards the size of small horses. The neighbors moved away and left them locked up in a rental house. They complained about how big they got. I asked them once if they ever looked at their paws; that would be a tip-off as to how big they'd get."

"Why leave them locked up?" Who thought that was a good idea? "Couldn't they take them to the pound or rescue or something?" I hated stories of animal cruelty.

"Jäger and Whiskey got a good home now. My grandkids love them. I think the dogs are secretly glad the kids don't live with us. They need rest time to build their stamina before the next play date." Quatro checked his watch. "I've got another stop." He waved and got in his truck.

"I've started my own gig." Ben handed me a card. "You got any more jobs, call me direct. Spoon still sends referrals."

"I'm also happy to give you a reference. Every job you've done for me has been excellent."

"I met your mother, she's a live one." Ben gave me a half smile nod of his head. "Gave me a cigar. A little strong, so I smoke two, three puffs at a time."

My phone rang. I looked at the screen and groaned. "Zach." I pushed ignore. "See you at the grand re-opening."

"I'm with four fingers. The only time this place had a lineup had to do with illegal business and nothing to do with clean cars, more about getting their hydro before it ran out. That's good quality pot in case you didn't know."

"Considering I don't use them, I know more about drugs than I ever wanted to know."

Chapter 32

On my drive to The Cottages, I wondered how bad the lecture from Zach would be for ignoring his phone calls and being late. I swung into the driveway. Everything looked quiet, no lurkers on the street or in the driveway. I could see through my windshield that there was a note taped to the office door.

I bet myself a dollar it read, "At the pool."

"I win," I said to no one.

Mac and Shirl were sunning by the pool in two-piece bathing suits. "'Lifeguard' is not one of your job duties," I said to Mac, letting the gate bang behind me.

"I've got a dress I can pull on if any paying people show up." Mac said before she pointed to a piece of cloth bundled up over a chair.

"I haven't forgotten about you," I said to Shirl, pulling up a chair. "Fab and I will retrieve your belongings this week."

"Ronnie doesn't get to keep your stuff," Mac huffed. Ronnie was Shirl's ex, and apparently not happy over the breakup.

I kicked off my flip-flops, got up, and put my feet in the pool. "How about a raise?"

"That depends, is it legal?" Mac looked at me over the top of her sunglasses.

"My plan is to shuffle Jake's paperwork off on you. The books were set up by the CPA; same procedures are in place as The Cottage's books. And find Apple for me." I knew the mention of our favorite homeless drunk would peak her interest.

"About her," Mac started. "Apple came by here the other day. I gave her money out of petty cash when she confirmed the clean pee storyline and that Miss J is branching out, peddling her urine to anyone with cash."

Somehow I had to convince Miss January her new entrepreneurial spirit could land her in jail. "I thought Apple graduated from the half-way house and got a life. Is she back on the streets?"

Memories of Apple rolling around the floor naked with my ex-husband when I thought we were still happily married had receded. Then one day, I stumbled over her panhandling. I helped give her an option to get off of the streets by giving her the name of a women's shelter, but it had been up to her to make the first step.

"Apple left the program early. She hooked up with Angie and moved into a one-room apartment over the cleaners. No air conditioning. That's a nice feeling, sweat running down your body 24/7 in the summertime." Mac stopped to suck down the rest of her energy drink. "Everything was fine until Angie showed up for an 11:00 a.m., stinkin' drunk. Apple has given herself the title of 'Social Drinker.' They're one paycheck away from eviction."

I kicked water on Mac. "I've got a proposition for Apple and Angie that might keep them off the streets."

"Are you going to run hookers now?" Shirl belly-laughed. "Lordee, I'm funny." She slapped her thigh.

I fished my ringing phone out of my pocket. "It's about time. Where the hell have you been?"

"Can't a girl get a few minutes of peace?" Fab whined. "I'm on my way back to the house."

"I'm out of patience today," I warned her. "Meet me at Wino's. We've got a couple of jobs to discuss."

Wino's just opened recently, a wine bar for people who preferred their wine out of a bottle with a cork, as opposed to a screw top. The added bonus—outside seating.

"Why can't we do that by the pool?" Fab laid on her horn.

"Mother and Brad threw a pool party. The house is full of people; we wouldn't get a minute of privacy." I'd break the news about Zach in person, after securing a promise she wouldn't ditch me and move.

The screen lit up with Zach calling. I sent him to voicemail.

"How's Zach doing?" Shirl asked. "He was a big pain-in-the-ass patient."

I got out of the pool and slipped into my flip-flops. "How long before Zach's one hundred percent?" I asked Shirl.

"Bet he's milking his headache for all it's worth. The doctor told him to call and make an appointment if he had any lingering symptoms after a day or two. Then he'll need brain surgery." Shirl gave a shout of laughter. "Seriously, it was a very mild rap to the head. Dr. A rolled his eyes when he signed him out, mouthing, 'asshole.'"

"I'm glad I relaxed the rule on long-term tenants; you're working out." I pointed to Mac and reminded her, "One time only."

* * *

Here I was, a grown woman, worried that I missed curfew by a couple of hours. Fab had scored us a sidewalk table at Wino's. A glass of Cabernet awaited me.

Just as I stepped out of the car, my phone rang; this time it said "Mother." This could be a trick. I threw the phone on the passenger seat. I felt extreme guilt about being a crappy girlfriend who didn't want to sit and stare at her boyfriend all day. But not enough to go home just yet.

"We can skip the lecture about your disappearance, if you make me a promise."

"I went back to the condo for a second look around, are you happy?" Fab narrowed her eyes. "Before you ask, nosey, I found two keys that he stuffed inside a light fixture."

I gulped what was probably very good wine that didn't deserve not to be savored.

"Next time I ransack a place, I'll be sure to remember that tip. Any idea what they go to?" I clinked glasses with her, almost forgetting my wine etiquette.

"Not a safety deposit box, so that takes sneaking into a bank vault off the table."

Shoo, that sounded like a felony to me. "Hold up your right hand and best-friend swear to my promise." Being a good example, I held up my hand.

"Okay, what? You're so dramatic," Fab said.

"Promise me you will not move out." I had a horrible feeling that if Zach and I moved in together, that would be the end of my relationship with my best friend. I wanted to keep all of my friends.

"I knew this was weird," Fab hit her hand on the table. "What's going on?"

"Zach got into a car accident, has a concussion, and is recuperating for a couple of days at the house."

"Days? And nights too?" Fab shrieked.

I lowered my voice to a deep growl and mimicked Zach, "Get me a pillow, and water, hold my hand, stare at me. I can't take it already. My favorite is 'who's on the phone?'"

Fab gave me her creepy smile. "He won't last." Her phone rang and she answered. After a pause, she said, "I've been busy, what's up?" She hit the Speaker button.

"'Busy,' my ass. You were probably doing something illegal. You better not go to jail again," Mother lectured, "Do you hear me?"

"You could be a little nicer, I've had a bad day."

"You know I love you and nothing better happen to you. Do you understand me?"

"Yes, Madame." Fab sounded sincere but she smirked at me.

"We're having a family party and you're not here. Bring my other daughter and get the hell over here."

"I don't...."

"Don't bother lying. You suck at it. Fifteen minutes and I want you both walking through the front door." Mother hung up the phone.

"Is she going to ground me?" Fab asked.

I laughed at the look on Fab's face. She had no control over Mother and that frustrated her.

"How mad was Creole after I snuck

out?" Fab handed me my wine glass. "Gulp this down and let's go."

"Cut the man a break. He's been generous in giving you information; you need to return the favor. Have you noticed he helps us every time he can?" I finished off my wine. "Creole was livid and he took out his frustration on my lips."

Fab whistled. "How was that? Oh, don't give me that innocent look," she said. "You sample that and you'll be thinking, 'Zach who?' Do you notice that Creole, for the most part, doesn't care what you do?"

"I'm in love with Zach," I said, but I didn't want to give up half my life to be with him.

"Then why did you just suck down the last of the wine? You could be home playing sexy nurse to his annoying self," Fab watched me closely. "Who's better, Zach or Creole?"

"They're both good, but very different." I fingered my lips. "We've only got five minutes before the second deadline of my day comes and goes."

Chapter 33

Fab got bored driving the speed limit and sped by me, so I arrived long after her. I walked by the kitchen window and Spoon gave me a quick wave and resumed washing dishes.

"Took you long enough," Fab said after she opened the front door with a big smile. "Didier's back. Ha-ha, Zach's not enjoying the party."

I took a deep breath, pushed my bag into Fab's arms, and walked into the living room. Zach sat rooted in the same spot I left him in, a look of thinly-disguised fury on his face. "Sorry it took so long." I bent and kissed him on the lips. "Good news, re-opening the carwash is just days away."

Zach's gaze wandered to the kitchen where Didier joined Spoon, who was putting dishes in the dishwasher. "The party got bigger after you left."

"No one will bother you in the bedroom," I said, hoping he realized if that was what he chose that he would be entertaining himself. I had zero plans of sitting in my room like a disobedient child.

"What I really want is a beer," Zach snapped, rubbing his temples.

"Probably not a good idea. Hanging out by the pool always makes me feel better." I ran my fingers across his cheek and brushed his hair back.

Zach grabbed my wrist and pulled me down next to him. "Tell me about your involvement in Clean Bubbles."

Fab cut in, pulling on Zach's arm. "Come on invalid, we're moving the party outside and that includes you. Get your ass up or I'll tell Madeline on you." She turned to me, saying, "Go put your bathing suit on."

Relieved for a getaway, I flew off the couch and up the stairs. I sighed, leaning against my bedroom door. I was happy to not be grilled and have to check my response before it came out of my mouth.

I slipped into my new turquoise tankini, tying a sheer colorful wrap around my waist, low on my hips. I pulled my curly mess up into a ponytail. A swim would put me in the party mood. If I could manage to stop worrying over Zach's every sigh, he might loosen up and enjoy himself.

***

From the top of the stairs, I recognized Creole's back, talking to Zach. They had been childhood best buddies, but their friendship ended when Zach thought Creole had come back to town as drug dealing scum. Only after Mother forced them to talk did Creole fess up to being DEA assigned to the Miami office. The trust between them was tentative. It didn't help that Creole told Zach he was biding his time until Zach screwed up so that he could sweep me off my feet.

Zach had me in his sights, staring intently as I walked down the stairs. Creole turned around, winked, and stripped my clothes off with his gaze. Didier met me at the bottom of the stairs and offered his arm.

I spoke to Didier in my best French accent that I practiced in the bathroom mirror.

"So, you think I'm charming?" Didier whispered against my ear. "How about if I drive those two thugs over there crazy?" He motioned to Zach and Creole. Didier put his hand at the back of my neck and whispered in French.

I blushed and giggled. "You know, I didn't understand a word of that."

Didier laughed. "I complimented the way you look in your bathing suit and threw in something slightly naughty."

My cheeks burned. "I love that you and Fab are together. You are really good for her. She's softer, less intense because of you. Treat her good or I'll shoot you."

Didier glanced over his shoulder. "Which one is it going to be? Say the word, Fab will shoot one of them for you."

Fab put her arm around Didier. "What

are you two whispering about?" She had on three pieces of black material, held together with string.

"Didier was telling me how cute I am," I said.

"Do you think I'd have an ugly friend?" Fab looked horrified.

"That's shallow," I bit my lip.

Didier kissed Fab. "I love her bold honesty. I never wonder where I stand with her, she tells me, and sometimes quite loudly."

Mother yelled, "Listen up!" She paused until everyone stopped talking. "Dinner's ready and we're all eating outside. That includes you." She pointed to Zach.

I whispered to Fab as we moved to the patio. "We need to talk. We've got a job. A freebie."

"This side of the partnership doesn't work for free."

I poked Fab. "You tell Shirl you'll be sending her a bill."

"Shirl's a nurse who could come in handy. Make it clear—free for you, fine, but she owes me."

I had no intention of telling Fab that Shirl would be excited to "owe" Fab.

Mother pushed together the tables so that everyone could sit together. She had chosen all the shell-themed dishes from my collection and arranged all the side dishes, covered with wire mesh bug deterrents, on my latest backyard project—a new countertop installed by Ben. He added storage underneath and a small sink. I added my personal touch, ordering several bags of seashells to cover the entire top of the counter and overhang. After a few ugly starts, I finally got it right.

I sat down next to Zach and kissed his cheek, "See what you miss out on when you only show up in the middle of the night?"

He glared at me. "You didn't return any of my calls."

Brad set a huge platter of assorted barbequed fish in the middle of the table. They were sitting on a bed of rice with skewers of grilled vegetables.

"Guess what we saw yesterday?" Liam flopped in the chair next to me.

"Don't look at me," Fab said. "I know already."

I grabbed my chest and looked at Liam. "I'm the last to know?"

Liam laughed. "We went to an alligator farm, and a tourist showing off tried to pet it and got chunks eaten out of his arm, and blood spurted everywhere. At first, Mom said I couldn't look and then changed her mind. She pointed to the sign that said, 'No molesting the alligators.'"

"Did he croak?" Creole asked.

"The alligator was fine," Liam laughed.

I nudged him, "The dude."

"When he looked down and saw himself covered in blood, he passed out; but he woke up by the time they rolled him into the medic van," Liam said. "I'm a kid and even I know that petting the alligators is a terrible idea. I called Kevin to see if the dude died and he checked and said no, but he's in the jail ward of the hospital, since he got arrested for being a stupid ass."

Everyone at the table laughed.

"Remind me to talk to Kevin about how he describes his 'cool arrest stories,'" Julie said.

"How was jail?" Liam asked Fab.

That brought silence to the table, everyone looking uncomfortable. Zach laughed.

"Not a lot of fun, the food's terrible. Thank you for asking." Fab winked at Liam. "Hey, hotshot," she said, and looked at Creole, "my cellmate said she didn't murder anyone either and I believed her. Can you help another girl out?"

Creole banged the table. "You've got a lot of nerve. NO!"

"Just figuring that out?" Zach mumbled.

"We should talk after dinner," Fab said quietly.

Mother, Julie, and I glared at Creole.

Brad laughed at Creole. "You're so stupid. You need a couple of lessons dealing with Westin women."

"Why can't I say stupid?" Liam asked his mom. "Does Brad have to apologize?"

Julie turned her head and made what sounded like a cough.

Spoon deflected the conversation. "When are you coming by my auto body for a tour?" he asked Liam.

"We're coming soon." Liam sent a high five his way. "Brad's restoring a 1962 Corvette and needs parts. Joseph said you're the only man in The Keys who can get anything a person needs."

"I'll bet," Zach said under his breath.

Brad wasn't all that sold on Spoon as a suitable boyfriend for Mother. I thought the two of them working together on this restoration project was a good way to show they had more in common than differences. "What do you like most about Spoon, Mother?" I asked.

Mother kissed his cheek, a big statement to everyone at the table. They were no longer sneaking around; they just became official. "That's easy, how often does a woman find someone to enjoy a Jack on the rocks and a cigar with who makes her laugh?"

I glared at Brad with a warning look that said, *Do not upset Mother.*

Brad shook his head, not convinced. "And you, Spoon?"

"Miss Madeline accepts me for all my flaws and doesn't hold my past against me. Emphasis on past," Spoon said.

Well done Spoon, he easily held his own. "Time for dessert." I stood up. "Fab and I will clear these plates." I followed Fab into the kitchen.

Julie trailed behind us. "Your mother just asked Zach when she'd get to meet his family."

The three of us stood at the island. "He's going to think I put her up to that," I groaned. "What did he say?"

"Not until you committed to something more than sleeping together," Julie said. "That brought the conversation to a halt. I thought Brad would punch him."

"Did you meet the Lazarro family?" I asked Fab.

Julie looked surprised. "Did you and Zach...?"

"We had sex a long damned time ago," Fab said. "The last time I met a boy's family was in high school. Both families prayed the romance would be short-lived."

"What about Gabriel's family?" I asked, wrapping up food.

"Gabriel's family tree consisted mostly of criminals. They loved me. His father helped me perfect my pickpocket skills. His mother, a true wino, sipped from morning until night and played board games in between. His uncle Leon, who lived with them, hit on me at every family get together."

"We're taking our dessert home with us." Julie cut pieces of Key Lime pie and put them on a plate. "The three of us are getting up early for a road trip. Liam's working on a class project."

A pair of male arms went around me. "I sense trouble in paradise and I'm keeping my eye on you." Creole kissed my neck. "I'm reminding you of your promise to right of first refusal." His hand traced my cheek, down to my shoulder.

Fab smirked and Julie's jaw dropped, neither said a word.

I had to push hard to step away. "Are you leaving?"

"Criminals don't keep banker's hours." Creole squeezed my cheeks together and planted a hard kiss on my lips.

"Before you go," Fab opened the junk drawer and handed him two keys, "I found these and have no clue what they're for."

I gave Fab a thumbs up behind his back.

Creole tossed them in his hand. "Do you mind if I take them? You have my promise you'll get them back. I have a colleague who'll be able to tell us what they unlock."

"Madison vouched for you," Fab warned.

"Are you worried I'll sneak out on you, lie to your face? Not my style." Creole's eyes narrowed. "Get me the info on your girlfriend from jail. I'll look into it." He left out the front door.

Mother came into the kitchen, hands loaded with dishes. "Mind if I spend the night? Spoon's driving to Orlando to pick up a Lamborghini in a few hours."

"See you later. Didier and I are going for a walk on the beach." Fab looped her arm in Didier's, who'd just shown up at her side.

With all the helping hands, we cleaned up the kitchen in record time.

"Where are you guys going tomorrow?" I hugged Liam. Brad and Julie waited at the door.

"We're touring Hemingway's House in Key West. Then I'm going to write a report for my English class," Liam said.

I wanted to follow everyone out the door. Instead, I stood in the entryway and hoped Zach and I weren't about to start a fight. I blew out a deep breath and joined Zach on the couch.

"Are we finally alone?" Zach asked.

"Not for long. Fab and Didier won't walk on the beach all night and Mother's sleeping over. Spoon's got a job."

He arched his brow. "Who works in the middle of the night?"

"You do, for one," I reminded him.

Zach gripped my arms and pulled me onto his chest. "I'm a terrible patient. I don't know how to sit and do nothing." He ran his fingers down my back and over my butt. He kissed me hard.

"Where is your mother sleeping?" Zach whispered.

"I'm not asking her to sleep on the couch," I giggled.

His mouth ascended on mine, his tongue flirted and teased, our mouths locked together. I wiggled against him while he kissed me into a coma.

The front door opened. "Hey, sis, I'm back. Look who I found on the sidewalk."

"We're in the living room."

Brad and Mother walked in together. "Mother lurked at the end of your driveway, smoking like a thug. Since we're leaving early for Key West, I thought I'd spend the night. What do you say, Zach, a slumber party?"

I buried my face on Zach's chest and laughed.

"You and me in the living room," Brad said to Zach. "We can stay up all night, get to know one another."

Zach's bad mood came back in full bloom. "Sounds great," he said dryly.

Brad went to the garage and started dragging in the blow-up bed.

Chapter 34

"What are you doing? It's dark outside," I grumbled.

Mother had gotten out of bed, turned on the light, and stuck her head out the bedroom door, back in two seconds. "Fab left a piece of string on her door."

I pulled the covers over my head and peeked out. "Didier's here, she's busy. Turn the light off."

"You're awake. I want to know what's going on. If I wait until breakfast, you'll eat and sneak out the door." Mother unplugged her phone.

"Who are you calling at this hour?"

"Don't 'what' me," Mother said into the phone. "Get in here; we're in Madison's bedroom."

The bedroom door opened. Fab came in and to my astonishment, closed it quietly. "There are two of you and neither can tell time?" Fab was wearing one of Didier's T-shirts and had the morning sexy look going for her, her hair tousled, no makeup, and tan legs under the shirt. I groaned that I never looked that good in the morning.

"This wasn't my idea," I said.

Mother pinned Fab with a stare, sitting

back on the bed. "What's the latest on your case?"

"No suspects, except for me. At least the cops know I didn't do it, although they're not letting me off the hook just yet." Fab climbed onto the bed, lying sideways at the foot.

"Why is Creole mad at you?" Mother continued her grilling. I didn't smirk at Fab because Mother would be questioning me next.

"It's all good. Madison convinced me I could trust him. He's on probation with me right now. We'll see how information sharing works out."

"I thought you two promised to keep me in the loop," Mother said.

"That was Madison," Fab said.

Mother glared at her.

Fab jumped off the bed. "Okay, me too."

Mother jerked the sheet off my face. "Sit back down," she said, pointing to Fab. "What's with you and a carwash?"

"Mr. Ivers is giving me half interest in exchange for evicting the road-kill specialists and getting it up and running again."

"What's wrong with cash?" Mother asked.

"My point exactly," Fab said.

I kicked Fab under the covers. If I told them it sounded fun to own a car wash, they might think I'd lost my mind.

"Honey, I hate to tell you this, but

nobody washes their own car," Mother said.

I was sick of hearing that argument. "You two just wait. And no, I'm not telling you my plan. I feel the definite lack of support."

"If this early-morning chat is over, I'm going back to bed. Next time," Fab said, "wait until after I've had my morning latte." When Mother stayed silent, she rolled off the bed. She opened the door and poked her head out. "What is wrong with you people? The guys are moving around downstairs."

"She's clearly not a morning person," Mother said.

* * *

Mother drove to The Bakery Café and brought back enough breakfast food to feed twenty. I wolfed down an egg soufflé and fruit.

Slice and Zach commandeered the patio for AZL business. I'd be surprised if Zach didn't sneak out with his partner now that he had the house to himself, unable to stand another day at Casa Madison. Brad left first to pick up Julie and Liam. They had plans to stop for breakfast in Islamorada. With people coming and going, it made it easier to drop a kiss on Zach's cheek, making my getaway with no questions.

"I don't get you and Zach." I looked at Fab. "You two have some kind of disagreement that neither of you got over?"

"Zach never wanted you and me to be

friends. Everything bad that happens to you he blames on me. Hell, I didn't even know that last psycho. Did I mention he hates sneaking out in the morning and seeing me lean against my bedroom door?"

My phone rang, Mac's name popping up. "I got an address for Apple. She and Angie have been evicted and they're camped out in an abandoned house. The bright coral one on Begonia."

"Does Apple still have a job?" I asked.

"She waitresses nights at Custer's," Mac said. "It's standing-room only every night with the locals."

I couldn't believe Apple made enough money from that bar, the first choice for hardened drunks. She'd never be able to move.

Fab and I headed to Ronnie's. Time to deal with Shirl's ex-boyfriend. We needed to check him out and size up the job.

"Personally, I'd like to kick the door in and bind and threaten him until he gives up the boxes."

Fab turned onto Plumeria, where most of the homes on the block were '50s style small block homes. A few had been replaced by two-story stilt homes that were now mandated by code.

"Moving truck in front of Shirl's old place; that can't be good," Fab pointed out.

"Do a slow drive-by. It's Mercy House

and the guys are loading boxes from the garage. I'll bet you it's Shirl's stuff." Mercy House is a women's shelter that runs a resale shop, selling used household items and furniture. I reached into my wallet and took out money. "You keep Ronnie busy and I'll buy a little information."

"Why me?" Fab looked at me. "Don't you dare channel your mother, I can't take anymore today."

I almost laughed. Fab just needed to get used to the idea that Mother would mind her business whether she liked it or not. "Whatever you do, don't threaten him or take out your gun. Shirl told me he has 911 on speed dial so he can complain on a regular basis."

Fab and I split up, she wiggled her butt up the driveway straight to the waiting Ronnie. His awestruck look said he thought he just got lucky.

Men are so easy. I cut around the far side of the Mercy House truck completely out of Ronnie's view. Two young guys rolled their dollies, piled high with boxes, up the ramp.

"What's up, sister?" The taller of the two asked, rivers of sweat running down his face, collecting in the rag around his neck. Both had Mercy House T-shirts and long jeans on, which mystified me; must be a safety issue.

I held out the money saying, "Answer a

couple of questions and you get one and your friend gets the other."

He looked me up and down, lingering an extra beat on my chest and legs. "Why should we?"

"If I have to blow time calling Wendy for permission, then no money. Any idea what's in those boxes you're loading?" I asked.

Wendy and I became friends after I needed her help on another weird case from Brick. Then I found out she and Spoon were friends and that sealed the deal.

The other one spoke up, "The man's wife died and he's boxed her belongings for donation." He grinned at the other man.

"Last stop, warehouse at the docks?" I noticed the first guy had pushed all the boxes up against the rear wall.

"Yep, one more stop and we're headed that way."

I handed over the money and a business card. "Stop by Jake's sometime and tell the bartender, free beer on Madison."

I raced back to the Hummer and jumped in. I leaned across from the passenger seat, laying on the horn. Fab was always happier when she drove, even though there were times it made me nauseous.

Fab opened the door. "Ronnie's disgusting. And another damned dog. All dogs hate me, except Grover. What? Do I have dog cooties?"

"Head over to Mercy House, we'll broker a deal with Wendy. At least we didn't have to break into the garage in the middle of the night."

"Terrible idea. Ronnie's boxer barked and growled when I walked up. Ronnie called him off, but I noticed he had to jerk the collar a couple of times. The dog stared me down."

"How did Shirl sneak into a cottage? That violates your no-long-term-tenant rule," Fab asked.

"I think having a nurse living there is a good idea. Since I have two tenants who are supposed to die any day, she could come in handy. For my own selfish reasons, I'd like advance notice of impending death. Like a hospital trip or something. I'm fond of Joseph and Miss January; it would break my heart if one of them keeled over. I need time for a quick good-bye to kiss their wrinkly cheeks."

"Do you suppose Joseph has chosen Svetlana's next husband?" Fab asked.

"Did you know she's anatomically correct?" I managed to ask with a straight face.

Fab put her finger in her mouth. "Eww. You don't suppose he...."

"Oh stop. Yes, I do think he does...whatever. And I refuse to think about it."

* * *

"How long is this going to take?" Fab grumbled. "Do I need to remind you this is another one of your free-ass jobs?"

"Rest up and get ready to use your muscle. We'll load the boxes and take them to The Cottages. Once I get the okay, I'll call Mac and have her bring her pickup. I refuse to ride in her truck. I'd have to throw myself on the seat and hoist myself in, which I'd never manage without showing my butt. We could stop and get your Ferrari. How many boxes could we get in there?"

Fab gave me a dirty look. "No boxes, no food, nothing in my car." She pulled up in front of Mercy House, getting the only empty parking space. "I'll wait here and watch for the truck."

Wendy waved when she saw me come through the doors. "I'm afraid to ask what brings you here." She closed the few feet between us.

I related the details of Shirl and Ronnie and how he'd just donated all of her lifelong possessions.

"That's not the first time that's happened," Wendy sighed. "Usually, though, it's the ex-wife who's been cheated on and left for the other woman."

"Look over the boxes, place a resale value on them, and I'll write a check," I said.

"I think you were sent here for another

purpose. We're due to have our annual employee dinner and this year the budget is tight. There are twelve of us, what if we come to Jake's and you give us a discount?"

"I can make that happen. If you'd like I can seat all of you out on the deck. It's nice out there with all of the twinkling lights. You could have it to yourself." After rebuilding the deck, the new tables and chairs were a fun purchase, ceiling fans every few feet. Every inch decorated with small white Christmas lights and tiki torches.

"That would be better than anything we've had in the past."

"Done," I said. "Write down the dates and I'll take care of the rest."

"Have you kept track of Apple?" Wendy's eyes looked troubled. "She started the sober program with some potential, then she got a job and old demons beckoned her with the promise she could drink a little."

Wendy had fast-tracked Apple into a detox program, although she didn't believe her to be the ideal candidate. Apple, out of options at the time, grabbed the opportunity. She hung in longer than I thought she would and surpassed my expectations.

"So far, Apple's been able to hold her life together. Her partner hasn't had such good luck. Angie just lost her job. Apple is a survivor. She survived life on the streets all that time, I couldn't have done that."

"Truck's here!" Fab shouted inside the door.

The doors rolled up, and the truck backed into the warehouse. Wendy met the driver. "Do you remember what boxes you picked up off Plumeria?"

I watched in horror as Mac screamed around the corner in her truck, using her brakes at the last second. "That's Mac, she's with me."

"The last stop only had two boxes and a load of toys." Ricky nodded to me. "We can unload them first."

Fab pulled on Ricky's arm. "You and your friend load these boxes in the Hummer and that black pickup, and I'll pay you." She stared at me.

I had the same thought but didn't say anything. My next words were going to be 'thank you.'

It took the guys less than ten minutes. They secured the boxes in the pickup with rope that Mac produced. Cash exchanged hands and both men smiled at Fab, another happy transaction.

I yelled to Mac who was in her truck, revving her engine like a teenage boy in daddy's truck. "We'll follow you, in case a box falls off; Fab can jump out and retrieve it!"

"I'll run over it, *oops*." Fab laughed at

her own joke.

* * *

"Didn't anyone in this neighborhood notice a couple of squatters moved in?" Fab asked. "Why do you want to talk to Apple anyway?"

They were in a regular neighborhood, a block from the Intracoastal Waterway. There was a mixture of well-maintained bungalow style and two-story homes where no one neglected their yards.

"I have a business proposition for her."

Fab pulled into the driveway of the vacant pinkish house, a little too much art deco in the paint colors. The other homes were more subdued. There was a 'Keep Out' sign posted prominently in the front window, and the doorknob had been removed and now padlocked top and bottom.

"Let's go around the back," I said. The front looked freshly mowed, probably by a neighbor.

The backyard told the real story of how long the house stood vacant. We tromped through the knee-high weeds. None of the windows had coverings, with the exception of one.

Fab looked around. "Your call. I'm here for back up, even though I don't think shots will ring out."

I brushed the small bugs off my legs,

went deeper into the weeds, and knocked on the bedroom window. "Hey, Apple!" I yelled.

"The neighbors know they have squatters now," Fab said.

The sheet moved slightly, then a hand unlocked the window. Apple stuck her head through the screenless window, her stringy hair hanging in her face. She had an odd pallor, looking as if I woke her from a nightmare.

"What's up?" Apple brushed her hair back with one hand, covered her breasts with the other.

"I've got a job offer for you and your friend, Angie. Can you be at The Cottages in an hour?" This had started out as a good idea, or so I thought.

Apple held up her hand and disappeared behind the sheet.

"Why Apple? She's the only one you could think of?" Fab asked.

Apple's hand reappeared in the window, this time not bothering with any modesty. "Angie and I will be there. Will you let us shower and do you have coffee?"

"I can get that all covered."

"Half hour." Apple waved and it took her two tries to bang the window closed.

"The mosquitoes are feasting on my legs in groups. Let's get the hell out of here." Fab took off. She had on shorts, showing off the long legs that she used to crawl into other people's windows.

I fished my phone out of my skirt pocket and pushed speed dial for Mac. "Can you make a pot of coffee? Apple and Angie are headed over. Let them use the office bathroom to shower."

"Cooties in my bathroom!" Mac shrieked.

"Aren't you current on your shots?" I asked. "They're on their way over." I hung up before she could tell me, "No way."

Apple and Angie arrived fifteen minutes after we did, huge backpacks slung over their shoulders, holding what I guessed to be everything they owned. They showered together and changed in record time. "Do you mind if we do our laundry?" Apple asked, sitting on the couch next to Angie.

Angie sat quietly, white as a sheet, hung over. She'd clearly been puking all night.

Mac glared at me and shook her head *no*.

"Sure. Sorry to hear you lost your apartment," I said.

"As soon as Angie gets a job we'll be moving out. I'm used to not having electricity, but the water was shut off last week and the water department put a lock on the meter. We're on the waiting list to get a room at Old Lady Jackson's rooming house."

Fab rolled her eyes and stood in the corner by the door, as far away as she could get without missing a word.

Five people crowded into the small office felt claustrophobic. "Let's go sit by the pool," I said.

Mac locked the office door after everyone shuffled out. "They used my bathroom, I'm listening in," she whispered.

I pushed opened the pool gate. "Have a seat." I motioned to the chairs around a table, pulling up another one.

Apple fidgeted. "I told Angie not to worry that your job offer probably had nothing to do with sex. I was right, wasn't I?"

Both Mac and Fab stared at me and laughed. It annoyed me that they both were enjoying my annoyance.

"Here's the deal, girls. I'm part owner of Clean Bubbles a block down from Jake's. It's currently self-serve. I want to offer full service. In the beginning, half will stay coin operated. I want to hire the two of you to wash cars and keep the place clean and stocked."

Angie came to life. "We get paid? Do we have to wear a uniform?"

"You get paid hourly and keep your tips. You wear what you want. A pair of shorts and T-shirt would be perfect. Shoes are a must for safety. No smoking in front of the customers, no showing up to work drunk, or getting drunk on the job." Only time would tell if this came back to be a butt-biter.

"Grand re-opening is next week. A new sign is going up, lots of balloons, free soda or water for anyone who gets a car wash. One more thing, you do one illegal act on the property, and you're fired."

"Let's talk, Apple." Angie stood and walked to the other side of the pool. Apple followed.

"Good idea." Mac nodded her head. "Every perv in town will stop to get their truck or bicycle washed."

"I'm impressed," Fab said. "I couldn't get anyone to put hard cash that you'd make a profit and you might actually now."

"I don't see them doing anything illegal except maybe a blow job or two," Mac said. "As long as they're smart enough not to quote a price and accept donations they'll be fine."

What a terrible way to supplement one's income.

"Ick." Fab made a choking noise. "Blow jobs by donation. Men will be lined up with their pocket change."

Apple and Angie came back to the table. "Are there set hours?" Apple asked. "Can Angie work by herself when I go to my other job?"

"I'm totally flexible. I'm sure you'll want to tailor your hours to when you'd make the most tips, such as afternoons and weekends," I said.

"We're in. It's going to be fun to roll in bubbles all day," Apple said. "You should get us T-shirts that say 'Clean Bubbles.' Get a smaller size; we both can squeeze into a large."

I had to admit Apple had a good idea. They were both well-endowed and didn't seem too embarrassed to use them as a selling tool. "Keep in touch with Mac. She'll have the details," I said.

Apple wiped her hand on her pants and held it out. "Sorry, I forgot," she said, and jerked it back. "Thanks for all your help. I really am sorry that I slept with your husband."

I winced. "Let's not bring that up again." I reached into my pocket and handed her money. "Go have lunch or something."

They both waved and shuffled out the gate.

"You two are suspiciously quiet." I wasn't feeling the love. "You were my first choice for the car wash job, but I know how busy you are," I said to Fab.

Chapter 35

Fab kicked the front door open like a breaking and entering criminal.

"Who's there?" Zach yelled.

I didn't expect to see my living room turned into an office. Zach had papers strewn all over the coffee table and he lay back on the couch with his laptop. "What's going on?"

Zach's phone rang; he put a finger to his lips and answered. From his side of the conversation, I could tell there were problems at the office.

I joined Fab in the kitchen, staring out the window. "There's a Mercedes sedan sitting out front. I've seen it before, as I recall it had no tags. Any reason someone would be surveilling us?"

Fab shook her head 'no.' "Nice ride," she said.

No one got in or out of the Mercedes, and it suddenly pulled away from the curb and disappeared from sight.

"Don't say a word to Zach," I whispered.

"Do you remember when you last saw the car?"

"A couple of days ago, I noticed it parked in the same place. I pulled in the driveway and when I got out it left." I took water from the refrigerator and handed one to Fab. "I noticed because it was brand new and I know it doesn't belong to anyone in the neighborhood."

"Once, maybe. Twice in the same place, and we need to be on guard," Fab said.

"What are you two whispering about?" Zach said.

"Does he ask what you're doing in the bathroom when the door's closed?" Fab gave him a disgusted look. "Be ready to be questioned like a perp."

Creole walked through the French doors. "Hey, ladies...and you," he said to Zach.

"How often do you stop by?" Zach demanded.

"Whenever I feel like it." Creole flipped him off. "I'm here to see Fab."

Fab swept past me. "Let's talk outside."

Zach grabbed my arm. "Don't get involved with whatever is going on there."

"Your phone is ringing," I told him, trying to hide my irritation. I hurried out to the patio and sat next to Fab.

Creole had the keys in his hand that Fab found while ransacking the condo. "My guy made copies." He handed her a small key. "He says this one is for a standard lock that storage unit places sell to new customers. Any idea which one?"

Fab turned the key over, and looked at it like it might speak to her. "No idea."

"If you do figure it out, I'll be your first call, right?" Creole lifted her chin to look at him.

"Yeah, sure. I mean, of course." Fab smirked. "The other key?"

Creole gave the other one back. "Not sure yet. But I'll give you the same courtesy you're extending to me. I'll call and let you know."

Zach leaned against the door jam. "What's going on?"

"Can you give us a couple more minutes?" Creole asked, sounding more like *get the hell out of here.*

Fab nudged me under the table. I didn't look up.

"Madison, can I talk you?" Zach motioned me to come inside.

"I'll be in, in a minute." I realized my jaw was clenched tight; I needed to stop doing that or my teeth would fall out.

Both Fab and Creole looked at me as though they felt sorry for me.

"Answer a couple of questions, and try telling the truth," Creole said to Fab.

"I was accused once of being incapable of telling the truth. Sure you want to give it a go?" Fab pulled her hair up, twisting it off her neck.

"I'm going to repeat myself here, in case you weren't listening the other times I told you. You can trust me. You give me something, I'll use it to develop my case, and I'll give you the same anonymity that I'd give any other informant." Creole searched her face. "Did you find anything else at the condo?"

"Asked and answered I believe," Fab said.

"Yeah, but I got this feeling. We went over the condo top to bottom and you found the keys." Creole's eyes never left her face. "How about a straight up answer; did you or not?"

I held my breath, not sure what Fab would say next. I was happy Creole wasn't staring at me; my face might give him his answers. Since the kiss, I felt off-balance around him.

Fab took a breath. "I found his briefcase," she said, blushing.

Creole hit his hand on the table. "I knew it. Damn, you're good. Where was it?"

"Right there in plain sight in the office. Not sure how you hotshots missed it. I'll go get it." Fab stood up and disappeared before Creole could say anything.

I knew that wasn't true. "This is a big leap of faith for Fab, you'd better not abuse her trust." I stared down his smirk.

Zach came through the doors and stared

at Creole. "Why are you involving Madison in a murder case? You know she'd do anything for Fab, and if she ends up getting hurt, it will be your fault, pal."

"Oh, stop. Fab is cooperating with the police investigation," I told him.

Zach laughed. "Sure she is. Be careful," he said to Creole. "She'll get bored and shoot you."

Fab breezed through the French doors, briefcase in hand, and sat down next to Creole, flipping the locks up.

"Do you mind?" Creole said to Zach.

I stood up and looped my arm in Zach's. "Let's go inside."

Zach scanned my face with suspicion. "You know what's in the briefcase don't you?" he accused.

"Contrary to what you think, Fab keeps a lot to herself. It looked like boring paperwork to me." It bothered me to be constantly evasive.

My phone ringing brought a welcome interruption. I pulled it out of my pocket and looked at the screen. I sent Brick to voicemail, not wanting to fight with Zach.

"Who's that?" Zach demanded.

"I never ask you who's calling when you get a phone call. It's business if you must know." I'd return the call much later.

My phone rang again. Looks like later

just arrived.

"You might as well answer. Must be important, they called back," Zach said.

"What's up?" I asked Brick

"Did you send me to voicemail?" Brick barked.

"And you didn't take the hint?"

"Oh, gotcha. You can't talk. Come to my office first thing, got a job for you." He hung up before I could come up with a creative excuse for being busy. If he called me first, Fab would never accept the job.

"Brick wants to see me in his office first thing in the morning." I tried and failed with the full-disclosure policy, but made the instantaneous decision to try again right now. I hated weighing every word, wondering if it would upset Zach.

"When are we going to have time together? Let's go back to my place?" Zach asked.

"Name one time I've not been available or said no to you, except when you've asked me to go to your place, which holds bad memories. Your job demands more of you than mine does. I'm home every night, you're not."

I didn't get my phone back in my pocket before it started ringing again.

Zach leaned against the back of the couch. "Your phone rings more than mine," he grumbled.

I answered, knowing that Zach planned to listen to every word.

"There's something you ought to know," Brad said.

"Hello to you too, and yes, I'm fine."

Brad laughed. "When I got to The Cottages this morning to pick up Julie and Liam, Liam informed me there were squatters out by the pool."

"I don't believe you."

"Two guys asleep by the pool; one in a chaise lounge, the other face down on the concrete. The upright guy, snoring loud enough to be heard down the block. The other one I thought maybe was dead, until I kicked him and he rolled over. I yelled good and loud for them to hit the road. Told them the only reason they weren't getting arrested was I had plans for the day."

"Impersonating a cop?" I chuckled.

Zach frowned.

"You and Liam," he whispered. "I wanted to point out that technically I didn't say that, not my concern what they believed. But decided that would make a sucky role model."

"Now your phone is ringing," I said to Zach.

"Not your usual direct self. The boyfriend listening?" Brad asked. "He sure knows how to milk a headache. The squatters won't be back. They were friends of Joseph's, but he didn't want them puking in his house."

I turned my back and told Brad, "The upside is you called me and not the sheriff. Thanks for the heads up." I used Zach's distraction to go back outside.

"Where did Creole go?" I asked Fab, and sat in the chaise next to her.

"This will be your fault if this sharing goes south." Fab fingered the key Creole gave back to her. "Where do you suppose he'd rent a storage unit?"

"Is there one located near the condo? Even if one were around the corner, you'd get caught if you go there and try to unlock every unit. Security cameras. What about at the condo unit itself? Even rich people have to store their Christmas decorations somewhere."

"Do you two want something to drink?" Zach stood just inside the patio doors.

Fab turned in her seat. "Go away," she told him.

The tension made me twitchy. "That's awkward," I said, and nudged her.

"Don't get comfortable with him underfoot."

Chapter 36

I tried to be as quiet as I could, consciously stopping myself from tossing and turning, not wanting to wake Zach. I stared at the ceiling, checking the clock for the hundredth time, then minutes later, checking it again.

I didn't think boyfriends were supposed to beg off hot sex with the "my head aches" excuse. It hurt my feelings when he turned away and, damn him, fell asleep. Slipping quietly out of bed, I pulled on a pair of crop sweats and a T-shirt I left on the chair used exclusively for clothing I was too lazy to hang up.

If I'd been alone in bed, I would've pulled out a book or turned on the shopping channel until I fell asleep. Instead, I sat at the kitchen island, chin on my hands.

Fab slipped quietly into the kitchen. "Why are you walking around in the middle of the night?"

I raised my eyebrows and stared at her.

"You know I'm a light sleeper, I hear every noise," Fab reminded.

"Insomnia," I sighed. "I got tired of the clock taunting me, the hours ticking by and no sleep. If I had a dog I'd go for a walk on the beach."

"I could drive you around until you fall asleep or cruise the only place open, the twenty-four hour donut hangout, for stoners who need their sugar fix."

"I haven't had a donut since they took them out of the gas station. I'm fine." I smiled at her. "Go back to sleep."

Fab grabbed my arm, pulling me off the stool. "Buckle on your flip-flops. I'm not a dog, but we can still walk on the beach."

We went out the French doors and squeezed through the space in the fence. Since I started using the path, I had all the weeds and overgrowth cleaned out and paver stones put down. We cut between the two houses, and the path ended at a set of steps that take you out to the water. The lapping of the waves on the sand was a soothing sound.

"You know how some of our ideas blow? This might be one, hitting the beach in the middle of the night," I said.

"Sit." Fab pulled me down on the steps. "Tell me why you're not banging Zach until you're exhausted. Makes me sleep like a log."

"He has a headache."

When I didn't say anything else she said, "Change of subject. Do you think Creole is banging the widow?"

"I never asked. That day on the island, they looked like lovers; that look of new intimacy. The happy glow, before you have your first fight and you get a glimpse of the real person."

Fab's phone rang. Good thing one of us was prepared, I left mine plugged in by the bedside.

"I bet that's not good news," I said. Could this night get any better?

Fab looked at the screen. "Hi, honey."

Didier couldn't have said more than a couple of sentences. "We're sitting on the beach steps behind the house, girl talking. Be back in a little while. Thanks for the heads up." Fab hung up. "Didier wanted us to know that Zach is awake wandering around the house."

I sighed. "I hoped to sneak in and out without waking him up. Our irritation with the other is at an all-time high."

"Reality check, he's getting an eye-full of life at Casa Madison and he's not liking it. Before you have a big fight and break up over whether the toilet seat is up or down, you two need to come to an agreement on expectations of the other."

"I feel like I've missed curfew and my dad's going to be waiting at the door."

"Did you sneak out of the house as a teenager?" Fab asked.

I could see the thought intrigued Fab. "Not to be with boys, but to go joy riding without permission, spy on our latest infatuation, and toilet paper their houses. That meant you were crushing hard."

"I missed out on that rite of passage. You didn't disobey my father. Embarrassing the family would've gotten me shipped to a convent." Fab's face showed no emotion. "You ever get caught?"

"One morning Mother announced at breakfast that I was to hurry up and eat, and get my butt over to Todd Peters' house to help him clean up the yard. His mother and mine were friends and she called, humiliated by all the toilet paper."

"Mother said, 'Don't give me that innocent look.' Then I squealed back something like, 'Todd will know. I like him.' Then Mother looked at me and said, 'You're not to confess one word. If Janet Peters finds out, you're grounded. She'll spread it all over town. Get a good story together before you arrive.' Then she pushed me out the door.

"I stopped on the way over, got my best friend, and we pretended to be walking by and offered our help. Todd acknowledged us at school after that with a hello and a wave, but that's it. Janet Peters looked down her nose at everyone, but she figured out I had a part in her humiliation and turned downright frigid. I never understood how Mother could have been friends with her. The last time I saw her I gave her the same condescending look she gave me, and was quite proud of myself."

"No boys were allowed, except for a special occasion like a school dance. And my parents wondered why I ran off with the first guy offering fun and adventure," Fab mused. "Did I mention my future husband had been pre-selected? You know, someone with impeccable lineage. Henri Ricard is a philosophy professor and head of the department at Université Pierre. He outgrew his pimples and, still nerdy, he married, had six children and a beautiful, intelligent well-bred wife who suffers through the endless parties, her small talk flawless. I bet Henri's family is relieved he never married me."

"It's funny how a single choice can change the direction of your life. Any regrets?" I nudged her shoulder.

"I've thought about that. But if I did I wouldn't be here, and honestly, I'm happy. I'm not so sure I could say that if I were Madame Ricard right now." Fab stood up, offering her hand.

"We should go back inside. If Zach is sitting in the living room with his arms crossed, you're on your own. I'm racing upstairs."

"Thank you, and Didier. I love these girl convos. Next one we'll do in the middle of the day."

Fab went into the house ahead of me

and looked in the living room. "Coast is clear."

"See you in the morning," I whispered, and followed her up the stairs.

Zach lay on his side, his back to the room. He never moved, though his breathing indicated he was awake. I swapped my clothes for a Miami Dolphins T-shirt and climbed into bed. I suppose if I didn't feel guilty, I'd snuggle up to his back and fall asleep. Instead, I kept to my own side of the bed.

Chapter 37

Zach woke up early, took a shower, and went downstairs without a good morning nibble on my neck. I feigned sleep until he left the bedroom, not wanting to start the day with any serious conversation.

Black storm clouds were rolling in across The Gulf, making me wish I could just snuggle under the covers until I had the house to myself. I forced my body out of bed and into the shower. With a full day ahead of me, I stepped into a white cotton skirt with big pockets and a bright coral sleeveless top. Carwash class day! The boss needed to learn to run all the equipment and for that, I grabbed shorts.

Fab's door was closed and nothing hung from the doorknob. Leaning against the stair railing, I saw Jazz curled up asleep, the living room to himself. Zach had his back to me, sitting at the kitchen counter.

"What the hell?" Zach yelled. "Put some pants on, asshole," Zach said to Didier.

Didier, clad in an apron and black briefs showing a peek of his cheeks at the top, had eggs in his hands. Setting them on the counter, he stuck his leg out and nudged the refrigerator closed. He pulled himself to his full height, he had Zach by a smidge, both over six feet tall.

"Go fuck yourself."

I figured Didier would back down, but the look on his face told me with the slightest provocation, he'd punch Zach.

"Good morning," I said way too cheerfully. "I'll start the coffee." That would be a trick since every person in the house liked their coffee different.

Zach pushed his bar stool back. "Just make yours and join me at the pool." He headed for the French doors.

I started my day with a French coffee mix and water nuked for two minutes; I couldn't tolerate the swill Fab called coffee.

"I'm sorry, Didier. You're making one of my favorites, save me a bite." I grabbed a piece of cheese.

Didier stood at the counter chopping ingredients for one of his masterful frittatas. "Bon jour, Madison." He winked. "You look lovely today."

I blushed and almost giggled. Zach would flip if he heard that come out of my mouth.

"Zach leave?" Fab suddenly appeared, kissing Didier.

"He's on the patio. I'm going out there now." I mixed the hot water into my cup and threw the spoon in the sink.

"He walks around in his underwear?" Zach demanded. "Where do you draw the line on offensive behavior?" The muscles in his jaw tightened.

I leaned across the table to kiss him. "Do you want to fight or could we maybe start over and enjoy our coffee together?" Now probably wasn't the time to remind him that Didier had an apron on.

Slice squeezed through the space in the fence, from the super-secret path everyone knew about and used.

"Hey, boss." He winked at me.

Zach glared. "Slice and I need to go over client issues," he said to me.

"Food, drink, help yourself," I said to Slice as he walked into the house. "I need to go to The Cottages. Mac and I are having our weekly meeting. I won't be home until later." I stood up and bent down to kiss Zach; it could be called lukewarm, since it lacked any participation on his part. "Why don't I get take-out tonight? We can eat out here by the pool and go swimming?"

"We can talk later." Zach didn't make eye contact.

Slice passed me coming out the door with a bottle of orange juice in one hand and a plate of Didier's eggs and fruit in the other. He sat opposite Zach and proceeded to wolf down his food.

I grabbed my tote bag and looked at Fab with green-eyed jealousy, sitting at the counter, Didier feeding her strawberries.

"I'll see you later," I called, closing the front door behind me.

* * *

"Where are you?" Fab asked when I answered my phone.

"Eating breakfast at The Bakery Café." I had finished my scrambled egg concoction and started on a pecan roll.

"Don't go anywhere." Fab hung up.

I scrolled the internet looking for storage units in the über-wealthy section of Miami Beach. They were everywhere, like hamburger stands. But would the rich allow them in their neighborhood? They didn't allow the fast food restaurants. With a little digging, I found one storage place within a mile, off the beaten path according to the aerial. It appeared to share a lot with a boat storage place. I typed the name of the condo unit, The Pointe, into the search box to check the amenities they advertised. Extra space to put your junk would qualify.

Fab set her laptop on the table. "Do you want anything?"

I looked at my watch. "What did you do, blow every stop light?"

A creature of some habit, she never passed up a double latte, skinny something, extra stuff, coffee. To me I might as well pour it in a hypodermic needle and shoot-up. The high would be great, but the down would suck.

"Didier told me to tell you he thinks you're fabulous and to have a great day."

"I apologize for Zach's rudeness. I could only risk a quick peek at those tight buns of Didier's—nice! Very impressed Didier stood up to Zach."

"You think Didier's a sissy?" Fab looked horrified.

"I wanted to yell, 'Go, Didier!' Such a beautiful face, and of course the rest of him. I can't see him throwing punches and rolling in the dirt."

"Why are you looking at The Pointe?"

"Got an architectural drawing of the place which includes the underground parking, nothing about extra storage listed anywhere. There's a storage place nearby, two others a couple of blocks away." I clicked on the file and showed her everything I found.

"Let's go check them out. We'll start at the condos. Gabriel wouldn't be that obvious but if he could use someone else's storage, he'd think that was clever. The cops would check the one associated with the unit, but they wouldn't get a warrant to check every one. It's not like they're looking for a body that's unaccounted for."

"Where is Gabriel's final resting place?" Maybe my invitation to a stranger's funeral had gotten lost in the mail.

"Dickie set him on fire and what was left got shipped back to France. His uncle footed the bill, according to our weird little friend."

"I thought you were going to be nice to Dickie since he helped you out in a big way," I reminded.

"There's a statute on that promise."

I shook my head. "First stop is Brick's; he's got a job for me."

* * *

Fab squealed into the driveway of Famosa Motors and slammed the brakes.

"I'm driving when we leave here," I said, thankful my seat belt never failed me, jerking me tightly against the seat.

"No you're not," Fab pitched a mini fit. After two or three unintelligible words, she took a breath. "Oh, okay, I'll slow down."

We walked through the front doors, Bitsy nowhere in sight. I couldn't remember a time when her pesky self hadn't been preening behind the desk.

"Hey, Brick, you up there?" Fab yelled.

Brick's head appeared in his office window, where he knocked on the glass and motioned us up.

We raced up the stairs, pushing each

other to see which one of us would get to the top first. Fab won with a last minute hip swing.

"I can't believe you have the balls to yell in my place of business!" Brick yelled back at Fab.

I grabbed the back of Fab's shirt before she jumped on his desk, kicking everything on it to the floor. "Where's Bitsy? Isn't she supposed to announce us?"

"She heard you two squeal into the driveway, ran and locked herself in the bathroom." Brick looked disgusted.

"That's what she gets for screwing us on a straight-up information transaction," I said.

"Easy!" Brick yelled again. "Whack job there," he said, and pointed to Fab, "pulled a gun on her, scared my girl."

Fab stood at his window and surveyed the car lot. From her view, she had a several-block view of an upscale commercial district.

"Bitsy got off easy," she said.

Brick tossed me a large manila envelope. "These eviction notices need to be served in two days. Get it done and then you'll have some paperwork you need to sign."

"Not so fast." I narrowed my eyes. "What's the trick?" I rested my butt against the corner of the desk and flipped through the envelope's contents.

"Simple job. I bought a new building and want the tenants out. Try for personal service, it makes it easier in court; last resort, tape it to the door."

"I'm going with her." Fab turned on Brick. "Neither of us better end up in jail."

"Both of you get out of my office. The damn phone is ringing and Bitsy needs to get the hell out of the bathroom."

Brick yelled, "BITSY!"

Fab slid down the banister and laughed when she veered off over the side. I cut around her, tugged on her shirt, and detoured her away from the women's bathroom.

"Hey, Bitsy!" I yelled. "You can come out now, we're leaving. See you next time."

Fab laughed. "Brick's standing in his office window, I dare you to turn and give him the finger."

I turned and waved up to him. "You didn't really think I was going to do that, did you?"

"A girl can hope."

I stopped at Bitsy's desk and took a huge handful of wrapped chocolate peppermints; I shoved them in my pocket and gave Brick the thumbs up. "You get me in trouble and Mother won't let us play together."

"Your mother would've given him the finger. She told me once it makes her face hurt to be nice to him, holding a silly smile in place."

I threw the envelope on the back seat.

"The Pointe for a quick look around?"

"Program that thing." Fab pointed to the GPS and said, "Quickest route so I'm not forced to stop at red lights."

"Who do you know with computer-hacking skills?" I asked. "We can't try the key on every unit at a storage place. Give your hacker the names Gabriel would use, and see if he has a unit anywhere. Get us the number. If we have to, we'll rent a unit close by while we check out Gabriel's."

Fab picked up her phone. "Gunz needs to get on that." He rarely answered his phone, so she left a message.

Chapter 38

The beach along Ocean Drive is spectacular, with endless white sand. I watched the joggers sweating on the jogging path. A barrier island of Miami Beach, in the heart of the art deco district, it dominates with its preserved buildings, outdoor restaurants, and shopping.

"We could stop and go for a walk," I said.

"The only time I did that, I wanted to shoot you, picking up shells every stinking step. I'll buy you a damn bag."

"You've promised that before and not a single shell, let alone a whole bag, showed up in the kitchen." I made a sad face at Fab.

"Your phone's ringing." Fab hit the brakes, just missing rolling over the biker who pulled into traffic without looking.

"It's Creole," I told her, looking at the screen.

"Why are you two headed to Gabriel's condo?" he asked as soon as I answered.

I caught my breath and hung up on him. "He knows we're headed to the condo. How? Is he behind us?"

Fab checked her side and rearview mirrors. "I always have an eye out for tail."

My phone rang again. "Answer it," Fab hissed. "Speaker." She shook her finger.

"Did you hang up on me?" Creole demanded.

"We get disconnected and you take it personally?" I rolled down the window so air would blow in his ear and he'd hang up.

"What the hell are you two up to now?" Creole asked.

"We're checking out the garage to see if they have storage places. Satisfied? In and out, less than five minutes."

"I can save you a trip. I've already checked out the garage from one end to other. Now turn around and go home," Creole said.

"You have my word," Fab spoke out. She pulled into the beach parking lot, jumped out, and started looking around the underside of the Hummer.

"Next time you put me on speaker phone, give me a heads up," Creole said.

"Here's a heads up — good-bye," I said. "What are you looking for?"

"Just a hunch." Fab grabbed a beach towel from the back and got down on the ground on her back. "Look what I found." She withdrew a small black box and threw it on the ground. "Tracking device."

Fab got behind the wheel and drove over it and then backed over it again for good measure. I picked up the flattened mess and got back in on the passenger side.

My phone rang as Fab inserted her card in the underground garage security box, the gate opening in response.

"You're a bastard," I told Creole. "You want to know what hanging up on you sounds like?" I pushed the End Call button and turned off the phone.

We drove around the garage and Creole was right, nothing but a couple of large trash areas. I looked around. "Don't you think it's odd that with a bunch load of units, there are only five cars parked down here? A couple of them junky."

"Beach pads for millionaires. Creole told me he checked out the owner list, most had questionable connections."

I looked at my watch. "I need to get back to The Cove for car wash class."

"I'm coming with you. You're not going to know something I don't," Fab said.

"Are you my driver today, because after the class I need to go out to Pigeon Key to see Mr. Ivers."

"That old man is going to walk all over you. Aren't you under budget on the renovations? And where's the money?" Fab stuck her palm out.

"I'm terrible at demanding money. What I really want is to buy the entire property from Ivers. I could own the whole block: trailer park, roach coach, that cute abandoned building, and the car wash. I already own Jake's."

"And do what with it?" Fab felt my forehead.

"It has potential." I knocked her hand away. "Watch where you're going! If someone puts a bullet hole in my vehicle from road rage, you're paying to get it repaired."

* * *

We pulled into Clean Bubbles and saw that the new sign had been installed. It would glow neon pink, white, and green at night, a Flamingo in the corner. The building itself was freshly painted turquoise and white, with a pink roof. All the equipment was new and shiny silver. The gang had assembled. Mac waved and put her phone away. Apple and Angie huddled together looking scared, poised for flight.

"Why did you hire those two train wrecks?" Fab asked.

"Who else do I know? Look at them, cut offs, butt cheeks showing, and tight T-shirts. Sexy looking girls sprawled across a hood, bubbles everywhere, now that will sell."

"You so owe me. Next sixteen jobs, you're my backup," Fab said.

"Stop with the faces. Everything is automated; we learn how the machines work and leave."

* * *

I grabbed Brick's manila envelope off the backseat. "This address is down by the docks, not far from Mercy House." I thumbed through the eviction notices. "Must be an old apartment building, there are twenty-five notices here."

"We'll drive by and check it out, but it might have to wait until morning." Fab cut straight across the two lanes of the Overseas, making a left turn.

The area was old and run down, mostly commercial. We turned the corner. The street ran along an inlet of water on one side, water views for abandoned buildings. The other side had a couple of dilapidated buildings that would blow down in the next hurricane. The building in question had a faded sign that read, "Rooming House." It was a three-story red brick building with plastic chairs lined up in the front, a couple of gray-haired men enjoying the cigarette they passed between them.

The building looked quiet, along with the neighborhood. No undesirables loitering. I walked over to the gentlemen enjoying the sun. "Do you live here?"

"Yes, honey, we do." One of the men smiled at me. He enjoyed a full head of hair and a friendly face; he's probably someone's grandfather. "You need help? We don't get anyone pretty in this neighborhood."

"Who lives in this building?" I asked, a bad feeling settling in the pit of my stomach. Looking up, most of the windows were open; a few with flowers on the sill.

"What's it to you?" the other man asked. A hard life stripped his charm, it showed in his heavily lined face.

I held up the envelope. "In here is a stack of eviction notices and before I go banging door to door, I'd like to know what to expect."

"Edward," the first man said, holding out his weathered hand. "We've been expecting them. How much time we got?"

Fab stepped up and shook his hand; I saw the confusion on his face. Fab leaned in and whispered to him, he smiled at her. "What's the story?"

The other man held his hand out to Fab. "Winston." He looked her over and liked what he saw. He hung on a little too long for Fab. She jerked her hand back and gave him her creepy smile. Winston laughed, clearly smitten.

"Turns out we're squatting on prime real estate," Edward told us. "Not sure when they made that decision. Last fifty years it's been a flop-hole for folks with limited means."

Winston lapsed into a coughing fit, hawking spit on the sidewalk. "Some developers bought up the block. The suits came in with big plans to run out the old folks and rehabilitate the area, bringing revenue to the city and fat cat builders. There's a bunch of greedy bastards in bed together."

I hated Brick. "Is everyone in the building a senior?"

Edgar nodded. "We've known about it for a while but affordable places are hard to find and rents are ridiculous. It's not the greatest building but we keep it up, fix everything ourselves, pooling money for parts."

"We don't have anywhere else to go, do you get that?" Winston asked, his face red from his coughing fit and now anger. "We'll be tossed out on the street. Happy then?"

"Do you have a lawyer?" I asked.

Fab caught my eye and shook her head. A warning look on her face that signaled, *Don't get involved.*

"We share an occasional cigarette; do you think we have money for a fancy mouthpiece?" Winston glared up at me.

"We had a retired lawyer helping us out, but he died," Edward said. He tried to light the cigarette again, nothing but filter left.

"What are the plans for this neighborhood?" I pulled my hair off my neck and tried to put it back in a ponytail, but the rubber band broke, forcing me to let it hang.

"Fancy boat marina, new docks, fish

market, restaurant, and a T-shirt store," Edward said.

"Didn't anyone official come by, offering relocation assistance?" I knew the law and they were entitled to moving expenses.

"Don't you get it, we can't afford it?" Winston wheezed. "Some of us are looking as far away as Miami at pay-by-the-week motels."

I motioned to Fab to get me a business card. We kept extras in the ashtray along with spare change. Fab handed me a bunch along with a pen. I scribbled my name on the back and handed one to Edward. "Write down your number. Maybe I can find some help for you."

"What about your notices?" Winston looked at me with suspicion.

"I'm not serving them. I can't promise the bastard who sent me won't hire someone else. If someone else does show up, call me," I said. "You'll have a couple days' reprieve because I won't tell my client I didn't do the job."

"You might get in trouble." Edward looked amused but worried. He knew his stay would be a short one.

"I'm going to try to bribe a lawyer to help you. If that doesn't work, I'll contact the Herald newspaper and see if someone is willing to do a front page story."

"You always such a do-gooder?" Winston snorted. "Give me one of them cards."

"No promises. I'll stay in touch." I walked around to the driver's side door. "Move over, I'm driving."

"You're mean." Fab sulked, crawling across the seat. "I take it you're going to call Brick and tell him to stick the job."

"I'm going to string Brick along until I can find them a lawyer." I squealed down the street, Fab style.

"Brick miscalculated big time. He should've sent me on this job," Fab said. "I would've taped the notices in the middle of the night and been gone. He probably thought I'd shoot an old person. Which I wouldn't do, just so you know. I could've told Brick sending you would turn into a long-lasting migraine."

I laughed. "I know you don't shoot people indiscriminately."

"You're prolonging the inevitable." Fab pointed her fingers frantically, doing her side seat driving, letting me know I could make a lane change. "Eventually, they'll all have to move."

Chapter 39

The Mercedes again. I recognized the car as the one sitting in front of my house on several occasions. Fab stood in the middle of the street, talking to a well-dressed man; must be a new client. Not a local, that's for sure. The man popped the trunk, motioning to Fab. Fab got within a foot of the car and jerked away. He produced a stun gun and pressed it to her neck; she dropped to the ground, shaking violently. In a swift movement, the man bent over, pulled her hands to the front of her body, cuffed them, and pitched her body in the trunk, slamming the lid. He brushed his hands on his pants and slid behind the wheel.

It happened so fast, I wondered how many women he'd kidnapped. I squealed around the corner after the rapidly disappearing car. My first instinct was to ram the back end, but Fab could end up seriously hurt or worse. I watched enough NASCAR to know that on the straight away I could spin him by hitting him in either rear corner. I jammed my foot on the gas and before he could turn the corner on to a main street of traffic, rammed the corner of the bumper. He went into a swerve, recovered, and shot out into traffic amongst screeching brakes and honking horns.

I struggled to keep up as he sped up the Overseas Highway, threatening to disappear at any minute. When the Mercedes veered off Highway 1, I breathed a sigh knowing he'd have to slow down, because it was a cop trap. Anyone from around here knew that stretch of highway to be lucrative for the city, in speeding tickets.

I hit speed dial and the phone started ringing on Zach's end. Two rings later, it went to voicemail. He diverted the call or it would have rang longer before going to voicemail. I hit the button again, hoping he'd realize it was important and pickup. No such luck; he turned his phone off.

"Wait until he asks me, 'Why didn't you call me first,'" I said to myself.

I settled in behind another car and followed the Mercedes up Highway 1 at a distance. I was clearly out of options, except for shooting out the tires, and that might land me in jail. I instantly hit Creole's number. He answered on the first ring.

"I need your help," I said, almost hysterically. "Fab's been kidnapped-- zapped with a taser, and thrown into the trunk of a black Mercedes, body style sedan, brand new, no plates, rear end damage."

"Where are you?" he yelled. "You're on speaker. I'm in Harder's office, he's calling it in."

"I'm following two cars behind on Highway 1, traveling northbound, getting close to Miami." Thank goodness for speed traps.

"Go home. We'll take it from here," Creole said.

"You can go f—That's my best friend. If I left, how would you know the Mercedes is about to get on the turnpike?"

"You got a description of the driver?" Harder chimed in.

"Not as tall as Creole, under six foot, jet black hair, overly tanned, and has an expensive-looking suit on in the middle of the day, even with humidity off the charts."

"Help's on the way," Harder said. "Creole just slammed out of the office. What's your friend gotten herself into now?"

"I've never seen the man before, but I've seen the car outside my house on several occasions, assumed he was visiting the neighbors. Fab's kept a low profile since her ex turned up dead."

"Hang on, this is probably Creole." Harder put me on hold and returned in less than a minute. "Wants to know where you are on the turnpike?"

"Mercedes just turned onto MacArthur Causeway. He's headed to Fisher Island. Does this have something to do with that double murder you can't solve?"

"This is probably a disgruntled, disreputable client that Miss Merceau screwed. Besides, we have our girl; we just need to build a case."

"Fab did not kill anyone!" I screamed. "How do I get on the ferry without a pass?"

"You don't. There's plenty of law enforcement around the ferry area to handle this situation. Have some faith," Harder said.

"Well, I don't." I threw my phone on the passenger seat.

I had too much on my mind to enjoy the drive over the bridge, with its pristine green waters. There were private islands on both sides of the highway, home to movie stars, sports celebrities, and trust fund babies.

Where were the flashing red lights? I knew Harder loathed Fab, but would he go so far as to refuse assistance? My stomach clenched. I knew first hand, if someone tasered you into submission, they had no intention of letting you go alive. It surprised me when the Mercedes turned into a parking structure not far from the ferry. A ticket jerked from the machine, the gate arm rising immediately after. I had three cars in front of me before I got into the parking lot. The Mercedes was nowhere in sight. The structure wasn't attached to anything else, so the car had to come out the way it went in... or did it? He had a head start on me and could be anywhere. "Where the hell are the police?" I mumbled, and retrieved my phone, calling Creole. It went straight to voicemail. I pulled over to the exit gates and the bank of elevators, backing into a space. If he were headed over to the island, he'd have to come out of the garage eventually.

A shadow passed by the driver's side window, then the sound of breaking glass, small pieces hitting my back and arm. I jerked around, at the same time reaching for my Glock attached to my thigh. The last thing I saw were bursts of electricity flashing before my eyes.

* * *

I moved my neck from side to side and opened my eyes, not happy to be unable to move my arms and legs I was bound with rope to a chair in what appeared to be someone's basement. Judging by the light that came in from the two small windows near the ceiling, it was still daytime.

"It took you long enough to come around. I thought you were dead," Fab said.

I turned in the direction of her voice. "What the hell happened? And where are we?"

Fab had her arms cuffed to the chair and her feet to each leg. "Bruno is our host. His party manners blow. No last name that he was willing to share."

"Who the hell is Bruno? And how are

you going to get us out of here?"

"No idea. My guess, he's the third party we've been speculating about. Don't piss him off, he held me up by my hair and did an invasive body exam."

"Any ideas what Bruno wants?" I looked around the large basement, the owner not big on clutter; it smelled of mildew and without the small windows, the darkness would close in on you.

"Bruno's short on conversational skills. He stopped to change cars and when he opened the trunk lid, and before he could stun gun me again, I got a sharp kick off to his arm," she groaned.

"Be careful down there. Then what happened?"

"He dropped the gun. I took a swan dive, my fingers inches away from the gun, but he kicked it away and slammed his fist into my stomach, pressed the gun to my neck squeezing off full voltage. I think I spasmed a couple of times."

"It's a weird feeling, that jerky drop to the ground." I shuddered, suppressing memories.

"I woke up in the back of a different car, drool and snot running down my face. I knew because I had kicked out one of the tail lights on the first car." Fab winced. "I'm working on these plastic cuffs. There's a jagged piece on the bottom of one of the chair's back bars, but its slow going."

Shaking my head didn't clear my thinking. I still felt twitchy from the electric shock.

"The next time I heard the key in the lock, I had my legs in position to kick him in the face. Imagine my surprise when you came flying into the trunk, passed out. 'You've been a bad girl,' Bruno said in his slimy accent. 'You won't be giving Bruno anymore trouble.' He dug his fingers into my breasts, half dragging me over the rim, putting a rag over my nose; chloroform, I believe."

"Being stun-gunned doesn't leave you feeling permanently stupid. It goes away. Hug if I could reach you." I twisted my ropes, hoping for leeway.

We stared at one another, thinking the same thing—were we going to get out of this alive?

Hearing her side of the story sent a chill up my spine. "I saw Bruno kidnap you and managed to stay behind a couple of cars all the way to the ferry." I related the details.

"You had to chase us down. Why not call the cops?"

"I did call the cops, Creole in fact. He was hanging with Harder who called it into Miami P.D. I got no lights, no sirens, and no police action. There were no cops at the ferry, either, as far as I could see, and there were only a couple of cars in line. Harder told me Creole donned his cape to come to the rescue. I stayed on with Harder until I got to the causeway, then he made me mad and I tossed my phone. He knew we were headed to Fisher but if we changed cars, they'll find the Mercedes and think we could be anywhere."

"So we're on Fisher." Fab frantically rubbed her cuffs on the back of the chair. "You couldn't shoot out his tires?"

The door at the top of the stairs opened, the light switch clicked. Bruno stood looking down at us with hate-filled eyes. Without a miracle, I knew we wouldn't get out alive. I hoped for something quick.

"Don't give up," Fab whispered.

Bruno clicked his tongue. "If only you'd stayed in jail, Miss Merceau. Then your friend wouldn't be in this predicament. Gabriel planned to frame you for the murder of Maxwell. He liked the idea of you rotting in jail. He didn't favor the death penalty; criminals are executed too swiftly in this state.

"Hi, ladies." The widow, Chrissy Wright, stood next to Bruno. "You were always so busy trying to break in, Miss Merceau." She shook her finger. "Now that you're my guest, how do you like the accommodations?"

"Why are we here?" Fab asked.

Bruno walked slowly down the stairs,

his mouth set in a hard line. "Let's kill them now."

Chrissy Wright gracefully descended the stairs, looking like she walked off the cover of a Miami glossy magazine, ready to greet her guests. "Why am I not surprised Gabriel's taste in sex partners turned out to be so common." She stood in front of Fab, raking a manicured nail across her cheek.

Chrissy had no idea how lucky she was that Fab was cuffed to a chair.

"We can come to a mutually agreeable arrangement and we'll leave. My skills could be quite useful to you," Fab said.

Chrissy ignored her and turned to me. "It's a shame you couldn't mind your own business, now you're going to die with your friend. Gabriel told me about Fab's puppy dog friend. 'Dumber than dirt' were his exact words."

"Are you at least going to tell us why you're willing to commit double murder?" I asked.

"Quadruple, but who's counting?" Chrissy laughed. "Gabriel," she sighed. "I will miss the sex. Afterward, lying in his arms, planning the robbery to the last detail." Her eyes glittered. "I made the list of items to steal, pieces I had become bored with and knew their value. Everything had been removed and transported that afternoon to a house rented for the purpose of storage on the opposite side of the island. It was so delicious, stealing my own property," she licked her lips. "Especially knowing I'd collect the insurance and continue to enjoy the pieces. I had tired of Maxwell and had no interest in giving him a settlement or cutting him a check every month. The bastard would never remarry if he had a monthly income," she sneered.

"You're one of the richest women in South Florida," I said. The greed astonished me.

Chrissy moved to me and looked straight down her nose. "Who has enough money? That's something rich people say to make you little people feel better about your vanilla lives."

"You will never get away this," I said angrily. "Creole, your current bed mate, will drag you to justice."

Chrissy slapped my face. "You really are quite stupid. I handle the men in my life and he will be dealt with. Where do you think I've been getting my inside information? That's why I know if this one disappears," she said, and pointed to Fab, "they'll stop investigating. She's their only suspect, and when she goes missing, they'll think she ran."

"The hole in your convoluted plan is that Creole will never give up," I said.

"I can be quite persuasive when I have a

man between my legs." Chrissy held my face between her claws. "Enjoy your last few hours together. At dusk, Bruno will take you out on the boat to the middle of the Atlantic and dump you both over. It's my idea that you be weighted down properly. With luck, only a bone or two will wash up on shore." She dug her nails in my cheeks. "Don't worry about Creole, I'll take care of him."

"Why shoot Gabriel?" Fab asked. "Didn't you have two more jobs planned?"

"Gabriel turned out to be a big disappointment. He couldn't be satisfied with one big job; he wanted to pilfer from the neighbors like a common thief. He had to go. Gabriel promised me your fingerprints would be all over the gun that shot Maxwell. Imagine my surprise when it turned up clean," she laughed.

Bruno grabbed her arm, but she twisted free. "Let's go upstairs." He inclined his head.

Chrissy continued to brag. "The sad part, Gabriel knew I would shoot him and he ran--ran for his larcenous life, forcing me to shoot him in the back. I could hardly let him get away. He'd never have gone away quietly suffering a double cross. In the end, he cheated me out of staring into his eyes when I pulled the trigger, watching him crumple to his death." Her face glowed as she relived those final moments.

"I thought the reason you were never a suspect is that you had an ironclad alibi?" Fab asked with more calm than I could muster.

"Bruno, my pet," Chrissy said, stroking his arm, "took care of all that. We dined out the night before at a friend's restaurant, catching it all on video. Bruno had the tapes swapped. He has numerous talents." She waved and started for the stairs. "See you later. If you make a sound, I'll send Bruno back down to knock your teeth out with a hammer. Shhh...." She touched her finger to her lips.

As soon as the door closed, Fab whispered, "Where are the cops? Creole? Harder? Anyone? We're stuck here with crazy bitch and time's running out."

"Last contact I had was on the causeway. Seems like if they're any good at their job they would've found us by now. Neither Harder nor Creole is stupid. I realize there are other islands along the way, but wouldn't they start with Fisher? And this house?" I asked.

"We're going to get out of here," Fab said.

"Who will take care of Jazz?" I twisted my arms, the ropes pulled tighter.

"You better not give up." Fab tipped her chair to the floor, landing on her side. "Oww," she hissed.

"What the hell are you doing?"

359

"I'm thinking I can drag my butt over to this steel-beamed column. See if I can work these zip ties on the sharp corners." She worked her core muscles and thighs and dragged herself, a little at a time, slow going.

"There's a reason to work out."

"Some strength training and a few less ice cream bars, and maybe, just maybe, one day you could kick my butt." Fab gritted her teeth.

"I'm not giving up, but if the worst happens, I'm going to bait Bruno into killing me. I don't want to drown." I struggled not to let the fear consume me. "You've been the best friend ever."

"After seventh grade I swore I'd never have another best friend, until I met you, and you were so pushy-insistent," Fab huffed.

"What was your best friend's name that turned you off the idea?" I asked.

"Danielle. I invited our little group of four over for a pool party. Mother caught us sunning in chaise lounges, smoking and drinking. Furious didn't quite cover the look on Mother's face. Dani jumped up, telling Mother I planned everything, and never let them know my dastardly plans until they arrived. She said the three of them were lambs led personally to the slaughter by me. Dani begged Mother, the other two chimed in. Word might get out and humiliate their families.

They were drawn in by the 'it' girl, they just wanted to be friends."

"Truth is, we planned it together. One girl brought the smokes, I supplied Father's expensive brandy. Mother grabbed me by my ponytail, about yanking my hair out of my head, slapped my face so hard my head ricocheted, and then ordered everyone to leave and never speak of the incident again."

"Dani played Mother and smiled at me as she left. I never had another best friend and relinquished my title of popular girl, never to be the 'it' girl again. I'd bet my life you'd have never done that to anyone."

"Dani never apologized, nothing?" I asked.

"Even better, she spread it all over school how Mother humiliated me in front of my friends. At first no one believed her, but then she started pointing out the bruise on my cheek left by Mother's ring."

"She was jealous of you. Dani needed a good ass kicking, but I don't suppose you ever got that satisfaction?" I pointed upward. "Shhh. Someone's trying to get the window open." The small glass panel was expertly popped out.

"Don't say a word until we find out who in the hell it is," Fab whispered. "You don't recognize the voice, don't say anything."

Chapter 40

I whispered back, "No human can crawl through that window and there's no door to the outside." I'd looked over every square inch while Chrissy had her eyes on Fab, telling her what a piece Gabriel was, as though Fab didn't know.

A flashlight swept around the basement, first landing on Fab lying sideways on the floor. It continued to scan, passed me by, and backed up. Creole poked his head in the window. "What the hell are you two doing down here? Is Fab dead?"

"No. She'd wave but her hands are cuffed. Get us out of here. Your lover is crazy."

"We've got enough for a warrant now. Be patient." Creole disappeared.

"He gets us out of here and I'll be nice to him," Fab said.

"First thing when we get out of here, we go to Aventura Mall, get drunk, and go shopping."

"We'll take your mother as our designated driver," Fab said.

The alarm system went off in the house. "I thought the alarm system was silent." The noise made me want to cover my ears. Rope burns and hearing loss.

"Zach's company installed it, so you know it's state of the art." Fab continued to wiggle on the floor. "My guess is that Zach is close by. Having worked with him, I know he has someone in the office that monitors the accounts twenty-four hours a day. Crap, two people to be nice to."

"Does this mean we're not going to die?" I asked.

"I'll feel more confident when we get out of here."

Two forceful thuds to the door at the top of the stairs and it flew open, slamming off the wall. Creole and Zach filled the doorway, each shoving the other down the stairs. Harder waved from the doorway.

Zach cut through the rope that bound my legs and arms and hugged me. I groaned. My arms ached from being tied so tight and at a bad angle. Creole picked up the chair Fab laid tied to, sitting it upright. He pulled an evil looking tool from the back of his belt and cut off her cuffs. He examined her wrists. "You'll live."

Zach pushed me away. "What the hell are you doing down here?" he yelled.

I opened my mouth and screamed in his face like a two-year-old. "I suppose you think it's my fault that I was tasered and chloroformed?" I started to cry.

"It's hard on her when she thinks she's

going to die." Fab covered her face taking a deep breath.

I buried my head on Zach's shoulder and made loud sniffing noises. All I wanted to do was go home. I sneaked a peek at Fab, winked, smiled, and made several more sniffing sounds. It was the best I could do for a pretend cry.

Fab walked over and put her arm around me. "Come on." She led me to the steps. "Well-played," she whispered. "I'm impressed."

* * *

"I don't know how you worked this out, but we both owe you," I told Harder from the back seat of his unmarked patrol car, Fab next to me.

"This is my case. Creole works for me and Lazarro is a nobody. They looked like they wanted to strangle you both. Who am I kidding? I loved sticking it to those two assholes, riding in like the white knight. Never had that pleasure, kind of liked it." Harder snorted.

"Where's the widow Chrissy and her lackey, greasy Bruno? Was she a suspect at all?" Fab asked.

"Being photographed at Miami jail. Neither has consented to a chat and we offered water in paper cups. Chrissy told Bruno to keep his mouth shut and called her high-price lawyers. Our first suspect is always the spouse, but we crossed her off the list when her alibi checked out. It wasn't until this past week when the lab reviewed the tapes and found one had been tampered with."

"Did you find the Hummer?" The last thing I wanted to do was negotiate another ride from Brick. I'd force myself to go to a real dealership.

"It's being swept for evidence as to your kidnapping. I'll tell the boys to tow it over to Famosa's when they're finished. Request Ernie in the body shop, he'll have your front end looking like new, he's an artist," Harder said.

"Would you hold off on transporting the Hummer? I may never get it back, even though I have signed docs that show I did a straight up deal. I screwed Brick and haven't had the pleasure of telling him I quit yet."

"What did Brick do now?" Harder demanded. He and Brick were longtime friends, not to mention, Brick's brother Casio worked for the Miami P.D.

I told him about the eviction notices for the seniors. "Wendy from Mercy House got them a pro bono attorney and I junked the notices."

"What an asshole," Harder snapped. "Why not relocate them? They have certain rights in regards to relocation, why not look like the big man and get a puff piece in the paper on why he deserved that stupid man of the year award."

"The problem is that rent isn't cheap. Finding a place to relocate them is frustrating; the rundown buildings are filled up."

"Don't tell him I told you this," Harder said, looking in the rearview mirror. "Threaten him with bad publicity and he'll come up with a win-win solution, like that." He snapped his fingers.

"Helping old people now," Fab grunted. "Guess I'll have to change my opinion of you. Where are you taking us?"

"To my office. You'll give a signed statement, and be out the door. You both will agree to make yourselves available for further questioning and no jerking me around." Harder glared at Fab.

Fab gave me her devil smile. That's exactly what she planned to do.

I shook my finger at her and said, "Don't worry, I'll give you my word for the both of us."

"No offense, Miss Merceau, but Madison's word keeps you from sitting in a holding cell until I'm satisfied you've given me every last detail, and that could take days." Harder pulled into an assigned space not far from the door. There appeared to be a shift change in progress, as a handful of officers pulled bulletproof vests from beneath open trunk lids. It gave me a shiver, reminding me that to protect and serve was a dangerous job.

* * *

"You are so lucky I don't have my gun. I'd force you out of this truck and make you walk!" I yelled at my brother Brad, hoisting myself into his testosterone truck. It annoyed me greatly that Fab didn't need the cheater bar.

Liam covered his face and laughed.

"You're a terrible example for a kid-- threatening violence," Brad said.

I had called Brad from Harder's cell phone. "Hummer has to be towed; can you give me and Fab a ride home?"

"Where are you?"

I remembered he had plans with Mother, Julie, and Liam. "Don't tell anyone. I'm at Miami Police headquarters. I'll meet you in front."

"Madison and her girlfriend got arrested," Brad announced, and I heard Mother shriek in the background.

"I did not get arrested," I argued. "And I'm going to hurt you, bad. I'm calling someone else."

"No you won't," Brad growled. "I'll be right over."

I reached over the driver's seat and cuffed Brad in the back of the head.

"Ow, damn it, we're not ten years old," Brad yelled. "I got here as fast as I could since I had to get directions. I've never been to the jail before for any reason."

"Brad told G that you said you hadn't been arrested," Liam said, his face full of excitement.

"Let me guess, Mother has you calling her G because she's out of like with Grandmother. Next time, try out Granny," I rolled my eyes.

Everyone laughed.

"You have no purse, no phone," Brad said as he flipped me his. "Call Mother. This ought to be good."

I tossed the phone to Fab.

"I'm not calling her." Fab handed Liam the phone as if it burned her hand.

"Liam, you call and make something up." I winked at him.

"Next time you have a problem, Liam, think about what those two would do," Brad said, and pointed to the back seat, "and do the opposite. Or call me."

I flicked Fab's hand when she started to raise her middle finger. I put my head down and covered my face. I should feel terrible telling Liam to call. There were three adults in the car and not one of us willing to step up with the news.

Fab put her arm around me. "This is low," Fab whispered.

Liam waved off the phone; he had his

own with Mother on speed dial. "We're on our way back to The Cove," he said when she answered. "They haven't told us yet." He paused and twisted in his seat. "I think Madison's crying," he said in a stage whisper. "Love you back." Liam ended the call.

"We've had a bad day," Fab announced. "We both got kidnapped at separate times, tied up, were about to be dumped in the Gulf, and got rescued. Happy now?"

"I love your stories," Liam knuckle bumped Fab over the back seat.

Brad groaned. "I guess I'm going to tell you I love you every time I see you, just in case."

"I love you, too." This time, real tears filled my eyes.

Chapter 41

I walked into the kitchen where Didier had Fab's back pressed hard against his bare chest, one arm holding her tightly. He sucked on her neck while cooking up one of his egg creations. They were the picture of hotness, he in a pair of shorts, Fab clad in one of his dress shirts.

"I'm hungry," I said before I poured myself a glass of orange juice and sat at the island.

"Mon cher," Didier winked. "The two of you almost dying is unacceptable and will not happen again." He shook his finger. His words were gentle, but his eyes snapped with anger.

My eyes filled with tears. I looked down and took a deep breath; I would not cry.

Didier came around the counter with Fab, pulling me off my stool and into a three-way hug. "I love you both." He kissed my cheek and kissed Fab hard on her mouth. He lifted my chin to meet his eyes. "Where is that boyfriend of yours?"

"He's angry with me right now, very angry," I whispered.

The timer went off. Didier put eggs and fresh raspberries on three plates. We were going to enjoy breakfast in the kitchen.

"We're alive, now that's a happy ending," I said. "And neither of us ended up in the hospital."

Didier looped his arm around Fab's neck, squeezing her, and she leaned into him. He pressed a forkful of egg to her lips. "Open up."

Watching this intimate scene play out in front of me made me needy for a hard hug from Zach. I jumped off my stool. "What are you wearing to Mother's party?" I asked Fab.

"We're not going." Fab crossed her arms, glaring at me.

"Does Mother know?"

"I'll call her later," Fab huffed.

Didier worked on a knot in Fab's hair with his fingers. "You will not." He stared at her. "She's wearing my favorite black dress and stilettos."

To my surprise, Fab didn't argue. I'd never seen her look so content. Didier held on to her the entire time I'd been in the kitchen.

"I'll see you later. I'm going to Jake's and then I'll be back for a nap." I picked up my keys and phone and left. I looked in the kitchen window and Fab and Didier were locked together in a kiss. My guess, they wouldn't make it out of the house until tonight.

* * *

I waved to Phil. I already hated the day

she'd graduate from law school and I'd have to find a new bartender. The perfect employee didn't happen twice in a row.

Phil motioned to the deck. "I told him you were on your way."

Zach waved to me from his table in the corner. His face a grim hard line, not a hint of a welcoming smile. I didn't think I could take another lecture on my shortcomings without bursting into tears. Phil handed me a bottle of water and I shuffled in his direction. If only he could get mad, yell, and get over it. Not Zach Lazarro, he kept it inside.

He stood and held a chair out for me. "You look good for someone who has had yet another brush with death."

I sat down. It surprised me that he slid back into his chair without so much as a kiss on my cheek.

"I left you a message," I said. "Mother is having a party tonight."

He ran his fingers through his hair, pushing it back. "I'm not going to be able to make it. I've got something rather important that needs my attention tonight."

Something important? What? I realized he never really shared anything. "You stopped by to see me?"

His blue eyes darkened. "I think we need a break. I finally get the message. All the times I've asked you to move in, the answer is no. And now, it might be too late."

Too late for what?

"You want to see other people?" I pinched my thigh hard and held on tight. I didn't care about a bruise, stopping the tears from rolling down my face was my only thought. "That's it, no warning, just good-bye?"

"I want to come home at the end of the day, enjoy a quiet dinner without one damned interruption, and watch a movie. Not to a girlfriend running around 'helping' the riff-raff or having to share the remote with a half-dressed Frenchman."

"When do you have time for that?" I tried to smile.

"Maybe I'd make it a priority if I knew you'd be there when I got home. Your life is chaotic. You're a Fab in the making. I've had that kind of relationship and I'm not repeating that mistake. Do you see this relationship as having longevity? I don't. I want a family and kids, do you want that? I liked the woman I fell in love with, where did she go?"

Kids! That scared me down to my toes.

"If I agree to get rid of my best friend, sell The Cottages, and be a stay-at-home girlfriend, we can get back together and you'll be happy?"

He sighed and downed the last of his coffee. "Time apart will be good for us. I need to take the time to sort out some personal issues. I know I don't want a woman who sleeps with a Glock."

Knowing full well it was bad luck to toast to water, I held up my bottle in salute. "To friends." My heart broke at his painful words. I needed to get out of here with my dignity intact and go home and crawl into bed. The last couple of days had been the worst.

Zach stood up, looking me in the face. "I hope if you were ever in trouble, you'd call me. If you need Slice for anything, call him, he'll never tell you no."

I shook my head yes, afraid to speak. He never one time touched me. I looked away as I heard his footsteps move toward the front door. I finally let the tears go that had been threatening to roll down my face.

* * *

My alarm woke me up from a sound sleep. I felt like crap, my muscles sore, and I had a slamming headache from too much crying. I had snuck back into my house quietly, Fab and Didier in her room, the ribbon on the knob. I peeled off all my clothes and climbed under the cool sheets, turning off my phone and sobbing myself to sleep.

I dragged myself off the bed and into my closet. How many times had I told myself not to wait until the last minute to decide what to wear? I couldn't compete with stilettos, but I could wear something barely covering my ass with a smaller heel and not look dumpy.

I jerked a dozen dresses off the closet rod before deciding on a short black dress with a plunging neckline that tied around my neck, and was backless, with a full skirt that hit mid-thigh. I picked up a pair of alligator looking slides and a handful of jewelry and tossed everything onto the bed. I headed for the shower to let the jets of cool water beat on me. I used special relaxing body wash, rubbing it onto my neck and shoulders, and stood under the waterfall until the stress washed away.

Cheap therapy.

Tonight would not be the night I told my family about Zach. Mother loved her parties, and she planned everything to the last detail. Nothing would spoil this dinner. I would tell them he had to work, an important client. I'd confide in Mother tomorrow and she could spread the news. Then she'd show up with something sweet to eat and put her arm around me; she had experience nursing a broken heart or two in high school.

I blew my red curls out, and pulled my hair off my neck, fastening it in a messy up-do with a tortoise shell hair clip. I twirled in the mirror and added bracelets and earrings, no necklace to distract from the neckline that plunged just below my breasts. Thank goodness it had built in cups that pushed the girls into a revealing cleavage.

When I passed by Fab's door, the ribbon was still firmly tied in place. I'd bet money that she was using every trick in her arsenal to not have to go to dinner tonight. Didier had mystery control over her that was fun to watch. My guess they'd be late but they'd be there. I laughed softly. Oh, Fab, you've met your match and you're in love.

Chapter 42

The drive to Islamorada, along the Overseas, was beautiful as the birds crisscrossed the highway. I cranked up the music as a much-wanted distraction from thinking too much. Mother had chosen a brand new "in" restaurant, Water's Edge, which had garnered rave reviews. I pulled in next to her car. I was happy I had on low heels, since it was a hike from the parking lot down the boardwalk to the restaurant that hung out over the water. If one were drunk they'd have to walk barefoot.

Word had gotten around. The restaurant had a waiting list and the bar was full. People sat around outside, pagers in their hands, waiting for them to glow red, the sign their table was ready. Mother, the consummate hostess, had arrived early to see to last minute details. She reserved a large table on the outside deck, just steps from the beach; you could wiggle your toes in the sand. It would be a perfect night to sit outside—clear skies and a light breeze—and watch the sun go down. I breezed past all the people patiently waiting. Mother stood just inside the door, next to the eight-foot long aquarium filled with exotic specimens.

Mother rushed over. "You're the first to arrive." She kissed me.

I hugged her tight, a little longer than usual. "I could use a drink." We both laughed.

"I had your favorite shell store make a centerpiece. You can play with the shells during dinner and then you get to take them home."

"You hate it when I make a mess at the table." I smiled, brushing my finger along her cheek.

"I'm so happy you're alive, you could throw a tantrum in the middle of this restaurant, and I wouldn't threaten you."

I groaned. "Please tell me I never did that."

"Your father and I were very lucky. You and Brad were well-behaved in public and at other people's houses--not so much at home."

The owners had gone to some expense: muted-blue walls, upscale bamboo furniture, ceiling fans, and small palm trees, ficus trees, and flowering cactus plants all well maintained.

"Everything is ready for your party, Mrs. Westin," the manager announced to Mother, offering his arm to walk her to the table.

I followed behind. We walked through the dining room, passing by floor-to-ceiling windows that overlooked a private saltwater lagoon and the Atlantic Ocean beyond. I looked into the eyes of Zach, sitting at a table for five, an older couple I just knew were his family, father and son carbon copies. Zach had his arm draped across the shoulders of a stunningly beautiful woman with waist-length black hair, huge brown eyes, and flawless olive skin. A young boy under five colored furiously on the paper provided.

"Too late," Zach had said earlier. He failed to mention he'd already moved on. The woman was not a relative, judging by the adoring look on her face, and she just kissed his cheek. I knew in my heart that if he didn't have impeccable manners he would've chose to ignore me. My body went stiff, pains shot up the back of my neck and I struggled to breathe. I should've kept walking but I had to know.

"Hello, Zach," I stopped in front of him.

"Madison," He nodded. We stared at one another, neither one of us saying anything. I could see in his eyes he wanted me to keep moving.

"Where are your manners, son?" His father stood, extending his hand. "Anthony Lazarro." He took mine and pressed his lips to the top of my hand. "My wife, Carlotta and this is Lucia Lazarro and our grandson, Anthony III."

I blinked hard. "You're married?" I

asked Zach. My legs felt like they'd give way any minute.

"We wish," Carlotta gushed. "But soon, maybe," she said, and winked at Lucia.

Mother walked up behind me. "Hi, Zach. Your parents? We finally get to meet. I'm Madison's mother, Madeline."

"You smoke?" Carlotta Lazarro said in indignation.

Mother held a small cigar holder in her hand. "Would you like one?" she said to Carlotta. Anthony extended his hand to Mother, also kissing her hand. "Clients of Zach's? I'll have one." He smiled at her.

Zach finally spoke up. "This is...Madison, she and I dated. And this is her mother."

Mother bristled. I squeezed her arm.

I felt him before he spoke. "Hello, everyone." Creole stood behind me. He kissed Mother's cheek. "Long time no see, Lucia."

"Papa," said the little boy, looking at Zach, "I need more paper."

Creole's arms went around me, holding me tight, keeping me from falling.

"So, you're a couple," Carlotta said to Creole. "You boys have shared a lot of things over the years." She looked relieved.

"Not officially, Carlotta, but I'm working on it. I have to overcome the hurdle of her last crappy boyfriend," Creole smiled.

Zach stared icily at Creole and me. "That's the worst idea ever, you two getting together."

"Oh, shut up," Mother whispered behind him.

"Long way from Italy, Lucia." Creole looked at her.

She said something to Zach in Italian. Both Carlotta and Anthony looked surprised.

Zach turned and glared at Creole. Creole glared back. "Thanks for stopping by to say hello," Zach said. "I know you're having a party. Thank you for the invitation and sorry I couldn't make it."

"Congratulations, you two," Carlotta said to me and Creole.

Creole's hand had moved up my back, holding me hard by the back of my neck, one of his perp-walk skills. He whispered, "Give them a big smile, say nice to meet you, and then I'm going to walk you away from here."

I wanted to sag against his side, but he held me firmly upright. I did exactly as he whispered. Good to his word, he led me to my chair, pushing me down. He leaned down and kissed me hard on the lips.

"If you even look like you're going to cry, I'm going to stick my hand under your dress and do some exploring." He took my face in his hands. "You understand me?" I nodded and he kissed me again.

Creole sat me down with my back to the window, so I wouldn't be tempted to stare at the unfolding family scene. I reached for Creole's hand in his lap and laced my fingers between his and held on tight.

"I had severe punishment in mind for you if you hadn't shown up." Mother hugged Fab.

Fab stared at my hand, and gave me a long look. "Later," I mouthed.

Didier kissed Mother's cheek. "You look beautiful, Madeline. Like mother, like daughter."

It brought a smile to my face to watch Didier charm Mother.

"Get your hands off my woman," Spoon growled. He turned Mother around and laid a long, hard kiss on her lips.

"Really, Mother," Brad said. "Not in front of the grandchild."

Brad and Julie looked happy, smiling, holding hands. All of the women rocked a variation of "the little black dress," and with accessories, we managed to look different.

Liam ran around the table and gave me a big hug. He knuckle-bumped Fab. Mother waited until we all had our drinks and stood to make a toast. "To Madison and Fab, I love you both. To the rest of you, this is an awesome family."

We traded good stories, laughed, ate,

and I drank too much. Creole winked at me. His hand moved slowly up my inner thigh, I parted my legs. I wiggled my finger to him, and he leaned forward. I said in his ear, "Stop. I've had too much to drink and I won't stop your fingers from going wherever they want. But when I wake up in the morning, I'll be angry with you."

"Can I at least kiss you?" His blue eyes twinkled.

"Not in front of my family. But later, one kiss." I held up one finger.

He put his lips on my ear and laughed.

No one asked about Zach and I was relieved, but surprised. Creole got me through the evening, squeezing my hand, encouraging me to eat, keeping me present in the conversation. Spoon had already delivered a couple of parts on Brad's Corvette restoration, and they seemed to have bonded over the experience.

"Give me your keys." Spoon held out his hand to me. "Why did you drive down here by yourself?"

"You were supposed to come with us." Fab glared.

I fished my keys out of my purse. "Catch." I tossed them at Spoon and he caught them easily. I turned to Fab. "And be late? I don't think so."

"We're working on getting places on

time, aren't we?" Didier asked her.

"No we're not." Fab frowned at him, bringing laughs from around the table.

"When you two wake up in the morning," Spoon said, indicating Mother and me, "your cars will be ready and waiting."

"You're riding home with me," Creole said quietly. "If you dare get in someone else's car, I'll drag you out and throw you over my shoulder."

I giggled. "A little caveman is...huh...." My cheeks turned red.

"You can ride with us." Didier smiled at Creole.

When no one was looking, Creole gave Didier the finger and Didier laughed.

When I stood and turned around for the first time, the Lazarros were long gone. The table had been set, ready for the next set of diners. What a day. I let out a long sigh.

Creole leaned over. "You okay?"

I reached across the table, grabbing the last of my drink and downing it. "Who cares if I have a hangover?"

Mother pulled Creole to the side and they spoke for several minutes. My ears should be on fire. We walked out to the front and everyone kissed good-bye.

"Swim party this weekend," I said to Brad. "You bring the food."

We waved and Creole and I walked to

his truck. The only way for me to get in by myself was to pull myself up onto the seat, my dress riding up, leaving nothing to surprise. I stopped and looked at him.

"This pains me greatly to do this," he said, and swept me off my feet and sat me in the front seat, buckling my seat belt. "I would've rather watched you crawl across the seat."

He got behind the wheel, and pulled my face to his and kissed me lightly. "What the hell happened back there, you didn't know?"

"I saw Zach earlier today; he said he wanted to take a break. I thought eventually we'd kiss and make-up, we've been through a lot. I didn't know he'd already left. A wife and a son. I would've never gotten involved with him."

"Lucia and Zach got divorced five years ago. She's beautiful, but high maintenance, and demands, and keeps on demanding. I caught a little of what she said in Italian, I don't think she's been here long."

"Zach said something about it being too late and I guess this is what he meant. Did he not know that he had a son? There is no Zach and I anymore, whatever his feelings for Lucia, he'd never walk away from his son. He asked me today if I wanted children. I practically broke out in hives."

"I can make you forget his name."

Creole twisted my hair in his hand, forcing me to look at him.

"You deserve better than being someone's rebound lover. You're excellent for a girl's ego, but I need time. I wish I'd heard about Lucia and Anthony from Zach. Wished he didn't look embarrassed to say, 'we dated.' I didn't realize until today how unhappy he'd been. I wonder for how long?" I told Creole about the conversation, Zach doing all the talking, and leaving out a few important details.

He tugged on a curl. "You can have all the time you want, but remember your promise. I get first right of refusal."

My eyes filled with tears.

"What did I tell you about that?" He rubbed my eyes with the pad of his finger.

I took his hand in mine and kissed his fingers. "Thank you for everything. I couldn't have made it through tonight without you infusing me with strength. If I had melted down, I would've ruined everyone's evening." I ran his hand across my face and kissed his palm.

"Look, we made it back before anyone else," Creole said, pulling into my parking space in the driveway. He turned my face to his. "I'm walking you to the door, collecting my kiss, and keeping my promise to be a gentleman."

I nodded.

He unbuckled my seat belt, slid me across the driver's side, and out the door into his arms. He spun me around, making me laugh before setting me on my feet. "Where are your keys?" He held out his hand.

"Spoon. We're locked out."

Creole laughed and reached into his back pocket, extracting a lock pick. He had the door open with the same speed as Fab. He carried me across the threshold, kicking the door closed, and sat in the double chair, pulling me into his arms. He slipped my shoes off, dumping them on the floor. He tipped me back, cradling my head in his arm, and clamped down on my mouth. His other hand freely roamed up my skirt, running up my thigh, across my butt and up my back, holding me firmly.

He groaned as he ran his tongue against my lips. "I want to make love to you until you scream my name, but not tonight. When you're ready to be with me, I'm not letting you go." He picked me up and carried me upstairs, putting me on my bed. "Sleep," he ordered. "You need anything, I want to be your only call." He trailed his finger down my neck and cleavage, his mouth slamming over mine.

Chapter 43

Creole forced some aspirin on me before he left, so my hangover the next morning was not as bad as I thought it would be, but I needed coffee. I heard voices from the top of the stairs so I knew I had guests. Fab saw me first and put my coffee cup in the microwave. I was the coffee lightweight in the bunch.

Didier, Mother, and Creole sat in front of a couple of pink bakery boxes at the island.

"Why aren't you cooking?" I looked at Didier.

He closed the space between us and gave me a bear hug, whispering French into my ear. "Mother and I love when you do that," I blushed.

I took my coffee from Fab's outstretched hand and stood between Mother and Creole. Mother set a pecan braid in front of me.

Creole ran his hand over my sweat shorts, squeezing first one ass cheek hard and then the other. I almost jumped.

"Good morning," he said as he stared at me.

Here I was, surrounded by people who loved me. They all knew what happened and they were going out of their way to give me a sense of normalcy, and to make me laugh.

Zach wanted me to give this up, and I didn't want to, and would never want to. It was time for me to figure out if I liked the woman I had become, and where I would go from here. I could make my own decisions, without having to hide a part of myself.

"I thought I'd spend the night," Mother said.

"I'd like that. We can lie in bed and you can tell me stories." I smiled at her. Thank God for mothers. They know everything, especially how to kiss your owies and make the pain go away.

* * *

Enjoy a preview of the next
Paradise novel, Book Five

GREED
IN PARADISE

Deborah Brown

Chapter 1

I leaned back and breathed in the fresh scent of the rain that beat relentlessly on the tin roof overhead, bringing welcome relief from the heat. The walkways were puddled with water. Looking for any excuse to avoid the paperwork in front of me, I stared at the inlet that ran along the back of Jake's bar. Since buying Jake out, I evicted the roaches and became the owner of my very own dive bar. We served the best Mexican food and margaritas in town, which were two of my personal favorites.

My new routine consisted of showing up to the bar every morning to check shipments in and organize receipts from the previous day. Rain or shine, I could be found sitting at the corner table on the deck enjoying my coffee. A dreary, gray day outside was a good excuse to turn on the white Christmas lights that wrapped around the railings, the roof overhang, and flickered in the palm trees.

It surprised me to hear heavy footsteps coming up the back stairs. Jake's wasn't even open yet. Even the hardcore drunks were still asleep, and we still had another few hours before the lunch drinkers arrived.

A man with several days' worth of facial

hair, mean slits for eyes, and dark hair standing on end appeared at the top of the stairs. A chill rolled up my spine.

"We're closed." I tried to smile.

"Hands up," he said as he whipped his gun from behind his back. "Now!"

Furious at myself for leaving my Glock in the nightstand next to the bed, I said, "I'm sure we can work something out without anyone ending up hurt or dead."

"Twenty-five thousand and I'll be on my way." His eyes flitted around and, popping his head inside, he saw the bar was empty. He screamed in desperation.

"We don't keep that kind of money on the premises. I can give you about a thousand dollars," I said, my voice calm; it wasn't the first time I'd had a gun stuck in my face. If I was able to get the safe open, a loaded Beretta sat inside.

"Jake owes my boss and I'm here to collect." He shook his gun at me. "I know he always has piles of cash on the premises."

Damn Jake.

"He's no longer the owner and I don't run anything illegal out of here." Jake had run out of town, knowing he'd been marked as a dead man over his non-existent repayment plan for his massive gambling debt. A few other attempts at collection had been made by other gun-toting thugs, but I'd been able to convince them that the bar was under new management and they went away quietly.

"Get up, let's go and check out that safe of yours. You'd better be lying about not having cash. Boss man is tired of waiting on payment that is long overdue."

I stood up.

"Why me? I'm not Jake." After being on the run for months, Jake had finally made contact and I bought out my silent partner. We used our shared CPA to construct a fair deal and he helped me set up private, legal financing. I had several illegal options, but passed.

"Bet you'll find the money if I tie you to a chair and listen to you scream while I slice off various body parts. How many will it take, one, two...?" He whipped a blade from his back pocket, kissing it tenderly and shoving it in the front of his pants.

The chilling, matter-of-fact way he threatened me scared me more than his gun. Out of the corner of my eye, I saw Phil, the bartender, drop behind the bar. I hoped she had the sheriff on speed dial.

"Just know that if you touch me, Jimmy Spoon will track your ass down and kill you. You do know Spoon don't you?" I asked.

Jimmy Spoon was *the* badass of the Keys and claimed boyfriend status with my mother. He was reformed from his criminal days, but still inspired fear amongst the low-life element. I also knew this man would die a slow death if Spoon got ahold of him, but I stayed focused on getting out of this alive and with no missing body parts.

He laughed. "Get moving."

Inside, as I moved slowly across the wooden floor, he knocked me in my lower back with his gun, and I felt hot pain spidering up my back. I reflexively turned, jumped, and kicked him in the arm. When he dropped his gun and scrambled to retrieve it, I hopped to my feet and headed for the door, where I tripped.

"Damn."

Phil popped up from behind the bar and racked her shotgun. "Drop the gun, asshole." Thankfully, Jake left behind his Mossberg when he split town.

The man snaked his fingers out and, pulling his gun back into his grasp, rolled onto his back. He pointed the barrel toward Phil, but she pulled her trigger first. There was blood everywhere from a gaping stomach wound and he lifted slightly off the floor just before he died.

I leapt up. "Are you okay?" I fished my cell phone from my pocket to call Kevin Cory, a local sheriff. I only had his number because his sister, Julie, was dating my brother, Brad.

"You never call, what's up?" Kevin

asked when he answered.

"There's been a shooting at Jake's. No need for an ambulance; call the coroner." I wouldn't tell Kevin this, but I was glad the shooter had been dispatched to the afterlife, or he'd get out of jail and be back.

"Who'd you shoot this time?" Kevin asked. "Don't touch anything, we're on our way."

I hung up abruptly before he started to lecture. I'd tell him we must have gotten disconnected when I saw him. "I'll be upset if you quit over this," I said to Phil, taking a seat at the bar.

Curvy, blonde Phil, short for Philipa, had walked into the bar one day wanting to be the new bartender. A straight A second-year law school student, she was good for business in her butt-cheek baring jean shorts, tank tops, and tennis shoes. She handled the overly-obnoxious in an efficient manner; she'd had to ban a couple of men permanently.

"My daddy didn't raise no quitter." She laid the shotgun on the bar. "Wait till I call him tonight and give him the grisly details, he'll be bragging to his friends. Hell, he taught me and my brother to shoot—refused to have a helpless girl for a daughter."

Tarpon Cove is a small town that sits at the top of the Florida Keys, so the sheriff could get from one end of town to the other in a matter of minutes, depending on tourist traffic. Sirens could be heard in the distance.

"We'll need to close today," I sighed.

"I'll put out a sign: 'Death in the restaurant.' There's an upside — dirtbag's death could bring in the gawker crowd and it'll be good for business."

Phil grabbed two waters and shoved one across to me. "What did he want anyway?"

"Jake owed him money." I downed half my water, twisting the cap back on and rolling it across the back of my neck. "Maybe I need to put up a big neon sign that says: 'New owner.'"

"I've had a few collectors in here. Explained to them in small words that Jake left town, comped them a beer, and they left."

My hair clip snapped in half when I rolled on the floor, so I scooped my long red hair off my neck and fashioned it into a makeshift ponytail.

Kevin and his partner, Johnson, rushed through the door, two paramedics with a stretcher right behind them. "They don't listen very well. I told them the dude was dead," I said to Phil.

"Madison Westin, you're nothing but trouble, aren't you?" Johnson eyed me with his tight-ass smile firmly in place.

Johnson was the most uptight sheriff on

the force and he even looked the part. We had a well-documented dislike for one another. It frustrated him that I never gave him an excuse to cuff me and drag me to jail.

"He walked in, pointed a gun in my face, demanded money, and threatened to cut off body parts. Phil saved my life. End of story," I said.

Phil walked around the bar, extended her hand to Johnson. "Philipa Grey." She turned to me. "I advise you to call your lawyer before answering any more of the officer's questions, since there seems to be animosity between the two of you."

"Is that all you have—annoying, snotty-ass friends?" Johnson glared.

Kevin cut in. "I'll question these two, Johnson. You make sure the paramedics don't screw up the evidence. Jake's is closed today."

While Johnson stomped away, I gave the middle finger to his back. Kevin slapped my hand down and shook his head. Kevin had two personalities. Personally, I liked the out-of-uniform, easy-going, laughing, beach-boy good looks Kevin. Johnson turned back. "Madison, sorry to hear your boyfriend left you for that beautiful Italian model."

I sucked in my breath, but ignored Johnson. "Would you like something cold to drink?" I asked Kevin as I walked behind the bar.

Kevin nodded. He questioned Phil and I separately and took very few notes. He looked bored. "Dead guy is Carlos Osa—long, violent rap sheet. Good riddance."

"When can we reopen, capitalize on the bad publicity?" I asked.

"Once we haul his body out of here, we'll be done with our investigation. Pretty cut-and-dried," Kevin said. "I've got a crime scene cleaner on speed dial."

"I used him once at The Cottages. He did a good job; you wouldn't know the stain was blood unless someone told you." I owned a ten-unit building on the beach that had seen more than its fair share of excitement.

"Try being nice to Johnson, he'll come around," Kevin said.

"I'll bake cookies," I said, struggling not to make another inappropriate gesture. "I'm going to send everyone home and I'll be out on the deck until you're done."

* * *

ABOUT THE AUTHOR

Deborah Brown is the author of the Paradise series. She lives in South Florida, with her ungrateful animals, where Mother Nature takes out her bad attitude in the form of hurricanes.

Visit her website at
http://deborahbrownbooks.blogspot.com

You can contact her at Wildcurls@hotmail.com

Find me on Facebook:
https://www.facebook.com/
deborahbrownbooks

On Twitter:
https://twitter.com/debbrownbooks

Deborah's books are available on Amazon

48189773R00229

Made in the USA
Middletown, DE
12 September 2017